D1084819

SWEET DREAMS

SWEET DREAMS

PETER LEONARD

Rare Bird
Los Angeles, Calif.

THIS IS A GENUINE RARE BIRD BOOK

Rare Bird Books
453 South Spring Street, Suite 302
Los Angeles, CA 90013
rarebirdbooks.com

FIRST HARDCOVER EDITION

Set in Dante
Printed in the United States

10 9 8 7 6 5 4 3 2 1

Library of Congress Cataloging-in-Publication Data

Names: Leonard, Peter A., author.
Title: Sweet dreams / by Peter Leonard.
Description: Los Angeles, CA : Rare Bird Books, [2020]
Identifiers: LCCN 2020014145 | ISBN 9781644280959 (hardback)
Subjects: GSAFD: Mystery fiction.
Classification: LCC PS3612.E5737 S94 2020 | DDC 813/.6—dc23
LC record available at https://lccn.loc.gov/2020014145

ONE

O N HER FIRST DAY as a deputy United States marshal, Kate McGraw was leaving the city, driving home on Woodward Avenue. Just past Campus Martius she glanced right and saw a skinny black dude with dreads steal a woman's purse. The woman, white and well-dressed, fought, yelled, and took off after the guy. Kate hesitated for a couple beats, wondering what she should do knowing this wasn't exactly in the Marshals Service purview. But she couldn't ignore a crime in progress.

She punched the accelerator, pulled past the bandit sprinting along the sidewalk, the stolen animal print designer bag contrasting with the dude's tank top and jeans worn below his narrow hips, exposing six inches of white briefs. Kate parked on the side of the street, got out of the car, and waited for him. She could feel the adrenaline kick in when he was about forty feet away, drew her weapon from the shoulder bag, held it with two hands, and said,

"Deputy US Marshal," for the first time in her professional career. "Stop right there."

The dude glanced at her and cut right toward Cadillac Square, knowing she wasn't going to shoot him. Kate, still gripping the Glock, chased the guy for half a block, and when his low-rider jeans dropped to mid-thigh, he tripped and went down.

She cuffed his hands behind his back and patted him down, searching for weapons the way they'd taught her at Glynco. He was clean. She took his wallet out of a back pocket and sat him up on the concrete, people walking by, others stopping some distance away to see what was going on, checking out this girl with a Glock 22 in her hand.

The thief's name was Rashad Butler, twenty-three, her age, lived on Chalmers Street in Detroit.

"Who're you?" he said, looking up at her.

"I told you, I'm a deputy US marshal."

"Like on TV, huh? Think you gonna bring me in all by yourself, little thing like you?"

"Rashad, I have bad news and good news. The bad news: you're probably going to the Wayne County Jail. The good news: you get free room and board."

Rashad Butler grinned now, showing straight white teeth.

"Why're you out on the street stealing a woman's purse?"

"Thought it look good with my outfit."

"You have any warrants, ever been arrested?"

"No, I clean." He paused. "Yo, when this over, want to hang out?"

Now the woman whose purse was stolen rushed into the scene. Her hair was blonde, but gray along the part. She picked up the bag, opened it, looked inside, and said, "I'm a litigator at Miller Day. What you did is considered a felony. Do you understand?"

Rashad Butler looked away with a bored expression.

"This is Dolce & Gabbana," she said, indicating the bag. "Cost more than you *steal* in a year."

Rashad didn't seem impressed, his gaze fixed on something in the distance.

"Look at me when I'm talking to you," the lawyer said in her arrogant tone. "You're going to do time for this. Do you have anything to say for yourself?"

Rashad looked up at her from his seat on the concrete. "Yeah, will you please shut the fuck up?"

Rashad was the bad guy, broke the law, but Kate's sympathy went with him over this female lawyer who was so full of herself. Kate glanced toward Woodward and saw a police cruiser, a marked unit, lights flashing, park behind her car and felt relieved. Kate, a federal officer, could hand Rashad Butler over to the PD and go home.

•••

EIGHT FIFTEEN THE NEXT morning, Kate was nervous sitting across the desk from Chief Cliff Doven. He was fifty, but still looked fit and capable. "So, tell me, McGraw, how was your first day in the Marshals Service?"

"It was good, sir. I was excited to begin. I still want to pinch myself when I think I'm really a deputy US marshal. The day was interesting but uneventful, until I was on my way home."

"So I heard. You know the man you caught has two felony warrants against him?" Chief Doven glanced down at a piece of paper on the desk. "Aggravated assault and criminal possession of a loaded firearm." The chief looked up at Kate. "You're lucky he wasn't carrying."

"Or he was," Kate said, regretting it as soon as it came out of her mouth.

The chief's granite jaw relaxed, and he smiled for the first time. "Tell me what happened."

She did, giving him the details in straightforward sequence.

"Why'd you join the Marshals Service?"

"When I was fourteen my mother was arrested for selling marijuana, and I decided I wasn't going to go that way. I was going to do something meaningful with my life."

"Where was your father?"

"I don't know. He took off when I was six," Kate said. "I liked the idea of helping people and that attracted me to law enforcement." She took a breath, met the chief's gaze. "What did it, though, a US marshal came to my high school and talked about all of the things the marshals do. I was impressed. That's what convinced me to apply. A few years later I filled out an application, sent it in, and surprise, I was accepted." Kate didn't tell him the real reason was because she'd seen *Silence of the Lambs* five times and identified with the main character, a female FBI trainee.

"Based on your actions yesterday, Deputy McGraw, I think you're going to have a long and successful career with the Marshals Service. I like the cut of your jib."

"Thank you, Chief."

"You've already made a name for yourself."

Kaye gave him a puzzled look.

"They're calling you Quick Draw. It's a compliment."

She hoped it was temporary, a passing fancy, but everyone in the office continued to call her that, or QD.

In spite of her inner protests, Kate never voiced any disapproval about the name; it wouldn't have done any good anyway. Everyone had a nickname, more to protect their identity than to be cute or frivolous.

TWO

THREE YEARS LATER IN a donut shop parking lot, Kate and the other members of the fugitive task force team stood around the hood of her G-ride going over details about the ex-con killer they were after.

There was Terrell Reed, a former Detroit cop on the gang squad everyone called "Cornbread." Next to him was Sam Dodge, a six-foot-four Alabaman whose street name was Buck. And eating his third donut was Charlie Luna, the supervisor, a former combat Marine with a drooping, bandit mustache who answered to Paco.

Kate passed out eight-and-a-half-by-eleven wanted posters of the fugitive they were looking for—front and profile shots of a twenty-five-year old black male with a high-top fade. "His name's De'Ron Griffin." She glanced at Cornbread. "Is that how you pronounce it?"

"Not even close, QD. It's Day-Ron. That's how you say it."

Kate grinned. "Here's what we know for sure. Day-ron," she let it hang, glanced at Cornbread, "just got released from I-Max after six years for attempted robbery. Out less than a month, he carjacked a pregnant woman at a gas station. Stole her Chrysler 200 and robbed two liquor stores."

Cornbread said, "He back on the ye-yo?"

"That seems to be his pattern." Kate glanced at the wanted poster. "Says here De'Ron's got a tat, left forearm, that says, *Get it bitch*. And a screaming demon troublemaker on his chest.

"He's armed and dangerous," Kate said. "And exhibits violent tendencies."

Buck said, "QD, you referring to the knucklehead or yourself?"

Kate smiled. "Me, of course."

"Based on his moves so far," Cornbread said, "I got to believe it's the dude's final run. He's goin' out with a bang."

Kate said, "De'Ron's called Shakena Howard—his ex—fifty-two times in the past week."

"Find the hole," Buck said, "you'll find the pole."

Charlie said, "You run her?"

"All the way around. Arrested for soliciting in '16. Clean since," Kate said. "Everyone know where we're going?"

Kate sat behind the wheel of her ten-year-old banged up SUV that looked right at home in this neighborhood of a-bans and blight. She picked up the binoculars and trained them on Shakena Howard's house three doors away and heard the radio crackle.

"QD, where you at?" Buck said.

"On the eye. Westphalia just north of McNichols."

"Any sign of S-2?"

"All quiet. Grab a slab."

"Fourteen."

Kate glanced in the rearview mirror, saw Cornbread's 2003 Pontiac Bonneville parked fifty yards behind her.

"You hear?" It was Cornbread on the radio. "Shooter hit again, Comerica Bank on Woodward—number five, you're counting. Different disguise but same MO. Six minutes later, he walked out with eighteen thousand and disappeared."

"Sounds like he's trying to make top fifteen," Kate said.

Cornbread said, "I think he's already there."

She picked up the binoculars, focused on Buck's F-150 facing her one hundred yards down the street, and just beyond it was Charlie Luna's dented minivan. Kate's partners all had more time in the Marshals Service, but De'Ron Griffin was her case, and they backed her.

A BMW pulled into Shakena Howard's driveway. Kate picked up the radio handset. "Looks like S-2's home." Kate held the binoculars on a dark-haired girl, early twenties, as she walked to the front door and went inside.

Kate slipped the heavy vest over her head and felt adrenaline geeze through her system.

The team pulled up in front of Shakena's Tudor in their mismatched G-rides.

Kate and Cornbread went up the front steps; Buck and Charlie Luna, carrying AR-15s, went along the sides of the house to the back, forming a perimeter.

Kate knocked on the front door, Cornbread next to her, and said, "US Marshals."

A woman's voice said, "What you want?"

"Are you Shakena?"

"I might be, might not, depends what this about."

"All we want to do is talk. You're not in any trouble."

"Yeah, why you here with all those guns?"

"We're looking for De'Ron Griffin."

The deadbolt retracted and the door opened. Shakena Howard looked nervous, standing back a couple feet in the dim light of the foyer. Kate said, "Is De'Ron Griffin in the house?"

"No, he ain't," Shakena said, eyes fixed on Cornbread. She was a pretty girl with a lot of black curly hair down past her shoulders, wearing black tights and a gray short-sleeve top showing a couple inches of tight midriff.

Kate said, "When's the last time you saw him?"

"When he got out. Shows up here, he on the rock, says, 'Daddy home, come over here my pretty princess, give your big brown bear some sugar.' Crazy con gettin' all silly and such. Said, 'come on, Shak Shak, what up with you? Ain't you glad to have me home?' I said, 'De, I ain't seen you in six years, you come here all fucked up. I don't need this.' Tell you the truth, I was ill at him for that."

Kate said, "What did you do?"

"Told him to go," she said, eyes on Cornbread.

"Have you seen him since?"

"Few days ago."

Kate said, "Where was that?"

"Right there where you standing at."

"De'Ron tell you what he was up to?" Cornbread said. "Tell you he robbed two liquor stores?"

"Told me he wasn't going back to prison. Told me he was gonna take out any motherfuckers got in his way. Told me that."

Kate said, "What else did he say?"

"Wanted to know, did I still have feelings for him, so on and so forth. Was I still his baby boo, his munchkin butt? I said, 'De', you been gone six years, you think I'm sittin' around waiting for you? Like you got something special no one else got?'"

Grinning, Cornbread said, "You don't mind if we look around, do you?"

"Let me see your warrant."

"If you're aiding and abetting De'Ron Griffin," Kate said, "we'll take you to jail and have you prosecuted as an accessory to armed robbery. How's that sound?"

"Like *bull-shit*," she said, stretching the word. "Say you just want to talk, come in threatening me in my house. You want to look around? Look the fuck around."

Kate called Buck and Charlie in, and the three of them searched the house while Cornbread kept an eye on Shakena.

Twenty minutes later, walking to their cars, Cornbread said, "I wanted to spend time with an irate woman, I'd a stayed home."

Kate said, "What was her deal?"

"Has a strong dislike for law enforcement."

"Think she's seeing De'Ron?"

"Hard to say. She was either puttin' on an act or she's really moved on."

THREE

KATE WAS ON HER way to De'Ron's mother's, drinking her warm Vernors, when she got the call. A man fitting De'Ron's physicals had robbed and shot a dude at a Chase Bank on Livernois just north of Puritan.

There were two Detroit police cruisers, marked units, at opposite ends of the ATM lane next to the bank when Kate arrived. Between the cars and two long strips of crime scene tape was a white Chevrolet Cruze. Kate got out, took off her heavy vest, and walked into the scene wearing her duty belt and Marshals star on a chain around her neck.

Two Detroit Police homicide detectives were standing next to the car. She knew Avery Rison, a big bald black man who reminded her of Steve Harvey. "Avery, how you doing?"

"Not bad, McGraw. How 'bout yourself?"

"Hanging in there."

"This is Bob Dunn." Avery nodded at a short guy with a goatee and a crooked nose.

"When they start letting high school kids in the marshals?" Dunn grinned.

Avery Rison glanced at Kate and rolled his eyes.

"Same time they let midgets join homicide," Kate said.

Avery laughed. Dunn lost the grin.

"Now, are you going to tell me what happened?" Kate said. "Although it looks obvious enough."

Avery Rison said, "The driver, Fabin Wojak, a Polack from Hamtramck, age fifty-six, was robbed and shot."

"Know what the brothers call that?" Bob Dunn said, pointing at the entrance wound in the victim's left temple. "The fo' sho.'"

Dunn was showing off now, telling her he could talk the talk. Kate could see spatter from the exit wound that had turned the interior into a horror show, and the shattered side window where the bullet had done further damage and had enough left to keep going and probably hit a house across the street. "You want to see it? It's all on tape, recorded by the bank surveillance cameras," Bob Dunn said, now giving her a measure of professional courtesy.

Kate showed Dunn De'Ron Griffin's wanted poster. "This him?"

"No doubt about it."

Avery Rison nodded. "'Less the brother has a twin."

"De'Ron Griffin just graduated from armed robbery to murder," Kate said.

"And just got paroled, I hear," Avery Rison said. "Society is turning to shit at a high rate of speed." He paused. "I arrested a bandit one time, said God was sending him a message. First the dude found a note on the ground that said, *This is a hold up, give me your money*. Then the dude said he was walking by a field and found a loaded gun. Next thing, he was in a bank standing in front of a teller, God directing him to steal money. You believe that?"

Kate said, "Trying to justify his actions, huh?"

Cornbread, Buck, and Charlie pulled up and got out of their cars, walking toward the crime scene. All three nodded at the detectives and followed Kate into the empty bank.

The bank manager, Mr. Porter, was a big man in a three-piece suit, well-dressed and well-groomed, with an aura of cologne that clung to him and filled the room. Kate sat next to Porter on one side of the table—Charlie, Buck, and Cornbread on the other— and watched what had happened an hour earlier on the security monitor.

Kate saw a white Chevy drive into the frame and park next to the ATM. She saw the man reach his arm through the open window, slide his credit card in. Now, from another angle, a black Chrysler sedan turned in and parked behind the Chevy.

In the next frame, the man in the Chevy took his money, retrieved his card, and slid it in his wallet. De'Ron Griffin got out of the Chrysler, holding a matte black semiautomatic down his right leg as he walked to the Chevy. Kate knew what was going to happen and still tensed up when De'Ron aimed the gun, took the man's wallet, and shot him. No hesitation. De'Ron went back to his car, got in, and drove away.

Mr. Porter turned off the monitor and glanced at Kate and then Cornbread, Charlie, and Buck, holding his gaze on each of them for a beat. "An innocent man murdered for fifty dollars. What's the world coming to?" Porter shook his head. "You know who the son of a bitch is, why don't you go arrest him?"

Kate said, "We know *who* he is, not *where* he is. Taking De'Ron Griffin off the street is our number one priority."

•••

KATE, SITTING AT HER desk in the bullpen, saw Cornbread wave her over. "Check this out." He turned the computer monitor so she could see the screen. "What I was telling you about earlier."

It was footage from inside a bank. A priest in a black clergy shirt carrying a briefcase crossed the lobby to a teller window. "He opened the case and handed the cute blonde teller a note," Cornbread said. "Says give me everything you got and no dye packs."

Kate said, "Ever seen a priest carrying a briefcase?"

"Watch this."

The priest pulled a pistol out of the case and fired a round into the ceiling.

"Now he turns," Cornbread said, "yells, 'everyone on the floor,' and takes off with eighteen thousand dollars."

Kate said, "Anyone see him leave the bank?

"No," Cornbread said. "That's what's so strange. Man walks out, and poof, disappears like he a genie or something."

"I've got one for you. Where'd the shooter get his priest outfit?"

"Clergy Supply. Been dressing stylish men of God since 1893." Cornbread said it straight, trying not to grin. "Black, long-sleeve clergy shirts are going for eighty-three dollars. Collars are eleven seventy-five. They also have cassocks, chasubles, and clergy accessories."

"What's a clergy accessory?"

"You know, like vestment hangers and cope clasps."

"Oh, cope clasps, huh? I'm not even going to ask."

•••

TWO FIFTY-SEVEN P.M., KATE parked on Blaine Street, just west of De'Ron's mother's house. Her name was Bettye Lewis. She lived in a brick two-story bungalow with a front porch, a two-car garage in back, and a vacant lot next door.

It was another neighborhood filled with a-bans and blight. Two houses across the street had plywood over the doors and windows and lawns with grass better than two feet long. There were a couple cars parked on the street behind her and zero traffic.

She could see Buck park in the driveway of one of the a-bans, with a rearview eye on the Lewis home. Cornbread was at the end of the block, his car facing her. Charlie, parked in the minivan, was in her trunk.

According to the Department of Motor Vehicles, Bettye Lewis drove a 2005 Buick. According to the Michigan Unemployment Agency, Bettye Lewis had been let go from her job at Douglas Cleaners and was collecting twelve hundred a month. And according to cell phone tower records, Bettye Lewis had received half a dozen calls from De'Ron Griffin in the past couple days.

Kate could see the mailman approaching in her side mirror and then moving past the car. He continued along the sidewalk and stopped at the Lewis residence, took a stack of envelopes out of his bag, and stuffed them in the mailbox next to the door.

A few minutes later Kate noticed a woman on the porch, getting the mail. She picked up the radio. "Got a visual on S-3. Let's go."

On the porch, Cornbread nodded and Kate rang the bell. A black woman stood at the front window looking at them before she opened the door. "US Marshals. Are you Bettye Lewis?"

"Why don't you leave the poor boy alone? Just got done doin' his time. Let him be. I'm a God-fearing Christian woman prayin' on his behalf."

"Not hard enough," Kate wanted to say, but said, "Is De'Ron in the house?"

"He come by when he get release. Ain't seen him since."

"But you've talked to him."

Bettye Lewis looked at Kate but didn't say anything.

"While you were praying for De'Ron, he carjacked a pregnant woman. She went into labor and had to be rushed to the hospital," Kate said.

"Oh, Lord, oh, Lord. Lord have mercy," Bettye Lewis said, curlers in her black hair, fingers of her right hand holding the lapels of her robe closed.

"In the past few weeks De'Ron has robbed two liquor stores."

Bettye Lewis said, "Jesus have mercy. I have not come to call the righteous, but sinners to repentance."

"Hour and a half ago De'Ron murdered a man—"

Bettye Lewis cut her off with more scripture. "If we confess our sins, he is faithful and just to forgive us our sins, and to cleanse us from all unrighteousness."

Kate heard Buck's cowboy boots on the wood porch behind them. He came in the house and said, "QD, better check this out."

The garage door was up. One space was empty, and in the other was the Chrysler 200 she had seen earlier in the ATM robbery/ homicide video. Charlie Luna was checking the inside of the vehicle. Kate turned and looked at Bettye Lewis standing behind her. "When did De'Ron come and take your car?"

"For whosoever shall call upon the name of the Lord shall be saved."

"One more word of scripture, you're going to jail." Kate paused. "Where's your son?"

"I don't know."

"He's got your car, doesn't he?"

Betty Lewis didn't respond. Kate cuffed her and escorted Bettye to Charlie's G-ride that had a cage in back, and Charlie took her to the Wayne County Jail. Letting De'Ron use her car made Bettye an accessory.

Kate and Cornbread searched the house. Only thing they found was a statue of Jesus in one of the dark upstairs bedrooms.

Cornbread said, "Thought it was him, De'Ron. Almost shot Jesus."

"Are you putting me on?"

"You didn't think the scripture-quoting woman would have a Jesus statue?"

"No, that doesn't surprise me. I didn't expect the mother of a fugitive to play the religion card."

"Card? She played the whole deck."

"All right, where is he?" Kate said. "Where's De'Ron?"

"Getting his fix. I think he's still around. In a motel, maybe, or a dope house. He's gonna be out of money or out of product— one or the other or both—be back on the street. And when he is, De'Ron's gonna be driving a red 2005 Buick with a personalized plate says BETTYE. Shouldn't be hard to spot. There's a BOLO on De'Ron. We're gonna catch him." Cornbread paused. "Got time to look at more footage of the Shooter? That one's hot too."

"I can't. I've got a date."

"This the same dude you been seein'?"

"We've gone out six times. It might be a new record."

"What're you, hard to please?"

"No, I'm just looking for someone to hang out with, have fun. That shouldn't be too difficult, should it?"

"This current dude must be confident, huh? Step out with a marshal."

"We'll see."

"Come on, you got to be more positive." Cornbread shrugged. "Loosen up a little. Maybe you're too tough. Don't wear your duty belt on dates."

Kate smiled. "I'll remember that. Thanks."

"And don't pull your weapon less he really gets out of hand."

"Cornbread's dating tips. What would I do without you?"

"Diss me all you want, but I believe I qualify—all the ladies I been with." He said it matter of fact, not boasting.

Kate held him in her gaze. "But you found one and settled down, right?"

Cornbread frowned.

"Or have you?"

"Quick Draw, you gettin' in my lunch?" He flashed his big white teeth.

"Well, you are engaged, aren't you?"

"Yeah. But she got a cat. There's cat hair all over everything. I hate that shit."

"You can work it out, can't you?"

"You don't understand. It's between me and the cat, I'm gonna lose."

"I've got to go. Anything happens with De'Ron, call me."

FOUR

AN HOUR AND A half later Kate was chewing her first bite of grilled Hawaiian Big Eye Tuna rubbed in Togarashi when her phone started beeping. She took it out of her blazer pocket, glanced at the screen. "I've got to take this," she said to Adam, her date.

Kate walked outside and stood on the sidewalk, pressing her finger against her ear so she could hear over the traffic. It was Cornbread. "Patrol car just spotted a red Buick with a BETTYE plate on Manning Street approaching Gratiot and followed it to the Cabana Motel on Harper. A black male fitting De'Ron Griffin's physicals, and a white girl, the officer said looked about twenty, are currently in room eight on the ground floor."

"Where are we going to meet?"

"Abandoned repair shop just south of the motel."

Kate disconnected, glanced across the street, and saw a man in a gray Honda staring at her. She'd swear she had seen the same car parked in front of her apartment that morning.

Kate went back in the restaurant and said, "Something's come up, I've got to run."

Adam gave her a hard look. "Again? Seems like every time we go out..."

"It's my job. I'm sorry."

She took a twenty out of her wallet and put it on the table. "Take my fish home and have it tomorrow, it's good."

Adam glanced at her but didn't say anything. Kate crossed the room and walked out the door, thinking this was another one that wasn't going to work, and she kind of liked him.

It was 7:45 and still light out when she got on the freeway heading downtown. Kate saw a gray car in her rearview mirror, cutting through traffic, coming up behind her. Was it the same one she had just seen? Was somebody following her? Kate merged right into the middle lane and slowed down. The gray car she now recognized as a Honda passed her and took off.

Kate got a quick glance at the driver—a white male—but she couldn't say with certainty what he looked like or how old he was. She took a lane, floored it, and got almost close enough to read the license number before the Honda cut across three lanes and took the exit at Eight Mile Road.

It was dark when she met the team at the abandoned auto repair shop parking lot two doors from the motel, plywood over the windows and doors, grass growing through cracks in the asphalt. Kate, still dressed for her date, joined Cornbread, Buck, Avery Rison, and Bob Dunn.

Dunn said, "You sure clean up. I didn't recognize you without your duty belt."

Kate ignored him, took off her blazer, slipped a heavy vest over her head, and adjusted the straps. "Has anyone ID'd S-1 since he checked in?"

"I showed the manager De'Ron's picture," Buck said. "Man said it's him, no question, and the mother's car with the BETTYE plate is parked in front of the room."

Cornbread said, "Dispatch called, said De'Ron just ordered from Lucky's Pizza. Driver's gonna stop here in about twenty minutes. Who's gonna do the delivery?"

"I am," Kate said. "I'm going to give De'Ron his food and cuff him."

Avery Rison said. "What about the girl?"

Kate said, "What do we know about her?"

"Based on the police officer's description, she could be this twenty-year-old kid from Birmingham. Evidently, she came downtown, went to a party, and got hooked on crack," Avery Rison said. "Girl was arrested, bonded out, didn't show up for her hearing, and now has a fugitive warrant against her. Hangs around Gratiot and Seven Mile, bangs street trash to get money for her next fix. My guess, she has no idea who she's shacked up with."

Kate said, "What's her name?"

"Gretchen Conway," Rison said.

When the pizza man pulled in the lot, Kate walked over and met him. He was a scraggly white guy, late thirties, nervous seeing cops and marshals holding Remington 870 pump-action shotguns and AR-15s. She said, "I need to borrow your jacket." It was dark blue and had a *Lucky's Pizza* logo on the upper right side.

The pizza man took it off and gave it to her. He opened the hatchback and handed Kate a plastic delivery bag. "And you're gonna need this." She rested it on the hood of her G-ride, took out the pizza, opened the box and helped herself to a slice that looked like cheese with pepperoni and black olives.

Bob Dunn said, "Hey, what're you doing?"

"Having dinner," she said with a mouthful of pizza.

Kate pulled into the Cabana Motel parking lot, creeping, looking for room number eight, saw it and parked in front, Cornbread and Buck crouching behind the SUV. She got out wearing the Lucky's Pizza jacket and carrying the delivery bag and moved to the door. Kate knocked, glanced at the window, and saw the drapes rustle.

Seconds later the door opened a crack, held by the security chain. She heard the laugh track of a TV sitcom and saw De'Ron Griffin in a stained white T-shirt, right arm hanging down his leg. Kate couldn't see a gun but knew he had one. De'Ron unhooked the security chain, swung the door open, looked at her car with the Lucky's Pizza topper on the roof, stepped over the threshold, looked right, then left. He motioned Kate inside, closed the door, and refastened the security chain. Her heart was pounding. The girl on the bed, watching TV, glanced at her. The room had the sour smell of sweat.

Kate said, "Where do you want this?"

"Right there," De'Ron Griffin said, indicating a small table with two chairs against the wall. "The fuck took so long?"

"Sorry. It's been really busy tonight. The pizza's on us. No charge for the inconvenience."

"I think the whole thing should be on you. What kind a business you runnin'?"

Kate, with her back to De'Ron, placed the delivery bag on the table, and opened the Velcro flap, looking at her primary, a Glock 22.

"Leave everything where it's at," De'Ron said.

"I want to confirm your order: one pizza supreme," she slid the pizza box out, "eight wing dings, and a shrimp basket. Is that right?"

De'Ron Griffin started across the room. "Let me see what else you got in there."

Now Kate saw the semiautomatic he was holding down his leg.

"I'm starving," the girl said. "I want some pizza." She was pale and thin, her fingertips black from the crack pipe.

As De'Ron got closer Kate handed the pizza box to him. He took it in his left hand, turned, and gave it to the girl. "Okay, here you go. Don't eat it all."

The girl opened the box. "Hey, there's a piece missing."

De'Ron glanced at the pizza and back at Kate as she was bringing the Glock out of the delivery bag. "US Marshal. Drop your weapon."

De'Ron raised his gun in a split-second motion and fired twice. Kate felt the first round punch the center of her vest and knock her back against the wall. The second round hit higher and stung her collar bone. Without realizing it, Kate was firing back, squeezing the trigger, the hard blasts of the gunshots filling the room. De'Ron Griffin was on the floor when the door burst open, Cornbread and Buck charging in, aiming shotguns at the fugitive on the floor and the girl on the bed.

Kate was lightheaded, sitting in the chair. She could see blood streaming down the front of the windbreaker and wondered where it was coming from. Cornbread stepped closer to her, a look of concern on his face. "QD, you okay? Stay with me now." He touched her neck, feeling for a pulse. She was starting to fade as Cornbread grabbed his phone. "Shots fired, Cabana Motel, officer down, suspect down. US Marshal McGraw was shot but breathing. Scene is clear. Send EMS."

Cornbread's voice was the last thing Kate heard before she passed out.

•••

KATE, STARTING TO REGAIN consciousness, heard a whooshing sound, and the constant beeping of machines. She heard voices on the intercom and felt something in her nose and something in her arm and opened her eyes. She was in the hospital, her Aunt Elaine sitting in a chair next to the bed, worried but trying to smile.

"How do you feel, honey?"

Kate wondered why her aunt was whispering.

She glanced at the window; it was light out. "How long have I been here?" She tried to sit up, felt a sharp pain in her shoulder, touched the bandage that was high on the left side. Aunt Elaine got up, tears in her eyes, held Kate's hands, and said, "You're not supposed to move. You've been shot."

Kate's mind drifted back to the scene in the motel room, seeing De'Ron Griffin raise his gun, hearing the loud reports of the gunshots. She didn't remember firing back but De'Ron was on the floor as Cornbread and Buck entered the room.

"You've been here since last night," her aunt said, bringing Kate back to the present. "I've been worried sick."

"I'm fine," Kate said, letting out a breath. The pain in her shoulder was like a hot poker stabbing her.

"You could've been killed." Now her aunt was crying.

"But I wasn't. We're well-trained. We know what we're doing," Kate said, trying to calm her.

"Promise me you won't go back to the task force. You have to transfer to another department."

"Can we talk about this later? I'm really tired."

Next time Kate opened her eyes, Cornbread and Buck were in the chairs next to the bed. "Where's De'Ron?"

"DOA," Cornbread said. "You put him out of business."

"He almost put me out." Kate took a breath. "How about the girl?"

"In custody," Buck said. "Going to rehab, try to turn her life around. Avery was right. She's twenty, lived with her folks in Birmingham. Went to a party downtown, tried crack and liked it. What a surprise, huh? Started hooking to support her habit. Said she was on her own, a renegade, didn't have a pimp. Stayed in a motel on Gratiot."

"It was just a matter of time," Cornbread said. "Someone took her in, turned her out, laid down a quota. You know how it works."

Kate, looking at both of them, said, "What else is going on? Where's Charlie?"

"Took his wife and kids to a Tigers game." He paused. "I don't know as I should tell you this or not." Cornbread hesitated. "Shooter hit again. That's six banks in two months."

"What's his hurry? Is he using, strung out?"

"Doesn't appear to be desperate. Still no idea who he is. All we know for sure, dude's white and has his shit together."

Now Kate noticed a vase filled with orchids on the table next to the bed. She smiled at Buck and then Cornbread. "Aww, you shouldn't have."

Cornbread said, "Shouldn't a what?"

"Brought me flowers."

Buck looked embarrassed. "I wish," he said in his Alabama drawl. "Wasn't us. Sorry, QD."

"Is there a card?"

Buck walked over, checked the vase. "Don't see one."

"Come to think of it, there was a dude walking out of your room we were coming down the hall," Cornbread said.

"What did he look like?"

"Dark hair going gray, six feet, give or take." He turned to Buck. "How old would you say he was?"

"I don't know—late forties, fifty, maybe."

"Doesn't ring a bell," Kate said. "Was he a doctor?"

"Wasn't dressed like one," Cornbread said.

"I wouldn't worry about it," Buck said. "Whoever it is will likely be coming back." He had a bulge of tobacco under his lower lip, picked up a paper cup, and spit in it. "Sorry. I didn't mean to gross you out. How're you feeling?"

Cornbread said, "Yeah, how you feeling after seeing that?"

"Not too bad."

"Took a nine just over the vest, just missed your collarbone. Through-and-through." Cornbread paused. "Girl tough as you, I bet you heal fast, though—be back with us in no time."

"Give me a couple days, will you?"

FIVE

KATE AND CHARLIE LUNA were walking down the hall, passing rooms, passing patients and hospital staff, Kate pushing her IV pole on wheels. "You know they're gonna ask me if I think I can still cut it, tell me I don't have to go back. That I can take a break from the task force for a while, or forever."

"Yeah, but it's something they've gotta do," Charlie said, pulling on his bandit mustache. "They've gotta make sure you're okay, you can still do the job. I think that's reasonable."

Kate stopped at the doorway to her room. "Here we are." She went in, pushing the IV pole, sat on the side of the bed, and slid over with her back propped up against pillows. She picked up her cup and sucked water through the straw. "What are they going to ask me?"

"You feel bad about killing De'Ron Griffin?"

"It was him or me, and almost both of us."

"Do you need help, want to talk to someone?"

"No, thanks." She imagined herself being questioned by a solemn pipe-smoking psychologist with a beard, a stereotype based on characters she had seen in movies.

"I think you'll be okay. You know how to do this."

"My aunt wants me reassigned. Said she can't go through it again."

"Yeah, it's tough when the family's involved." There was a shyness about Charlie she had never seen before, but then she had never spent any time with him outside of work. Her feelings weren't romantic. Kate just liked him. He was a friend.

"You don't have to decide right now," Charlie said.

"You think I could handle cellblock duty or sitting in a courtroom all day after hunting fugitives?" Kate could feel herself stressing over it. "Are you kidding? I'd go out of my mind."

"Getting shot has a way of changing you." Charlie sat at the end of the bed by her feet. His sport coat opened and she could see the Glock on his hip.

"How do you know?"

"I came back from Afghanistan with two gunshot wounds."

"Well, you're still at it."

"Yeah, but I'm crazy. I've seen what it can do to a normal person. Good friend of mine, tough guy, became a cop and was shot twice by a perp fleeing the scene of a robbery. The vest saved his life, but being that close to death fucked him up. He couldn't get it out of his head and ended up quitting. Got a job working security at a mall."

"He's probably making more money."

Charlie smiled and pulled on his mustache.

Kate said, "You think this's gonna change how I do things?"

"I don't know. You'll find out when you go back, if you do. You don't, no one's gonna think any less of you."

Sure they are, Kate thought. "This is bullshit. It's my decision."

"'Course it is." Charlie stood up and came closer to her. "Take it easy, will you? You're supposed to be relaxing, getting better. Anything you need, anything I can bring you?"

"Where's my primary?"

"With investigations, standard procedure anytime you're involved in a shooting. You know that."

"I've never been involved in a shooting." Kate leaned back against the pillows, tried to get comfortable. "Just bring me my backup, will you? It's in the G-ride, compartment between the seats. But wait till I go home. I don't want to scare the nurses."

"Anything else?"

"My blazer, it's on the back seat. Oh, and my work computer." Kate took a breath. She was still weak. "Charlie, thanks for stopping by."

"Just so you know, QD, I want you back with us soon as you feel up to it."

Four days later Kate was discharged. The pain in her shoulder had lessened considerably, and she could walk down the hall and back without getting tired.

An orderly helped her out of a wheelchair into the car. Aunt Elaine leaned over, smiled, and squeezed Kate's hand. "Look at you. My God, you look so much better. You have color."

"I feel good. Happy to be out of there."

Elaine looked over. "Ever find out who sent you the orchids?"

Kate shook her head.

"Well, it's sure a mystery, isn't it?" Elaine smiled. "Think you've got a secret admirer?"

Kate said, "It's probably Adam, this guy I've gone out with a few times." Although she hadn't heard from him since their last date was interrupted and ended on a bad note. There was no other man in her life.

"Why didn't he leave a card?" Elaine gave her a look. "Doesn't make sense."

"Maybe he couldn't think of anything to say."

They rode in silence for a few minutes.

"You know I'm happy to stay with you, help out, till you're back on your feet."

"I'll be okay." The thought of Aunt Elaine, the drama queen, hanging around her small apartment, checking on Kate constantly, sounded awful.

"Have you decided what you're going to do?" Her aunt frowned now. "I mean, you can't go back to the task force. I hope you understand that."

"I don't want to talk about it." Kate could feel herself getting angry. "Please don't interfere. It's up to me. It's my decision, okay?"

Her aunt's face tightened. Elaine wouldn't look at Kate, and that was a relief.

•••

AFTER A HOT BATH Kate stood in front of the mirror. She loosened and removed the bandage covering the left side of her collar bone. The entrance wound was raw and bruised with stitches through the center. Now she turned her back to the mirror, looked over her shoulder, and studied the exit wound that was larger and had more bruising and more stitches.

Kate turned, staring at her face in the mirror and started crying, letting go for the first time since killing a man and being shot, holding in all that emotion for days and now letting it out.

The next morning Kate sat at the kitchen table sipping tea, eating a piece of toast, glancing at the sports section. Cabrera had hit two home runs in the game last night. The Tigers beat the Yankees and were in first place in the American League

Central, five games ahead of the Royals. That made her feel a little better.

She got up, opened the sliding door, walked out on the balcony, and rested her coffee cup on top of the railing. It was a nice sunny day. She looked down and saw a gray Honda parked across the street, looked away, and stepped back in the kitchen.

Kate ran into her bedroom, grabbed the binoculars hanging on a hook in the closet. From the kitchen, she crawled out to the balcony, sat behind the half-wall railing and waited. When the Honda pulled out a few minutes later, she raised the binoculars and zoomed in on the license plate: DZH 2871.

Kate heard a knock on the apartment door. She moved into the living room and heard a key in the lock. The door opened and Elaine entered, beaming, carrying a casserole dish. "I made one of your favorites. Chicken and lima bean hot dish." Kate followed her into the kitchen, regretting that she'd given her aunt a key to the apartment.

Elaine set the casserole dish on the counter and took off the tin foil cover. "Doesn't it look yummy?"

Kate forced a smile. It was tough to get excited about chicken and lima beans submerged in cream of mushroom soup.

"I'll heat it up for you," Elaine said.

"No, I'd rather save it for dinner."

"I've been thinking." Elaine paused. "Wouldn't it be nice if I moved in for a few days and took care of you?"

It was the last thing Kate wanted. "Thanks for the offer, but I need some time alone. I really need to rest."

Charlie Luna stopped by a little later carrying Kate's computer in one hand and her blazer on a hanger in the other.

"Come in, have a beer, will you? Tell me what's going on."

They walked into the kitchen. Charlie set the laptop on the table and hooked the hanger on the back of a chair, the blazer hanging almost to the floor.

Kate said, "You forget something?"

Charlie pulled her Glock 27 out of his jacket pocket and handed it to her. "Feel better?"

Kate ejected the magazine.

"It's all there," Charlie said.

Kate popped the magazine back in. "Just checking."

Charlie leaned against the counter, glancing at the casserole, and made a face. "What's that?"

"Chicken and lima bean hot dish. Want to take some home to your family?"

Charlie winced and shook his head. "No offense—it looks awful."

"I'll tell my aunt."

Charlie's face turned red.

"Take it easy. I'm kidding." Kate sipped her tea. "How are Buck and Cornbread?"

"Buck's been singing Hank Williams, Jr. songs the past few days. 'A Country Boy Can Survive,' among others. Getting ready for the concert."

"I didn't know Buck could sing."

"He can't. And Cornbread's in a disagreement with his girlfriend. Something new, huh? See what you're missing?"

"Any good busts? Come on, give me something, will you? I'm bored out of my mind."

"You miss it, huh? Miss the action," Charlie smiled. "That's a good sign." Now he looked out the sliding door to the balcony and back at Kate. "Okay, I got one for you. Remember Willy Batz?"

"How could I forget him?"

"A CI tells us Willy's living at Lloyd's Mobile Home Park in Trenton, even has the address." Charlie leaned against the island counter. "Nine the next morning we pull in, surround the trailer. I'm at the front door with Cornbread, I knock and see someone moving inside. So we bust in, look around, find Willy in the shower, dumping an ounce of heroin down the drain. We bring him out naked, sit him down dripping wet. He's got a giant swastika on his chest, and Nazi symbols inked all over his body. He'd just blasted off, needle still in his arm, eyes rolling back, face red. I don't think he knew what was happening. I looked across the living room and saw all these toys piled up against the wall. While the kids are away at camp Daddy's mainlining a Schedule 1 narcotic."

"That's a nice, heartwarming story. I'll tell that one to my aunt and uncle on Thanksgiving." Kate paused. "Need help with anything, let me know."

SIX

W HEN CHARLIE LEFT, KATE sat at the desk in her home office, booted up her computer, and accessed the Justice Department Information System. Entered the plate number, state, and make of the car.

It was registered to William R. Thompson, 23724 Davey Ave, Hazel Park, MI 48030, DOB: October 17, 1967 SSN: 382-58-4669.

Next, Kate entered his name in the NCIC database and uploaded mug shots of Thompson from 2007 and his criminal history. He had dark hair and a Fu Manchu in the front view. Sideburns and big ears in the profile view.

> **Name:** William R. Thompson
> **Race:** White
> **Gender:** Male
> **Hair color:** Partial Gray
> **Eye Color:** Blue
> **Height:** 5' 11"

Weight: 165
DOB: 10/17/67
Status: Released
Discharge Date: 9/12/16
Scars / Marks / Tattoos:
>   **Scar:** Surgical scar lower abdomen—hernia
>   **Tattoo:** Back—Only God can judge me
>   **Tattoo:** Left Forearm—4 Aces; Lucky
>   **Tattoo:** Right Forearm—Life or Death
>   **Tattoo:** Chest—Praying hands with rosary

Kate picked up her cell phone and recorded some notes. "Bill Thompson had been convicted on a Weapons charge—Felony Firearm in 1995—did three years in the Southern Michigan Correctional Facility, paroled in November 1998. He was convicted of bank robbery in 2007 and did nine years in the Federal Correctional Institute in Victorville, California, paroled in September 2016."

Thompson had either been clean since then or he hadn't been caught. She didn't know him. But she was going to find out what he wanted. Then she thought—wait a minute—could Bill Thompson be the serial bank robber? His physicals resembled those of the suspect in the newspaper. Thompson was about the same age, and he had gray hair. She opened the newspaper and compared Thompson's mug shots to the surveillance images of the suspect. They weren't a perfect match, but they were in the ballpark.

Kate went in the bedroom, took off her shorts and tank top, and put on Levi's and her light vest and a buttoned a blue work shirt over it. She slid the Glock 27, her backup, in the Longchamp shoulder bag along with a spare magazine, OC Spray, and handcuffs. She grabbed her car keys and went out the door.

Kate felt an adrenaline rush as she got in the Audi, fastened the seatbelt, and looked at herself in the rearview mirror. *Are you out of your mind? What're you doing?* She wasn't supposed to drive a car till she was cleared by her doctor. And she wasn't supposed to carry on her duties as a deputy US marshal until she was cleared by the Marshals Service Medical Department and reinstated by the chief. But most important: you never go after a fugitive by yourself. You wait for back up. You form a perimeter around the suspect's residence and go in with the team.

It was six twenty as Kate drove along Davey Avenue in Hazel Park, looking for 23724. It was a treeless neighborhood with small cookie-cutter houses on both sides of the street. According to Cornbread, this blue-collar town was also known as *Hazeltucky,* based on the high percentage of methed-out, southern hicks populating its environs. His words, not hers.

She rolled by the Thompson residence, a paint-chipped bungalow with houses crowding it on both sides. Bill Thompson wasn't a gardener or a handyman, that was obvious looking at the exterior. The front door was closed, shades pulled tight over the windows. The cracked, empty concrete driveway extended to a single-car garage.

Kate drove south a few houses, turned around, heading north now, parked on the street behind a red Chevy pickup, and waited. A couple preteen boys in basketball shorts rode by on Stingray bikes with banana seats. A few minutes later, a pregnant girl about Kate's age pushed a stroller past her, Kate wondering if she would ever have children. The way her relationships had gone it seemed unlikely.

Across the street Kate could see someone in the front window of a redbrick bungalow, looking out, and then there was a guy with a long, braided goatee on the porch staring at her.

Kate fixed her attention on Thompson's house. She wanted to check the garage, see if there was a gray Honda Accord inside.

The guy with the goatee walked across the street and stood at her side window. Kate turned, looking at a wild-eyed tweaker, early twenties. "Who are you?" he said through the glass. "What you doin' out here, spyin' on us?" The kid was obviously high and paranoid. Now two more tweakers came out of the house and moved toward the street.

Kate reached for her bag on the passenger seat, slid a hand in, feeling for the canister of OC Spray in case the tweaker became violent. She lowered the window a couple inches. "I'm a real estate agent. I have a client looking for a house in this neighborhood."

The tweaker looked at her and smiled, showing decaying nubs that had been his teeth. "Why would anyone want to live in this shithole?"

The encounter with the tweakers had attracted attention, several neighbors coming out of their homes to see what was going on. She backed up a couple feet, put it in gear, and swung around the pickup truck and took off.

Passing Thompson's house she saw a gray Honda in the driveway, two men sitting in it, but that was enough for today. Kate considered herself lucky. She hadn't done anything embarrassing or egregiously stupid but was close on both counts. She drove back to her apartment wondering what her next move should be, and decided to play it cool, relax, take it easy—what she should've been doing all along.

SEVEN

IN THE MORNING KATE sat on the balcony with a cup of tea and the newspaper. It was already seventy-five degrees and humid at eight thirty in the morning. A headline on the front page caught her eye.

Serial Bank Robber Strikes Again. Detroit Police Department is reaching out to the public for help identifying an armed serial bank robber responsible for robbing six banks over a two-month period. The suspect— seen on security images released to the media—is described as a white male, mid-forties, just under six feet tall and weighing approximately 170 pounds. Police are referring to the suspect as the Shooter due to a propensity to fire his weapon to gain control of the situation once he's inside the bank. Anyone with information about this individual is asked to call the Detroit Police Criminal Investigations or FBI Detroit Field Office at (313) 965-2323.

Detective Melvin Weston of the Detroit Police Department said, "Someone knows this man, knows his name, knows where he lives. But do not try to apprehend the suspect by yourself. He is armed and extremely dangerous. Call the police immediately."

Kate knew Melvin. He was a good guy, thirty-two-year veteran counting the days till retirement. She and Buck had once pulled a fugitive murderer off a charter flight bound for Mexico. Melvin had been after the guy for six months and flashed a big grin when they handed him over. "Owe you, McGraw," Melvin had said, nodding at her. "Ever need help with somethin', you know where I'm at."

Kate went into her office and called him.

Melvin picked up and said, "How you doing, McGraw? I heard all about it. Heard you sent the armed, cracked-up motherfucker to his grave. Well done."

"The armed, cracked-up motherfucker almost sent me to mine."

"But he didn't. All any of us got to do," Melvin said, "is stay one step ahead of the desperados."

"How've you been?" Kate walked out of the room, moving slowly, pacing around the apartment, trying to exercise.

"Counting the days till retirement." Melvin took a beat. "To what do I owe this?"

"I've missed you."

"Uh-huh. 'Cause I'm so pleasant and likable?"

"Forgot easygoing."

"Uh-huh."

"How you doing on the bank robber?"

"Tryin' to be funny, or what?"

Kate said, "You're calling him 'The Shooter,' huh?"

"That's right."

"You come up with the name?

"Uh-huh.

"It has your sound. Listen, you need some help? I've got nothing to do. I'm bored out of my mind." Kate sat on the couch in the living room and put her feet up on the coffee table.

"Got the FBI breathin' down my neck."

"And you're surprised? They keep score," Kate said.

"Ain't that the truth." Melvin coughed.

"Do you have a cold?"

"I got something. Okay, bottom line, this motherfucker doesn't exist. How're you at finding ghosts?"

"Send me everything you got." Kate let out a breath. "But keep it cool, keep it between us. I'm recuperating, not even cleared for light duty."

"At your computer? There's a mega-fuckin' file on each bank was hit. And I've got a video I want you to see. Still living in the same place?"

Kate made a cup of tea, blew on it, and walked out on the balcony. She stood at the railing, looked down, and saw a gray Honda Accord parked on the street. There was a man in the driver's seat.

She gripped her Glock, took the elevator down, and ran outside to see the Honda driving away. Thompson always seemed to be a step ahead of her. She had to come up with a plan, figure out what to do.

Back in the apartment, Kate downloaded the files from Melvin and printed surveillance photos of the robber from each bank and taped them to the wall in her office, studying the man in a different disguise at each bank. Next, Kate printed a map of Detroit and drew a red X at the location of each robbery and taped it to the wall.

An hour later Melvin arrived. She buzzed him in and stood at the open door as he came down the hall, a big man wearing a summer-weight suit and a porkpie hat that looked too small for his head. He was carrying a pile of file folders.

Melvin grinned and hugged Kate with his free arm. "You look good, 'specially for someone took a nine."

"What's that?" Kate said, eyes on the folders.

"Everything I got on the shooter."

"Yeah, you already sent it to me."

"Hey, I'm old school, got to have a hard copy."

"Come in. Can I get you anything?"

"I'm cool."

Melvin set the file folders on the credenza and studied the montage of photographs on the wall in Kate's office. "You don't waste any time, do you?"

"Tell me what you know."

"He's mid-to-late forties, just under six feet, between one-hundred sixty and a hundred seventy-five pounds. Got blue eyes. We've run his pictures through every crime database. Nothing. We've run his MO against known bank robbers and robberies in the past ten years. Again, nothing."

"Maybe you should go back further."

"Maybe I should."

Kate sat in her desk chair and let out a breath.

"You all right?"

"I get tired easy."

"We can do this another time," Melvin said.

"No, go ahead."

"As you can see, dude looks different in every shot. He's a mailman, painter, Tigers fan, laborer, priest, and businessman. He blends in. You don't give him a second look. But his facial features are the same in every shot."

Kate studied the faces as Melvin continued. "Same nose and ears, same mouth. And he's got crow's feet, so he's no spring chicken." Melvin handed her a DVD. "Check it out. Bank number six."

Kate rolled her chair closer to the computer and slid the disc in. A man in a fedora appeared entering the bank. He carried a briefcase and made his way to the counter, where deposit and withdrawal slips were stacked on shelves. The man wrote something on the back of a yellow deposit slip and put on a pair of surgical gloves. Now he approached a teller window. The teller smiled and greeted him. The smile faded when the man handed her the deposit slip.

"Note says to give him twenty-five grand and no dye packs or he starts shooting people. Watch this."

The Shooter pointed his gun at the ceiling, squeezed the trigger. The gunshot was loud and unexpected. Everybody froze. He turned, pointed his gun at stunned customers and a security guard and said, "Everybody on the floor."

"Teller puts the money in his briefcase," Melvin said. "He walks out, vanishes."

Kate paused the video.

Melvin said, "What we know: this one likes to take charge, likes to be in control, likes the element of danger."

Kate said, "What about the witness you mention in your notes?"

"You talking about Mildred Washington?"

"Is she the elderly black woman?"

"Claims she saw a well-dressed man with a briefcase climb in the trunk of a car on Parson's Street. It's across the street from the Comerica Bank that was robbed."

"Mind if I talk to her?"

"You feel up to it. I'll take all the help I can get."

"Just keep it between us."

"Feel better, McGraw. I'll be talking to you."

The woman's address and phone number were listed in the notes.

Kate called Mildred, introduced herself, and set up a time to meet at her house the next morning. Maybe Mrs. Washington would remember additional details that might be helpful.

Kate studied the images from each robbery, looking for a recurring face, an accomplice maybe, but that idea—like all the others—was a dead end. She studied the exteriors, the cars on the street at each bank, thinking the robber must've had a wheel man, someone driving him.

Outside the fifth bank that was robbed, a Bank of America on Griswold, there were six cars parked on the street: a VW bug, Land Rover, Mercedes convertible, Toyota sedan, Cadillac Escalade, and a minivan—and all of them had tickets on the windshields.

Kate phoned Melvin and he said, "Don't tell me you got something already?"

"Maybe, maybe not." Kate told him what she saw.

Melvin said, "You'd think that would've occurred to one of us. But no. I'll look into it and get back to you. Good work, McGraw."

"Don't thank me yet. Let's wait and see if it pans out."

EIGHT

KATE, WEARING JEANS AND a bra, sat on the edge of the examination table as Dr. Lambrecht checked her wounds.

"Everything looks good. No infection. Are you able to lift your arm?" Kate slowly raised her right arm straight up as far as she could. "Very good. Are you in any pain?"

"No."

"You're lucky it missed the nerve and bone or you'd be out for months. And you heal remarkably well. Let's take the stitches out."

Kate could feel a little tug every time Lambrecht pulled out a nylon thread but it didn't hurt. "When can I go back to work?"

"As far as I'm concerned, you're medically fit for duty. I'll send my report to the Marshals Service Medical Board and they'll decide."

The next stop was Mildred Washington's house. She lived on Fairfield Street in Detroit, across from Wembley, a small private school. Mildred, a pretty, well-dressed black woman in her fifties, answered the door. She led Kate through a series of spotless, meticulous rooms to the sunporch with a view of the sculpted gardens.

They sat in rattan chairs across from each other, a pot of tea and two cups on the table between them. "Cup of tea? It's oolong."

"No, thank you," Kate said.

Mildred poured herself a cup.

"Mrs. Washington, did you go to Wembley?"

"No, but I taught English there for twenty-eight years. Every one of my students knows grammar, knows how to diagram a sentence."

"I can see what you do with your free time. The gardens are beautiful."

"I have someone who helps with that. I am writing my memoir."

"The story of your life?"

"Parts of it anyway. I'll have to see how it goes." Mildred Washington sipped her tea. "Tell me again, for whom do you work?"

"I am a deputy US marshal."

"You look too young to be chasing criminals."

"I'm twenty-six," Kate said, like she was defending herself.

"How many women do what you do?"

"On the Fugitive Task Force? Just me."

"Are you the token female?"

"I would be if I didn't know how to shoot and hunt fugitives."

"Are you as good as the men?"

"I can hold my own."

"Oh my, and you're confident too. That's good." Mildred sipped her tea. "What can I do for you, Deputy?"

"On August fourth, at approximately two p.m., you were parked at a traffic light on Woodward Avenue. You said you saw a well-dressed man with a briefcase get in the trunk of a car parked on Parsons Street."

"I just thought the man was having fun, playing with whomever was in the car. I think it was a woman. She was in the driver's seat. What struck me as odd, it was eighty-five degrees that day and she was wearing a scarf over her head. In retrospect it looked like she was trying to conceal her identity."

This was the first Kate had heard about an accomplice. "Can you describe the woman?"

"She was small, petite."

"Why do you say that?"

"That's how she appeared to me, almost like a child pretending to drive a car."

"Can you describe the scarf she was wearing?"

"It was bright, orange and red with logograms—Asian characters."

"Tell me again about the man. What exactly did you see?"

Mildred picked up the teacup but didn't bring it to her mouth. "He was carrying a briefcase, walking east on Parsons Street. He approached the car from the rear and the trunk popped open automatically. He got in, pulled the lid closed. The car drove away."

"So that's why it looked like he was walking and then disappeared," Kate said. "What kind of car?"

"The police asked me that, and I don't know. I am not an automobile aficionado."

"Can you describe it? How many doors?"

"Four."

"What color?"

"Silver. I think it was foreign—Japanese, maybe."

Kate was thinking about the Toyota with a parking ticket she had seen on Griswold. Would the Shooter have used the same car for two robberies? "When did you call the police?"

"A few hours later after I heard the bank had been robbed."

"Thanks for your help, Mrs. Washington."

In the car Kate listened to her messages on speaker. The first one was from her aunt. "Kate, I made a pot of vegetable soup, your favorite. I'll bring you dinner." The next one was Cornbread. "Yo, checking up on wounded US Marshals. How you doing?"

Kate called Cornbread, listened to it ring half a dozen times, and heard, "What?"

"Did I catch you at a bad time?"

"Thought it was someone else. QD, don't tell me you're driving a car?"

"What else would I be driving?"

"You trying to get suspended?"

"I had to get out of my apartment."

"Don't let the chief find out."

"What's happening with the Shooter?"

"Nothing. Motherfucker strikes, disappears." She heard voices in the background. "Let me get back to you, got a smackdown in midtown. Ex-con with two homicide warrants." Cornbread disconnected.

Kate knew she should have gone back to her apartment to rest, take it easy, but she was too revved up. She drove by Bill Thompson's house in Hazel Park. The Honda was in the driveway. She parked on the street a couple doors away. It was 12:42 p.m. Kate was hungry; she could hear her stomach making noises.

At 1:17, a man wearing a baseball cap came out of the house and got in the car. Kate followed him to a bowling alley and watched him go inside. She waited for a few minutes, got out, went to the Honda, and tried the door. It was unlocked. She sat in the driver's seat, opened the glove box, and took out the registration. The car was owned by William R. Thompson and insured by AAA.

The bowling alley door opened a little after three. Thompson came out, shielding his eyes from the afternoon sun, and walked toward the car. Kate ducked down in the back seat as he got in and fastened the seatbelt. Now Kate brought the Glock up and pressed the barrel against the back of his head.

"If this is a robbery," he said, "you're going to be disappointed. I've got like eight bucks on me."

She could see his face in the rearview mirror under the cap brim. There was something familiar about him.

"How'd you like the flowers?"

Kate wasn't expecting that. "Who are you?" Although now she had a pretty good idea.

"You know, we even look alike."

She could smell his beer breath.

"I'm Frank Galvin—your father."

She had his blue eyes and small nose. "I don't have a father. He took off when I was six."

"I didn't plan it that way. Something happened that was out of my control."

"Oh, come on. You didn't want to be married with a kid. Did I cramp your style? Did I get in your way?"

"It had nothing to do with you. I made a bad decision, screwed up, and paid for it for eighteen years."

Kate lowered the gun. "What did you do?"

"Robbed an armored truck." He took off the cap. His dark hair was flecked with gray. "I was in federal prison till a few weeks ago. A place called Victorville."

"Why didn't you call, tell us where you were?"

"Your mother knew. But decided not to tell you, and I don't blame her."

"All this time I thought it was my fault. I thought you took off 'cause you had a problem with me."

"I didn't have a problem, I loved you. You were my little girl. I still feel that way."

Kate's eyes welled up. She took a couple breaths and got it together. "What's your connection with Bill Thompson?"

"He was my cellmate for six years. Bill's a good guy. Invited me to come and stay with him when I got out."

"Is he still robbing banks?"

"Been clean since he was released. Has no urge to go back to the trade."

"This is fun stuff—the good old boy bank robbers, ex-cons hanging out together. What's next? You going to tell me you're in a bowling league?" Kate paused. "I've seen you following me. What do you want?"

"At first I just wanted to look at you, see how you turned out. Then I wanted to contact you but couldn't quite bring myself to do it. I thought we could spend some time together, get reacquainted."

"What do you think this is, make believe? We forget everything that's happened, live happily ever after?"

"I don't blame you for being angry."

"I don't think that quite says it."

He took a pack of cigarettes out of his shirt pocket, shook one out, lit it with a plastic lighter, and lowered the window. "I could help you with this bank robber you're trying to catch."

"What do you know about it? You got caught."

Frank turned in his seat, eyes holding on her now. "I know who he is."

NINE

KATE SAID, "WHY ARE we meeting in a bowling alley?"

"You have something against bowling?" Frank picked up his beer bottle.

"If I'm playing a sport and there's a ball involved, I'd rather throw it, catch it, or hit it."

"Next time we can meet wherever you want."

"How do you know there's going to be a next time?"

"Then how am I gonna get to know you? Help with this bank robber."

"Who is he?" Kate said.

"His name's Ray Skinner. I met him at a party."

"Put a year on this for me."

"1995. I used to see him around. Skinner looked successful, dressed well, drove a nice car, always had a good-looking babe with him. Ray liked the Orientals: cute, tiny, quiet girls."

"Witness I interviewed said she saw the Shooter get in the trunk of a car driven by a petite woman wearing an Asian scarf on a hot day like she was trying conceal her identity. With what you just told me it now makes sense." Kate sucked Coke through the straw. "To catch him, what should I do, hang out at sushi restaurants?"

"That's not a bad idea."

Frank hoisted the bottle, drained the rest of the beer, and signaled the bartender.

Kate gave him a dirty look. "Making up for lost time, huh?"

"Something like that. What do you care?"

They sat in silence for several beats like strangers until Kate, trying to restart the conversation, said, "What were you doing in '95?"

"Trying to find a job," Frank said. "I was a gasket salesman and got laid off."

"You were lucky. Sounds like a terrible way to make a living."

"You don't think mechanical seals are exciting, huh?"

"Does anyone?"

"Engineers." Frank smiled. "They love gaskets. They get turned on talking about them."

The bartender put a fresh beer in front of Frank and took his empty. Frank eyed the beer, picked up the bottle, and took a drink.

"I ran into Skinner one night in a bar. I recognized him, and we started talking."

"What'd he do?"

"That's what I asked him. Skinner sipped his Crown on the rocks and said, 'I handle money.'"

"What does that mean?"

"I'm gonna tell you if you'll let me. I know where you get your patience."

"What patience?"

"You can blame me for that."

"I'm already blaming you for a lot of other things. We can let that one slide."

Frank hoisted the bottle and drank hard.

"Jesus. Take it easy, will you?

"You married?"

"No," Kate said. "Why?"

"You nag like a wife."

Kate frowned. "Well, aren't you a charmer." She took a beat. "Did Mom nag you?"

"She was a world-class nagger," Frank said.

"Is that why you left?" Still holding the bottle, he glanced at her but didn't say anything.

After a long pause, Kate said, "Get back to Skinner, will you?"

"Where was I?"

"You ran into him in a bar."

"Skinner took a wad of bills out of his pocket, peeled off eight twenties and handed them to me. I said, 'What's this?' He said, 'A loan.'"

"So, he was setting you up."

"I was into him for a couple thousand when he made his pitch."

"He robbed banks, huh? I can hear that coming." Kate drank her Coke. Still taking meds, she wasn't ready for anything stronger. She could hear the constant sound of bowling balls hitting pins. The closest bowlers were about forty feet from where they were sitting.

"Skinner said, 'Listen, you can keep getting deeper in debt, or you can start earning your keep.' Told me he robbed banks and could use a driver. I said, 'Are you out of your mind?'" Frank finished his beer and signaled the bartender.

"But something about it intrigued you."

"I researched the subject, found out how the famous bank robbers did it. Pretty Boy Floyd used a machine gun. Bonnie and Clyde were known to be unpredictable and vicious, but were glorified on the big screen. John Dillinger, I read, was something of a showman. He'd go into a bank with his gang and work the room. One of his famous lines was 'I rob banks. What do you do for a living?'" Frank's beer came, and he took a drink. "And then there was Willy Sutton, who used various disguises and robbed over one-hundred banks. I studied their techniques and methods. You can go in with a gun, threaten people and make a scene, or you can be discreet, inconspicuous, walk in, talk to the teller, and be polite."

"That's what you did, huh?"

Frank told her about his first robbery—nervous entering the bank, moving across the floor—a casual stride—to a teller window, flashing a smile at the frumpy woman behind the counter. "I said, 'How're you doing today? Boy, I'll tell you, that dress looks like a million dollars on you. I mean it.'" Frank took a beat. "The teller smiled, enjoying the attention, feeling good about herself. I said, 'Listen, ma'am, I don't mean to be rude, but this is a hold up. I'm out of work and have a family to feed.' I let that sink in and said, 'No dye packs if you please. And, of course, you know the money's insured, you're not gonna lose your job or anything like that.' The teller said: 'Well, here you go, sir. I hope your luck changes. All I've got is five thousand dollars, I hope it helps.' You believe it?"

"That's awful, taking advantage of the homely."

"You think it's funny, though, don't you?"

Kate shook her head. "But I can see how it could work. The gentleman bank robber. You gave her compliments, and I'll bet she didn't get many."

The bartender put a beer in front of Frank and picked up the empty.

"The teller felt for you; she was sympathetic. That's a good strategy." Kate sipped her Coke. "Did you point a gun at her?"

"I never used a gun. Didn't have one. I've never even fired a gun."

"Come on."

"I'm serious. Walked in unarmed, walked out with cash."

"Just relying on your wits, huh? Where were these banks you hit?"

"I started in Detroit and then moved around the Midwest and East Coast. Your mother thought I had taken another job as a salesman." He held Kate in his gaze. "Thing I've never told anyone except Thompson, robbing banks was fun." Frank gave her his gentleman-bank-robber smile.

"I can't believe you're telling me this. I'd think you'd be sorry and embarrassed."

"I paid for it, so I guess I can say whatever I want."

Kate said, "How did you get caught?"

Frank drank his beer. "Broke my one rule: always work alone. Most I ever got at a bank was seven thousand five hundred dollars. This was a chance to get into the big leagues. One score, take you and your mom to LA, start over." Frank sipped his beer. "It was an armored truck heist. Ray Skinner came to me with the plan and it was a good one. The armored truck with two guards was going to be carrying the concessions and tickets sales from a week of games at Tiger Stadium. Skinner knew the pickup time and the route the armored truck would take to the National Bank of Detroit building at 611 Woodward Avenue."

"Were you carrying a gun that time?"

"Skinner offered me a .38, but I didn't take it." Frank tilted the beer bottle up and finished it. "The armored truck would be coming down an alley behind the bank building, and that's where one of Skinner's girlfriends was in a station wagon blocking the way. Poor girl didn't know what she was doing, didn't know she was breaking the law."

Kate said, "Did you know her?"

"I'd never seen her before. The armored truck had to stop. One of the guards, seeing this innocent-looking Japanese girl, got out to help her. Tried to push the car but couldn't do it so he waved at the driver to help him. While the guards were busy, we got in the armored truck. Skinner put it in reverse, turned around, and we drove away."

"What'd the guards do?"

"Ran after us."

"What happened to the girl?"

"She started the station wagon and took off. I never saw her again. Skinner drove to an abandoned building he had rented."

"How much did you get?"

"Four hundred fifty thousand dollars and change. We each took twenty-five grand and agreed to split the rest the next day. The police were waiting for me when I got home. They found the armored truck but not the money. They thought I hid it." Frank signaled the bartender for another one. "You can see why it's personal between us. You can see why I want to help you catch him. Skinner owes me eighteen years and two-hundred grand, plus interest."

"You really think you're going to get the money?" Kate's cell phone rang. She took it out of her purse, looked at the screen, and put it back. "Why did Ray Skinner return to Detroit?"

"I don't know that he ever left. He was set for quite a while."

"What can you tell me about him?" Kate said.

"He liked to play the horses. He used to hang around the stables, got to know the jockeys, paid them for the names of the fastest, most reliable horses."

"Where was this?"

"Hazel Park Raceway. Is he still at it? I have no idea."

"Well, it's a place to start." Kate sipped her Coke "What else did he like?"

"Making the scene. Good food and booze. Show me what you've got on him, photos, surveillance footage, information that hasn't been in the newspaper, things only the police know. Maybe it'll trigger something. I'd also like to see the bank surveillance footage a couple days before each robbery. Skinner would always check out a bank before he robbed it."

"Is that how you did it?"

"You bet."

"What did you look for?"

"The general layout, where the guard was, where the cameras were located."

"What I don't understand," Kate said, "Ray Skinner's hit six banks in less than two months. You'd think he'd know not to press his luck."

"As I told you, Skinner gambles, needs money for his habit."

Kate was tired, took a breath. "How old is he?"

"I don't know, my age, maybe a little older."

"So we've got a middle-aged man hanging out with a petite Asian girl or woman? That's an angle that hasn't been mentioned yet."

"Let that out, Skinner's gonna run." Frank drank some beer.

"Is he from Detroit? Does he have family in the area?"

"I don't know."

"Where did he go to school? Where did he live?"

"He never said." Frank picked up the bottle and drank some beer.

"Tell me about the party where you met him. Was Mom with you?"

Frank's face went blank. "I don't remember." He didn't want to go there, admit he was seeing someone on the side, having an affair.

"It was at an apartment downtown. I was introduced to Skinner and we talked for a while. Ray was an interesting guy."

"That's it?"

"I'd run into him occasionally. As I said, he was a scene maker."

"Sounds like you were too. Where was Mom while you were out on the town?"

"Home taking care of you."

"So you were fooling around, huh? Now it all makes sense."

"What're you talking about?"

"Leaving us," Kate said. "Getting a divorce."

"The divorce was your mother's idea."

"God, you're unbelievable. Do you take responsibility for anything?"

"Listen, I've got to get out of here, have a smoke."

"Don't like what you hear, change the subject, huh?"

Frank ignored her and signaled the bartender.

"I'll get this. You're a philandering ex-con without a job." Kate put thirty dollars on the bar top.

"You don't hold back, do you?"

When they were in the parking lot, he lit up, inhaling like he craved it. "When're you going back to work?"

"Soon as I'm cleared by the Marshals Service. Next week, I hope. Give me your number, I'll text you when I have everything."

"I don't have a phone."

"Why don't you get one, it might come in handy."

"I can't afford it."

"Rob a bank. That might be the only thing you're good at."

"I was thinking about it."

Kate gave him a hard look.

"I'm kidding," Frank said, breaking into a grin.

"Are you?"

TEN

MELVIN CALLED EARLY THE next morning, saying the PD had checked and interviewed the owners of the six cars that had been illegally parked on Griswold Street the afternoon the bank was robbed. "Four belonged to bank customers running in for a couple minutes to take care of business. But here's where it gets interesting. One of the cars, a Toyota sedan, had a stolen plate on it from a Ford Flex registered to Katy Dudley of Bloomfield Village. I visited Ms. Dudley, who was genuinely surprised to learn that the license plate on her vehicle had been stolen." Melvin paused, "Got anything for me?"

"Not sure. I want to look at the surveillance tapes from the banks that were hit one, two, three days before each robbery. I think the Shooter cased them in advance, wouldn't you? And I think he might have an accomplice."

"Whoa, hang on. Where's this coming from?"

"Something Mildred Washington said."

"And you didn't call me?" Melvin sounded annoyed.

"And the get-away car from bank number six might be a silver Toyota sedan. Get me the tapes, I hope I'll be able to tell you more."

•••

FRANK STOPPED BY MIDAFTERNOON. "What's happening?"

"Checking to see if Ray Skinner's in the system." Kate logged onto the National Crime Information Center and typed in Ray Skinner. She glanced at Frank. "There are two possible matches. One is Raymond L. Skinner, twenty-nine, doing time for selling ten kilos of Mexican heroin in Tucson, Arizona. Number two is Billy Ray Skinner, who would've been sixty-eight if he hadn't been murdered in prison forty-three years ago."

Kate read his sheet:

"Billy Ray was a career criminal, in and out of prison his whole adult life. Arrested for grand theft auto when he was eighteen, and kept going, moved onto armed robbery specializing in supermarkets and convenience stores."

Frank studied the mug shots.

Kate said, "Does he look familiar? Could this be your buddy's father?"

Frank gave her a dirty look. "First of all, he's not my buddy. And, yeah, it's possible. Our Ray Skinner has a similar face and build and the same shit-eating grin."

"But unlike his dad, it appears as though our Ray Skinner has never been arrested." Kate raised her hands over her head and stretched. "Listen, I've got to run out and pick up a few things. I'm out of milk, eggs, and coffee cream. Want to come?"

Kate drove her estranged, ex-con father to a shopping center and parked in the lot. Frank looked wide-eyed at the store front. "What's this?"

"Target."

"What do they sell?"

"Everything. You've never heard of Target?"

Frank shook his head.

"Need anything?"

"Do they have underwear? I've been wearing Thompson's since I got back."

Kate made a face. "TMI."

Frank looked at her with a question.

"It means 'too much information.'"

They went in and Kate led him to the men's department. "Pick what you want. I'll meet you at the cashier."

Ten minutes later, Frank, who looked embarrassed, handed her two three-packs of Hanes boxer briefs. "Can you get these for me?"

"Sure."

"I'll meet you outside. I'm gonna have a smoke."

Kate paid for the underwear, groceries, and a mobile phone for Frank.

Back in her apartment kitchen, Kate reached in the Target bag, grabbed Frank's two three-packs of underwear, and tossed them to him. "I don't know how to thank you. This is the first thing anyone's given me in a long time."

"I have something else for you." She reached into the bag, brought out the phone, and handed it to him. "It's a Samsung Galaxy J7 with twelve hours of talk time."

Frank looked at her like she was speaking Chinese.

"New underwear and a new phone. You're ready for anything."

Frank said, "I don't have anyone to call."

"What about me?"

"Okay, you."

Kate said, "You're going to meet people."

"I am, huh? Where?"

"I don't know, the bowling alley."

Frank frowned looking at the phone. "I don't know how to use it."

"I can show you in two minutes."

Frank smiled and said, "Thanks."

Kate's phone beeped. She dug it out of her pocket and checked the message.

"I want you to see something. I just got an e-mail from Melvin Weston with the Detroit police."

They sat side-by-side at Kate's desk, staring at the laptop screen, studying time-coded surveillance footage she was able to speed up, Frank watching, drinking beer. It was boring and uneventful till he said, "Can you stop it right there?"

Kate froze the frame. "That's him." Frank pointed to a man wearing a baseball cap and a Detroit Tigers jersey, walking into the bank. She advanced the tape a couple frames and now Ray Skinner was standing at the island counter where the deposit and withdrawal slips were stacked on shelves.

Kate said, "Looks like he's subtly checking out the room. And he walked out without making a transaction."

Frank said, "When was it robbed?"

"Two days later." Kate opened another file. "This is footage from the second bank."

They watched for a few minutes until Frank, on the edge of his seat, pointed at the screen. "You see her? The girl in the scarf."

Kate rewound a few frames and froze the image. The woman stood at the counter in the center of the lobby with a phone in her hand.

Frank said, "What's she doing?"

"Wants us to think she's checking her messages, but I think she's taking photographs of the bank." Kate zoomed in on her face. "Do you know her?"

"She looks Asian, but it's too grainy to make out her features."

"I can have it enlarged and enhanced, but let's keep going."

The same woman appeared again in the third bank that was hit. This time she wore sunglasses, hair pulled back in a ponytail. She had her phone out again, presumably taking pictures. Kate zoomed in on her face but it was too pixelated to identify.

In various disguises the mystery woman also appeared in the other banks a day or two before each was robbed.

Kate said, "What do you think?"

Frank sipped his beer. "Sure looks like the same girl."

"Well, if I wasn't convinced, I am now," Kate said. "She's getting Skinner what he needs, minimizing his risk." She printed and scanned the images and emailed them to Melvin Weston.

Her cell rang ten minutes later, Melvin saying, "Okay, I give up, who's this out-of-focus babe you keep sending pictures of?"

"The Shooter's partner in crime."

"How you know that?"

"A confidential informant." Kate smiled at Frank. "You can see her in five of the six banks just before they were robbed."

"Why do I get the feeling you're not telling me everything?"

"You want me to compromise the identity of my CI?"

"Think I'd lose sleep over that?"

"Can you have the frames cleaned up and send them back?" Kate paused. "Let's see if she's in the system. Find her, you're going to find him."

"I'll see what I can do," Melvin said and disconnected.

They moved into the kitchen, Frank leaning with an elbow on the counter. She got him another beer and poured herself a glass of wine.

"Let me ask you something. Do you have a boyfriend? You're good-looking and you're fun to hang out with. They should be fighting over you."

"I date. At first guys like the idea of going out with a deputy US marshal. They want to see my gun and hear stories about arresting fugitives."

"Yeah?"

"Then something happens." Kate sipped her wine. "I think they get intimidated."

"Find one that's confident, that can handle it."

She could hear Cornbread saying the same thing. "Easier said than done. Believe me, I'm looking."

"What about the guys you work with?"

Kate shook her head.

"I don't mean to give you the third degree."

"It's okay."

Frank finished the beer. "I better go. I've got to get Thompson's Honda back. I feel like I'm in high school, borrowing my parents' car.

"Call me later on your new phone."

Frank smiled, walked to the door, stopped and looked back at Kate. "Thanks again. I like spending time with you. You're a lot of fun."

"I like spending time with you too. Just hang in there, will you? I've got a good feeling you're going to turn things around."

•••

IN THE MORNING, MELVIN called and said, "Get the files?"

"I'm looking at them." Kate had taped five enhanced, retouched eight-and-a-half-by-eleven images of the Asian girl on the wall and was studying them with a magnifying glass, different angles that captured the details of her face. Kate guessed the woman was in her mid-to-late twenties.

"She doesn't have a starring role on NCIC, that's the first thing I checked," Melvin said. "I showed the pictures to a dude at the

Japan American Society. He wasn't one-hundred-percent positive, but thinks, based on the girl's facial features, she's Japanese." Now Melvin was humming a tune.

"Melvin, you sound happy, what's up?"

"Countdown to *retirement*. Three weeks."

"What if we don't catch the Shooter, you going to stay on finish the job?"

"McGraw, where'd you get your wicked sense of humor at?"

"The Japanese guy say anything else?"

"Axed me why the police were looking for her. I said, she is very likely a witness to a bank robbery. I just want to talk to her."

"You give him the photo?"

"Didn't feel right. You see *Rising Sun* with Sean Connery?"

"No, I missed that one."

"Bottom line, you can't trust them. See the picture, you'll understand what I'm saying. Japanese got their own way of doing things."

•••

FRANK CAME BACK AT five thirty and drank a Stella, looking at the enhanced, retouched images of the Asian woman taped to the wall.

Kate said, "Is that her?"

"Are you asking is this Ray Skinner's girlfriend from 1995? No way. You see how young she looks."

"I think we should send these photos to the security heads at all the banks in the metro area. They see her, tell them to contact Melvin Weston with the Detroit Police immediately."

Frank said, "You know what times the banks were robbed?"

That was an important piece of information she hadn't considered. "I think all of them were midafternoon, which makes sense. It's after lunch and before rush hour."

Now Frank was staring at the map of Detroit on the wall showing the locations of the banks that had been hit, numbered one through six. "What's the date of the last robbery?"

"August fourth," Kate said.

"So it's been a few weeks. I think he's cleared out, moved on."

"Maybe he's taking a break," Kate said, "letting things cool down. Isn't that how you did it?"

"I moved around. As you've probably noticed there're banks everywhere." Frank picked up a photo of the Asian girl. "You mind if I keep one of these?"

"What are you going to do with it?"

"Look for her."

"If you find her, don't do anything. Call me."

"And I need a shot of Ray."

Kate shuffled through the photos on her desk and picked up a headshot of Skinner dressed as a priest. "This is the best likeness of him."

ELEVEN

Frank parked Thompson's Honda in the huge racetrack lot that looked about three-quarters full on a weekday afternoon. Thompson, protective of his eleven-year-old car, always asked where Frank was going and when he'd be back.

The enlarged photo of the Asian girl was on the seat next to him. Frank studied her delicate features one more time: small nose, high cheekbones, dark eyes, wispy lashes. Part of her face hidden by a scarf. Then he looked at the shot of Skinner in the black shirt and priest's collar, face solemn as if he was about to hear confession.

Frank fit the sport cap low over his eyes and went inside. He bought a racing form and took the escalator up to the concourse. There were people in line at the ticket windows that ran along one wall, and more people sitting, staring at computer screens in a bullpen full of cubicles, everyone trying to beat the odds, strike it rich.

Frank wasn't a gambler and had never been to the track. He went out to the grandstand, scanned the crowd with their backs to him watching a race in progress, horses coming around the turn, thundering past the seats, and began to understand the appeal. It was exciting, and if you bet on the right horse you could make a lot of money.

When the race ended, the grandstand emptied. People headed for the cashier windows, bars, and restaurants. Frank stood on the concourse off to the side, pretending to study the racing form, scanning faces in the crowd. He noticed an Asian woman, maybe thirty, and followed her to the Homestretch Bar. The woman sat at a table with an Asian man who was Frank's age, maybe a little older.

Frank took an elevator to the fourth floor, sat at a table in the Park Grill, and ordered a beer. He opened the racing form, looking at the names of the horses in the next race: *Roll the Dice, Justified,* and *Sky's the Limit.* The purse was two-hundred grand— guaranteed. Late pick four. The post time was 4:50, which was in fifteen minutes.

After finishing his beer he went back to the grandstand. This time Frank sat high on the far-left side and could see everyone who walked in and out. He didn't notice any good-looking Japanese babes or Ray Skinner, and after the race decided to call it a day.

As he was driving out of the complex, Frank saw the stables, parked, and went in. A steward moved by him walking a horse. He stopped the old slouching black man. "Where're the jockeys?"

"They in the jockey room," he said, a cigar wedged in the corner of his mouth. He pointed to a separate wing of the stables. "Over there."

Frank opened the door, walked in a big room that had lockers on one side and a lounge on the other. The jockeys, in various stages of undress, were little dark-skinned guys who weighed just over a hundred pounds and wore brightly colored outfits. "Hey, how're you all doing?"

One angry shirtless shrimp stepped toward Frank. "You not allow in here."

Frank unfolded the piece of paper and showed it to him. "I am looking for my friend who has disappeared. It is important that I find him," he said, delivering the lines slowly, accentuating every word, assuming English wasn't the jockey's first language.

The jockey glanced at the photo, shook his head, and passed it to the others. One by one they looked at the picture, a few shook their heads, but now a few were nodding. A jockey in a red outfit said, "He come here, want to know about the horses. Ask what are the bests."

"When was the last time you saw him?"

"Four weeks." A jockey dressed in bright green said, handing him the photo.

"You talked to him, Mr. Skinner?"

"Yes, I talk to him."

"Did he have a woman with him?"

The jockey nodded. "She outside."

"But you saw her?"

The jockey nodded again. Frank unfolded a surveillance photo from one of the banks and handed it to him. "Is this her?"

The jockey stared at the photograph and nodded a third time.

TWELVE

Eıɢʜᴛ ıɴ ᴛʜᴇ ᴍᴏʀɴıɴɢ Kate sat across the desk from Chief Cliff Doven. "How do you feel, McGraw?"

"Good as new, Chief." She was still aware of the wound in her shoulder, felt the tightness when she moved, a constant reminder of having been shot. But it didn't hurt.

"You've been cleared for full duty. You're fit physically, but you're the only one who knows for sure if you're ready to come back. Do you have any psychological issues? Any concerns about going back in the field, facing armed fugitives?"

After what happened Kate *was* apprehensive. She didn't know how she would react in a threatening situation. But she wasn't going to admit it. The only way to know for sure was to stay on the task force. "I don't think so, sir." Immediately wishing she had been more positive, more enthusiastic.

"Why don't you take a little more time, think about it and get back to me? If you have concerns, we can go slow, put you on light duty or have you reassigned."

"No, sir. I can't tell you how much I've missed the field. Believe me, I'm ready. I'm so ready."

"That's what I want to hear."

The chief swiveled his chair, picked up a Glock on the credenza behind him, and handed it to her. "Your primary. Cleared by Investigations." The chief stood. "Come with me; I want to show you something."

Kate followed him out of his office and down the hall to the conference room. He opened the door and Kate saw the team: Charlie, Buck, and Cornbread standing there, smiling.

"Gentlemen, let me present Deputy US Marshal Kate McGraw, reinstated and ready for duty."

The guys clapped, and Kate blushed.

Cornbread said, "Good to have you back, QD. Wouldn't have thought you'd dog it so long. What's it been, four weeks?"

"Well, you know what a slacker I am—anything to get out of work." Kate panned the guys with her gaze. "What's been going on?"

"Same old," Cornbread said. "No shortage of warrants. Dudes is still out there breaking the law."

Charlie glanced at Cliff Doven. "Chief, you tell her about the judge?"

"Not yet." The chief turned and looked at Kate. "There's been a threat on Judge Gant's life. He asked that you be involved, put on the detail. Bring her up to speed. I've got a meeting." Chief Doven walked out of the room.

"Who made the threat?"

"White supremacist murderer, name of Vernon Meeks," Cornbread said. "Judge sentenced him to life without the possibility of parole."

"You've got to see this," Buck said, turning to his laptop, which was on the conference table. He opened the file, playing footage from one of the courtroom cameras. Meeks, in yellow jail fatigues, hands cuffed to a leather transport belt, ankles manacled to a fifteen-inch chain, listened to the verdict without expression.

Judge Gant said, "Mr. Meeks, do you have anything to say?"

Vernon Meeks got to his feet and said, "You know what my verdict is? I'm sentencing you to death." Vernon started toward the bench. "Ain't nowhere you can go that's safe."

Sheriff's deputies took Vernon down and carried him out of the courtroom. The judge disappeared into his chambers.

Charlie said, "All right, you see what we're dealing with."

"Welcome back," Buck said and grinned. "What's the difference between God and a federal judge?"

"God doesn't think he's a federal judge," Kate said.

Cornbread said, "Judge Gant asked for you. You must know him, huh?"

"I worked court security for two years," Kate said. "Saw Steve 'the rock 'n' roll Judge' every day he wasn't sick or on vacation."

Cornbread smiled. "You there when he hit on the hot-looking defense attorney?"

"He didn't hit on her," Kate said. "He asked her out."

Charlie Luna said, "During a trial?"

"During her cross," Kate said.

Charlie said, "Come on. What'd he say?"

"Judge Steve said, 'Counselor, there's something different about you. What is it, your hair? That a new look?' Now clearly flustered, she said, 'With all due respect your honor, I'm in the middle of questioning a witness.' Judge Steve said, 'Let's have dinner.' She said, 'Your honor, I'm married.' Judge Steve said, 'I won't tell if you won't.'"

Cornbread glanced at her. "How's the man get away with that?"

"He's a federal judge," Kate said.

Charlie said, "How well you know him?"

"I've picked him up, taken him home. Had lunch with him, hung out in his chambers, watched him play air guitar. He has an extensive collection of albums. Big Brother and the Holding Company, Jimi Hendrix, Led Zeppelin. And His Honor gets high, smokes medical marijuana for his bad back."

Cornbread, eyes fixed on Kate said, "Judge Steve ever make a move?"

"He never stopped. He'd invite me to concerts, to his house for dinner. In his chambers he'd tell me I looked tense and needed a back rub. He'd change his clothes in front of me, and he doesn't believe in underwear."

Charlie said, "Why didn't you say something?"

"I wasn't worried. I kept my distance and never took him seriously. I'd say, 'Come On, your honor, let's be professional.'"

Buck said, "The judge buy that?"

"Are you kidding? He'd try again. You can't offend or embarrass him." Tired from standing, Kate sat at the conference table.

Charlie said, "You all right?"

"I'm fine."

"How old is he?" Buck said.

"Fifty," Kate said. "Seems younger 'cause of his attitude, thinks he's cool. Judge Steve's been married three times, currently divorced."

"Some dudes never learn," Cornbread said.

"Last I heard he was dating a stripper who works at the Bottoms Up Gentlemen's Club, which seems fitting," Kate said. "How credible is the threat?"

"You saw Vernon Meeks," Cornbread said. "Think he's playin'?"

"You know what people say after they're convicted," Kate said. "In the heat of the moment."

Charlie said, "Know anything about him?"

Kate shook her head.

"He's chancellor of a Neo-Nazi organization called the Aryan Knights. Shock troops for the hoped-for revolution. Buck opened another file. Vernon Meeks' face filled the screen. He had a shaved head, a swastika inked on his forehead, and hate in his eyes. "Vernon was convicted of murdering his girlfriend's husband. Here's the full list of charges: first degree murder, use of a firearm, and mutilation of a dead human body. First Vernon stabbed the poor guy four times with a kitchen knife and then shot him."

"What was the cause of death?"

"Lead poisoning," Charlie said. "They cut the poor man's private parts off, kept them in a mason jar in the refrigerator." Charlie made a face. "You believe what people do to each other? I'm always amazed."

Cornbread said, "Then they cut the man up while they were high on crystal meth. Took place over three days. You can look at it if you want. Vernon's naked the whole time except for his white socks. It's all on video. I've never seen anything like it."

"When this dude says the judge isn't safe," Charlie said, looking at Kate, "I think we better take him at his word."

Kate said, "What makes it federal?"

"Vernon's organization traffics methamphetamine across state lines," Cornbread said.

Charlie got up, eyes on Buck. "Take us through these, will you?"

"I want to show you Vernon Meeks's freedom fighters. If anyone's gonna be coming after the judge these are the ones likely to be on the first team." Buck opened a file and Kate looked at a face that was blue and green, ninety percent of his skin covered with tats. "This good-looking gent is Bud Teague. Did eight years for assaulting a homeless black man with an iron pipe. As Bud put it when he was arrested, 'I was drunk, bored, and decided to go fuck somebody up.'"

The next guy had a shaved head and a tat on his forehead that read *I am a white man.*

"Forgot one word," Cornbread said. "Dumb."

Buck said, "This matinee idol is Emmett Parnell, goes by Clyde. You would too, somebody named you Emmett."

"What's his claim to fame?" Kate said.

"Carrying a concealed weapon," Buck said, "drunk driving, and failure to pay alimony."

Kate said, "He sounds like an altar boy compared to the others."

Buck opened another file, brought up a photograph—this one showing a man from the waist up. "And the cream of the crop is Lowell Hodge."

Lowell wasn't wearing a shirt and had assorted tats covering his pale muscular arms and torso. "He did five years in the Florida State Prison at Raiford for armed robbery. Lowell was released and moved back to Michigan, where he was originally from. Then he was convicted for aggravated mayhem and battery and assault with a deadly weapon. Did eight years in I-Max and didn't come out any more agreeable."

"See that?" Cornbread said. "Got *skinhead* inked on his neck case he forgets what he is."

"They all look angry," Kate said, "or crazy. Probably both." She paused. "Has Judge Steve seen these?"

Charlie said, "I doubt it."

"I think it's a compelling argument for getting His Honor out of the city for a while," Kate said, "take him somewhere safe till things cool down."

Cornbread glanced at her. "Judge won't listen to us. Wants to stay in his house and won't change his schedule. He's full of himself."

"Doesn't know any better," Kate said.

"QD," Charlie frowned. "I don't want to put this on you, but you know the man. Want to give it a shot? Try to convince him to change his mind?"

No, Kate didn't, but she said, "I'll see what I can do."

THIRTEEN

Early afternoon Frank asked Thompson to come with him on an adventure.

Negative as always, he said, "Boy, I don't know. This sounds like trouble waiting to happen."

Frank guided them to the track. Thompson parked and said, "Okay, I give up. What the hell are we doing here?"

"I wanted to get you out of the house," Frank said.

"When did you decide you were in charge of my life?"

"You're a shut-in. Jesus. You don't do anything."

"I'm on the straight and narrow, trying to stay out of trouble."

Frank said, "How long are you gonna use that excuse?"

"It's been working for seven years," Thompson said.

"You've given up."

"What's it to you?"

"You need some excitement, you need to look at pretty girls, have a few drinks, let loose a little."

"This is your idea of having fun, huh?" Thompson said. The skin on his face looked bleached in the afternoon light, and his gray hair was almost white. "Think girls are gonna be interested in me, you better try again." He turned off the car and opened the door. "Well, what're you waiting for?"

It was four o'clock when they took the escalator up to the concourse. Frank stopped at a ticket window and asked what time the thoroughbreds ran.

"Listen," he said to Thompson, "we've got almost an hour till the next race. Let's have a drink." Frank took him to the Raceway Lounge, where races from different parts of the country were simulcast on a giant screen. The sat at a table and ordered beers. Horses were lined up in the starting gate. The race was about to begin.

Thompson said, "Where's this at?"

"How do I know?"

A rheumy-eyed old man at the table next to them said, "It's the Santa Ysabel Stakes for three-year-old fillies. Zippity Do-Dah's racing."

Frank said, "Who's Zippity Do-Dah?"

The man put his hand up to halt the conversation. Frank watched the race, one horse pulled away from the pack to win.

When it was over the senior fixed his attention on them again. "Where you been, the polar ice cap? Zippity Do-Dah's the unbeaten filly champion of 2018—just caught Not Now Mary on the wire. Talk about a grade one win. This year, as you just saw, Zippity's the best three-year-old by a pole. Youngster showing athleticism and gears."

Thompson finished his beer, and under his breath said, "I've heard enough horse racing bullshit for one day. Let's get the hell out of here."

They still had half an hour and went to the Homestretch, sat at the bar, and ordered beers. Frank looked to his left and noticed an over-the-hill blonde, early forties, sitting two seats away. She was drinking hard liquor and showing its effects. "How's it going? I'm Frank, and this handsome devil is Bill Thompson."

"Jesus, my lucky day."

She wore a tank top revealing a pair of tired knockers and had a starchy head of blonde hair that was being overtaken by her gray-brown natural color. She got up and moved next to Frank.

"What do you two captains of industry do?"

"We're retired bank robbers."

"I'm impressed." She shook the ice cubes in her empty glass. "I'll have Kessler's on the rocks."

Frank said, "What's your name?"

"Crystal."

"Crystal, huh? I guess we better handle you with care."

"That's original. Haven't heard that one since this morning." She brought the glass to her mouth, tilted it, and an ice cube slid in. "That's sarcasm, in case you don't recognize it."

Frank looked at the clock over the bar and said, "Crystal, we'd love to stay and get to know you. I'll bet you're a fascinating person, but we have to go. However, good luck to you."

"You cheapskate bullshitter."

"Well she's got you down," Thompson said as they walked toward the grandstand. "Why were you wasting your time on her?"

"I was doing it for you."

"Me?"

"When's the last time you got laid?"

"Couple years ago. I had something going with a woman in the neighborhood."

"What happened?"

"Her husband got released from county," Thompson said. "All I needed was to get on his radar."

"What'd he do?"

"She never said. I think it was assault with intent." Thompson took a beat. "What about you, how long's it been?"

"Eighteen years, four months, and five days—but who's counting?"

Thompson grinned. "I think you wanted Crystal for yourself. Handle with care, my ass. You could throw her out of a moving car and not hurt a hair on her head."

Frank led the way to the grandstand. He scanned the crowd top to bottom, section by section. At one point Thompson turned to him. "What the hell are you looking at? I thought you wanted to watch the thoroughbreds."

Frank wasn't listening. His gaze was fixed on a couple two sections over and a couple rows below them. It was the woman's hat that caught his attention, and as she turned her head to watch the horses coming around the turn, he could see she was Japanese, or at least Asian. The guy next to her was white and well-dressed, binoculars pressed to his eyes as the horses passed in a tight group shaking the building.

When the race was over, Frank said, "I've got to check something, meet you at the car in ten minutes."

Thompson said, "You going back to see Crystal, get her phone number?"

"You can see right through me, can't you?"

"All right. I'll pick you up in front. Just make it quick."

Frank watched the Asian girl and the guy walk up the stairs and followed them to the cashier windows, waited while they claimed their winnings, and when the guy turned, Frank felt a jolt of adrenaline kick in as he recognized Ray Skinner, Ray smiling, folding a wad of bills into his sport coat pocket.

Thompson's car was parked twenty feet from the door when Frank came out of the Club House. As Frank was getting in, he saw Skinner and the girl come out, Skinner handing a ticket to the valet.

Thompson put it in gear and started to pull away. Frank said, "Hang on a minute."

"Now what?" Thompson said.

"I need you to follow someone."

Thompson shrugged, gave him a puzzled look. "Is this a joke?" Now Thompson smiled. "Oh, I get it, you want to see where she lives."

"Just do me this favor, will you?" Frank pointed at a Cadillac driving by them. "There she is."

"That old bag drives a Caddy? No way," Thompson said. "I think you can do a lot better."

Thompson started to complain again as they drove into downtown Detroit. "Listen, I can give you a few more minutes but I've gotta stop before we run out of gas."

The gas gauge registered an eighth of a tank. "We'll make it," Frank said.

"You know where we're going?"

"Not exactly. But I think we're close."

Thompson sighed and shook his head. "You know how dumb that sounds?"

A few minutes later, Frank said, "Let's head back the other way."

Thompson made the turn and Frank saw Skinner's Cadillac creeping along in bumper-to-bumper traffic a couple cars ahead of them. And now Thompson saw the the big green sign and caught on. TUNNEL TO CANADA "I'm not going to Canada so you can get laid."

"Come on. I'll buy you dinner, take you to a strip club. When's the last time you had a lap dance from a naked girl?"

FOURTEEN

R AY SAW THE HONDA as they drove through the racetrack parking lot, one man getting in, another behind the wheel, saw it again on the freeway, and saw it a third time as he drove through the tunnel into Canada, the Honda a couple booths to his left, waiting to clear customs.

Was it the same car? Was he being paranoid? Ray didn't believe in coincidences, and that was one of the reasons he'd never been caught, had never been arrested. Twenty-seven years on the job and the police had never gotten close. Didn't seem to have a clue who he was or where he was gonna hit next.

When it was his turn, Ray stopped at the customs booth and handed his and Yumi's Canadian passports to a model-pretty brunette in a blue uniform, a matte black semiautomatic on her hip. She glanced at the passports and handed them back.

He went left on Ouellette Avenue and left on Erie Street, found a parking space across from Spago. "Are you hungry? It's a little early for dinner but I'm starving."

Yumi smiled. "How did you know? You read my mind. I was just thinking about linguine di mare and here we are."

Ray was thinking about the Honda as he looked in the rearview and side mirrors, watched several cars pass, didn't see it and opened the door. Yumi got out on her side, and they crossed the street.

It was crowded but Nick, the maître d', saw Ray and escorted them to a window table with a street view.

The waiter introduced himself and Ray ordered veal scaloppini and a bottle of Chianti and linguini ai frutti di mare for Yumi.

"I know you don't want to hear this," Yumi said. "We're out of money."

"What do you mean? I just won twelve hundred dollars."

"Are we going to rob another bank?"

"Unless we're planning to get jobs. Can you imagine?"

The waiter brought the wine. Ray tried it and nodded. The waiter poured them each a glass and walked away.

"Let me do the next one if you don't want to," Yumi said. "I can rob a bank."

"Whoa, hang on a second." Ray grinned, picturing this little dink of a girl—barely weighed a hundred pounds soaking wet—walking up to a teller window and drawing a gun. "Think you've got the nerve? 'Cause you've only got one chance to pull it off, or you're gonna spend the next twenty years in a federal penitentiary."

"It's easier than you think."

"Is that right?" Ray paused. "I forget, how many banks have you robbed?"

Yumi gave him a dirty look.

"Tell me how you'd do it."

She drank some wine. "I'd walk up to the teller, put a hand in my purse, and say, 'I have a gun. Give me twenty-five thousand dollars and no dye packs or I will shoot you and anyone who gets in my way.'"

"You know, that's not bad." He sipped some wine. "Let me see your game face."

Yumi gritted her teeth and fixed her dark eyes on him. She was convincing.

Ray smiled.

Yumi said, "Are you making fun of me?"

"No. I think you could do it, but we've got a system that works. Why change it?"

"I thought you were getting tired."

"Why would you say that?"

"'Cause it's been a few weeks," Yumi said, "and we're almost out of money."

"Let me worry about that."

"I am concerned about your gambling."

She wouldn't look at him, eyes on the table. That was the boldest thing she'd ever said. What was going on? Yumi'd been the model of Japanese subservience since he'd met her.

When the food came she dove into the pasta. Ray was preoccupied, sipped Chianti, glancing out the window, watching cars pass. Yumi said, "What do you keep looking at?"

"I think someone followed us from the track."

She put her fork down, her dark laser eyes boring into him. "Were you going to tell me?"

"Isn't that what I'm doing?" Where'd this new self-assertiveness, this new feminism come from? He'd always been partial to Orientals 'cause they didn't get in his business and did what they were told. Ray liked Yumi but he wasn't gonna take this.

"How would anyone know we were going to be at the track?"

"Unless they've seen us before."

Yumi frowned. "What are you talking about?"

"Take things for granted—that's how you get caught and sent to prison."

"Ray, I don't understand." Yumi dabbed her little mouth with the napkin. "You are usually so confident."

"It has nothing to do with confidence. It's about trusting yourself, trusting what you see, especially if it's out of context."

"Whatever that means."

Ray paid in cash, as always, and took a circuitous route to the apartment—no sign of the Honda. He checked the camera in each of the rooms, seeing only the two of them recorded that morning. He deleted the footage and turned off the cameras.

He walked out to the balcony, tilted the telescope, and scanned the street eight floors below from east to west, and then the parking area, taking his time, holding on each car before moving on. He didn't see anyone in any of the cars. Ray raised the telescope, focusing on the park across the street. There were couples holding hands and small groups of people cooking on the grills, making dinner.

Ray's first instinct was to run, but now thought he might be overreacting. The beat-up old Honda and the guys who were in it had looked too old, too desperate to be undercover law enforcement. But he kept going back to them and couldn't help but think that was the point. If you were a manhunter, you had to blend in; you didn't want to call attention to yourself.

Yumi appeared, coming into the living room in her robe. "Are you still worried about the men you saw?"

"No, I think I was wrong."

"If you want to go, I can be ready in five minutes."

Now, as Ray saw it, she was trying to make up for getting out of line earlier. He was thinking about what she'd said in the restaurant. "I can rob a bank." Maybe he should take her up on it. See how good she was.

Yumi untied the sash and now he could see she was bare naked underneath it. "Ray, let me help you relax, clear your mind," she said, showing a seductive side he'd never seen before.

FIFTEEN

KATE MET JUDGE GANT in his chambers after court, a rock tune on low volume in the background.

"You know who this is?"

Kate shook her head.

"Iron Butterfly. 'In-A-Gadda-Da-Vida.'" He turned up the volume and started singing: *"In a gadda da vida, honey / Don't you know that I love you?"*

"We have to talk." She waited, trying to get his attention.

Judge Steve rubbed his jaw and turned the music down. "McGraw, I think highly of you. That's why I specifically asked for you to be on my security detail."

"Your honor, I'm worried. I saw the footage of Vernon Meeks threatening you in the courtroom. I saw what Vernon and his girlfriend did to her husband. And I've seen the criminal histories of several of Vernon's associates."

"I know who they are. I saw them in court every day, mouthing off during the trial."

"Are you concerned?"

"Not especially."

"Well, I'll tell you the Marshals Service is. We'd feel a lot better taking you somewhere safe till all this blows over."

"Yeah, but I wouldn't. It's a big inconvenience. Do you have any idea how many threats I've received in twenty-three years on the bench?" Judge Steve lifted the robe over his head now and folded it on the back of a chair. "More than you can imagine."

"It only takes one."

"I'm in the middle of a trial." He combed his dyed dark hair back with his fingers. "There was a threat made by a gangbanger about five years ago. I packed my things and moved to a safe house for a month 'cause this wacko I put away said he was going to put out a contract on me. You know what happened?" Judge Steve paused for effect. "Nothing. He was all talk."

"You sound like you're disappointed. I'd say you were lucky. This time you may not be. Vernon Meeks's skinheads are bad guys."

"I've got you to protect me. Do what you have to do, but I'm not leaving my house." Judge Steve grinned. "Listen, I'm a good cook. I might even make you dinner."

"This isn't a social occasion."

"We can make it anything we want. We can sit around worried, or we can enjoy ourselves." Judge Steve winked at her and took off his white shirt and tie. He was wearing a *Protomartyr* T-shirt underneath. He took off his suit pants, standing there half naked. Kate turned her head as he slid into a pair of faded Levi's. Now he slipped on a summer-weight sport jacket and looked like a record producer. "What should we do, sit fearfully in a dark room with shotguns slung across our legs?"

That's not a bad idea, Kate was thinking. "Judge, I am asking you to work with us. Believe me, we have your best interests in mind." Kate took a beat. "I want you to leave your car here. I'll give you a ride home and someone will pick you up in the morning."

"I need groceries. I'm out of everything."

"Make a list; I'll have someone get what you need."

"You think I'm going to let somebody squeeze my melons?"

Nothing was easy with this guy, but Kate kept her cool. "You trust me, don't you?"

He ignored her and said, "All right, here's the way we're going to do it. I'll drive my own car. On the way home I am going to stop and pick up a few things at the market. You can come with me or wait in the parking lot, whatever you like."

"Judge, you're making it difficult to keep you safe."

"Maybe I need marshals who are more confident and better prepared."

That was classic Judge Steve, dissing the deputies putting their lives on the line for him.

Twenty minutes later, Kate, wearing her heavy vest and duty belt, met the judge as he pulled out of the parking garage in a Mercedes coupe. He stopped and lowered the window. "Judge, I'd like you to stay behind us." She pointed to Charlie Luna parked on the street in a minivan. "We're going to be the lead vehicle. And Deputy Marshals Terrell Reed and Sam Dodge will follow you." Kate pointed to Cornbread's Bonneville. "Where are we going?"

"Eastern Market."

Four thirty in the afternoon, Charlie was driving the speed limit on I-75 when Judge Gant pulled out of the convoy, passed them, and waved.

Charlie let out a breath. "You believe this guy?"

The radio crackled. "The hell's goin' on?" Cornbread said.

Kate picked up the handset. "The judge is playing by his own set of rules. Are you surprised?"

They caught him exiting on Russell Street and followed him to the market, the marshals' G-rides screeching to a stop behind the judge. Kate was standing next to his car as he got out. "Your Honor, what were you thinking? That crazy move compromised your security."

"Your friend was driving like an old lady. I think you're taking this a little too seriously. Lighten up." Judge Steve closed the door, locked the car, and crossed the street.

Kate stayed close, moving through the crowded open-air market, scanning the melting pot of black, white, Arab, and Hispanic people around her. She was keeping an eye on the judge as he wheeled his cart into the produce section. Steve examined the cantaloupes, caressing and smelling them. Charlie was twenty feet to her left. Buck and Cornbread were twenty feet behind her.

•••

"WANT TO SEE HOW good they are?" Lowell said to Emmett. "Look and learn." Standing just outside the market he saw Rooster make his move, walking across the congested floor toward the judge, Rooster in a tank top, arms and face inked with Nazi words and symbols. He had a wild shock of red hair, "Heil Hitler" on his forehead, and he held a hunting knife down his leg. Rooster attracted attention, and that was the idea. People noticed him and moved out of the way.

When he got close to the judge, the girl marshal did some kind of karate move, took the knife out of Rooster's hand, put him on the floor, and cuffed him while the other three marshals rushed to help her.

"Look at that, will you?" Lowell said. "The heavy hand of law enforcement violating the boy's constitutional rights."

"At times I feel like I'm living in a socialistic country," Emmett said.

Lowell had no idea what he was talking about, and let it go. The good news: he'd seen the judge's protection detail in action and wasn't impressed.

Lowell followed the judge and the four marshals in their three-car convoy to a house in West Village, a slick-looking neighborhood of old homes and mansions.

•••

FRANK SAT IN THE loud, crowded bar, drinking his second shot and beer. It had been a stressful day. An attractive, well-dressed woman, maybe forty, walked up to him and said, "Is this seat taken?"

"It's all yours."

She sat and he smelled perfume. "I'm Peggy."

"Frank."

She offered her hand and they shook. "What're you drinking?"

"Maker's Manhattan—up. What can I get you?"

"A martini with blue cheese olives."

Frank signaled the bartender, ordered Peggy's cocktail and another round for himself. "What do you do?"

"I'm a realtor. Residential, homes, and condos. I'm not used to going out by myself. I was married for twenty-six years. And now, thank God, I'm divorced."

"You sound relieved," Frank said.

"I'm free."

"I am, too."

"Did you just get a divorce?"

"No, I just got out of federal prison."

"Come on," Peggy smiled. "What were you in for?"

"Robbing an armored truck."

"Are you serious?"

The bartender brought their drinks and took Frank's empty.

"Listen, if you want to leave, get up and run, I don't blame you."

"Are you kidding?" Peggy smiled. "I've got to hear *this*."

•••

KATE AND CHARLIE SAT in Charlie's G-ride on the driveway apron behind the judge's house as the sun was setting. Cornbread and Buck were in front. The skinhead suspect they had taken down at Eastern Market had violated his parole and was in custody at the Wayne County Jail. His name was Ron Fleck. Kate was fairly certain that Ron's sudden appearance moving toward the judge was planned. He had purpose. The skins were trying to see how well-protected His Honor was.

"I'm gonna tell dispatch where we're at." Charlie picked up the radio handset. "Unit 125."

"Go ahead 125."

"We're sitting code at 2365 Seminole Street, West Village, Detroit. Negative ET."

"10-4."

Two hours later Kate could see Judge Steve in the kitchen window waving to her. Still not taking the situation seriously, he had asked her to come in twice, once to taste his coq au vin and the second time to hear a song. Her phone beeped. Assuming it was the judge calling again she said hello.

"How're you doing?"

It was Frank, and he sounded buzzed. She glanced at Charlie. "I've got to take this." Kate got out of the car, moved to the garage, and went in the side door, looking at Judge Steve's Mercedes in one space and an old Corvette in the other.

"Hey, you there?"

"You sound like you've been drinking."

"I've had a few," Frank said. "I got something to tell you, something important."

"I'm on duty. I'll call you in the morning."

"Wait…" he said before she disconnected.

Kate got back in the car.

Charlie gave her a look and said, "There a problem?"

"No. My father checking in."

"I thought he took off when you were a kid."

"He did. And now he's back. I'll tell you about it later." Kate's phone rang, and she thought it was Frank calling again. This time it was the judge. She listened and turned off the phone. "His Honor feels like a prisoner in his own house. Wants my help with something."

"You think he was gonna be this needy, this much trouble?"

"I think he's just getting started."

•••

CORNBREAD, SITTING LOW IN the driver's seat, Buck next to him, had watched people pass them walking their dogs, jogging, riding bikes, glancing at the car. Earlier, two concerned black dudes in suits—at first Cornbread thought they were Jehovahs—walked up to the car, stood at the side window that was down all the way.

"Who are you?" the one wearing black horn rims said. "What are you doing here in our neighborhood?"

"We're police officers," Cornbread said, showing his marshals star on a chain around his neck.

"There a problem?"

"Keeping an eye on His Honor, Judge Gant. You got nothing to worry about."

"All right, have a good evening, officers."

This was always a concern doing surveillance. People noticed a car they'd never seen before parked for an extended period of time. The marshals tried to fit in, look like they belonged, but it didn't always work.

West Village was an exclusive neighborhood back in the day. And now thanks to mostly young white and African American professionals renovating the stately old houses, the hood was making a comeback. This is where Cornbread would live if he could afford it.

They'd been sitting code four hours, watching the computer screen that showed different angles of the exterior and interior from security cameras that had been installed. And even after the sun went down and the windows were open, it was hot, Cornbread's wet ass sticking to the cracked leather seat of the Bonneville. He could feel sweat rolling down his body under the Detroit Lions T-shirt. He'd taken his vest off and draped it over the seat back. They were parked at the curb one house north of the judge's. Cornbread could see the rear end of Charlie's G-ride on the driveway behind the house.

Buck was eating a second cold Spam sandwich, washing it down with a can of Dad's Cream Soda, the smell of fried pork shoulder hanging in the hot humid air. Between bites, Buck talked about going to South Dakota on his next vacation to hunt Pronghorn antelope.

"You spend your work hours hunting fugitives," Cornbread said, "and then for fun you go hunt animals. Explain that to me, will you?"

"It's exciting."

"You got a high-powered rifle, what's the antelope got?"

"It can run fifty-five miles an hour."

Cornbread glanced at him in disbelief. "Come on."

"I'm serious. But you got to find them first, and when you take the shot you're usually a few hundred yards away."

"Where you stay at?"

"In a tent."

"Where you take a shower at, like a campground?"

"You don't." Buck grabbed his crotch. "After a few days you start to get gamey."

Cornbread made a face. "How long you do this for?"

"A week, sometimes ten days."

"And you're volunteering. Nobody's forcing you, huh?"

•••

KATE HEARD "WELCOME TO the Jungle" and got a whiff of high-grade hydroponic as she stepped into the kitchen—her third time in the house. Judge Steve was on the other side of the island counter, eyes closed, lost in the moment, playing air guitar. "Want a hit?" He came around the counter, offering her the joint.

"Will you put that away, please?"

"I have a card. It's perfectly legal. He brought the joint to his mouth and blew out smoke. "Relax, will you? How about a glass of wine?"

"Do you remember why we're here?"

•••

NOW CORNBREAD WAS WATCHING QD and the judge on the laptop monitor and saw light glance off the rearview mirror, headlights approaching from behind. A slow-moving car stopped in front of the judge's house for several seconds and then came toward them, beams of light angling through the interior as the car passed. It was an old Crown Vic.

"See who was in it?" Buck said.

Cornbread shook his head and looked at the clock on the dash that read eight-forty-two. "Could be another neighbor checking us out. We'll see." He flipped the tac vest over his head and adjusted the straps. Headlights lit up the mirror again. He gripped the Glock holstered at his side. Buck turned, looking at the approaching car. It slowed in front of the judge's again before passing them, the same Crown Vic. "That's twice. Get ready for an encore." Cornbread picked up the radio. "Got company coming, stay alert."

Charlie said, "How many perps?"

"Unknown," Cornbread said.

Cornbread saw another car approaching, and unholstered his primary. Buck pulled the charging handle on the AR-15. Expecting the Crown Vic, Cornbread was surprised when an old rusted-out Chrysler passed them.

•••

KATE'S PHONE BEEPED. IT was Charlie. "We got trouble. Take the judge to his bedroom and lock the door. I'll come up and get you when it's safe."

"I have to take you upstairs."

"I thought you'd never ask."

"Listen to me. There are men here to kill you. Do you understand?" Kate locked her arm around the judge's and pulled him across the kitchen into the foyer.

"I don't believe I've made it with a female marshal."

"Is that what you think this is about? Your Honor, will you do me a favor? Get your head out of your ass and go up to your room."

He grinned again. "Are you grounding me?" He held onto the banister going up, Kate nudging from behind, trying to hurry him. At the top of the stairs Judge Steve went left into the master bedroom. She followed him and locked the door. The room was huge, thirty-by-forty, extending from the front of the house to the back. There was a four- posted king-size bed, and a furniture grouping in front of a fireplace. "Stay away from the windows." Kate turned off the light on the bedside table.

"What am I supposed to do?"

"Go in your dressing room and don't make any noise."

"I have to use the bathroom."

"All right. Do it quick. Don't turn on a light, and stay away from the windows." Kate crossed the dark room, stood at the side of a front window, glancing down at the street, and saw Cornbread's Bonneville. She went to the rear window, looking down at Charlie's G-ride on the driveway apron. Her phone buzzed. Charlie said, "What's your status?"

SIXTEEN

BUD TEAGUE RODE PRESIDENTIAL, occasionally leaning between the front seats. "Why'd you boost this rust bucket?" Lowell said in the front passenger seat. "Couldn't find anything older, huh?" He had the shotgun barrel angled on the floor mat, stock leaning against the seat.

"You said pick something that'd blend in. That's what I done. I'd a checked with you there was time," Bud said. "Got your approval."

"You getting smart?" Lowell said, glancing over his shoulder.

Bud didn't say anything. Boy knew when to keep his mouth closed.

Emmett pulled over behind a parked car on Orleans Street and cut the lights. Toad came out of the shadows and got in next to Bud.

"Hello, hello," Toad said.

Lowell said, "Ready to rumble?"

"Oh, yeah."

Toad was a chubby, bug-eyed redneck who felt a profound kinship with Vernon Meeks' skins. He was all for purging the mongrels from our great country, and if he had to, he'd lay his own life down for the *cause*. Lowell wished he had a hundred—no, make that a thousand—more like the Toadster. Jesus, they could kick some serious ass.

A few minutes later they were passing dark houses on the dark street. Everything looked different from when they'd come by that afternoon. Emmett, behind the wheel, glanced across the interior and out the side window. "That's it right there, I'm not mistaken." Emmett slowed the car and stopped.

Lowell could see lights on in the downstairs rooms. They continued on, passed the judge's house, and Lowell saw the sedan with the two marshals parked on the street. "See 'em?" he said to Bud Teague. "Mr. John E. Law and his partner still waitin' to surprise us. I got an idea—let's surprise *them*."

Emmett said, "How do you know for sure the judge is even in there?"

"He was earlier," Lowell said. "You were with me. You did see him, didn't you?"

"Yeah, I seen him."

"Then what's the problem?"

"They could've moved him."

"Uh-huh," Lowell said. "Then why've those two marshals been settin' there almost five hours?"

"Throw us off the trail," Emmett said, smiling like he was proud of himself.

"That what you'd do, you was plannin' this operation?"

"I don't know," Emmett said. "I'd have to think about it."

"While you're thinkin', go around the block and turn off the lights." Compared to Emmett, Bud and Toad were neurosurgeons.

Bud Teague opened the rear door, looked at his watch, and said, "Okay, we hit at quarter till." Lowell watched him walk between two houses that had lights on to the fence that bordered the judge's backyard.

Headlights still off, Emmett went back around the block, eased the Chrysler to the curb, and killed the engine. Lowell looked at the judge's house and then straight ahead at the three parked cars in front of them, trying to see the old Pontiac the marshals were in. It was still there about seventy yards down the street. Lowell looked at his watch, four minutes till the action was set to begin. "Sure you can handle them?"

"Do chickens have lips?" Emmett racked the High Standard Flite King twelve gauge.

Toad said, "Mr. Hodge, what do you want me to do?"

In all the commotion Lowell'd forgot about the Toadster. "I want you to go to the south side of the residence." He pointed. "See that porch?"

"Yes, sir."

"Break in the house, find the judge, and kill him."

"Sure, no problem."

Lowell handed him a Ruger Nine.

"I've got this too." Toad held up an Elk Ridge hunting knife that had a brass pommel. "The judge, you want me to gut him, skin him, or carve him?"

"That's up to you. But you're gonna have to do it fast."

Toad got out and crouched along the chest-high shrubs between the judge's house and the neighbor's. When he reached the screened-in porch, he looked back at the street, saw Emmett strolling past the parked cars forty yards from the target with two minutes to go. He walked to the edge of the house, where the side and back met, saw a car on the driveway apron, couldn't tell if someone was in it or not. And then Bud Teague appeared, shotgun leveled, standing partially concealed by tall shrubs in the garden. Toad checked his watch—a minute and a half to go.

•••

KATE HEARD THE TOILET flush. The door opened, and Judge Steve came toward her. "This is ridiculous. I'm sitting up here like some kid who's being punished," he said, a hard edge to his voice now. "I'm going down to get a drink."

She'd had enough of Judge Steve's attitude. "No, you're not. You're going to do what I tell you. You're going to go in the dressing room and not make a sound."

He ignored her, moving toward the door, reaching to unlock it.

"Walk out of this room, I'll tase you."

"You wouldn't dare," he said with his back to her.

Kate slid the Taser out of a vest pocket and aimed it at him, thinking she should have done it earlier. He opened the door. "Ever been tased, Judge? It hurts like hell, knocks you down and takes your breath away." Kate had experienced it at the academy with the other recruits.

Judge Steve turned, now glaring at her. "McGraw, I'm going to report you for this."

"The skinheads are coming for you. You want to live? Listen to me."

He finally seemed to understand the seriousness of the situation. He went into the dressing room and closed the door.

Kate stood at the bedroom window, looking down at the street, studying the scene and thought she saw something. It took a couple seconds for her eyes to adjust to the darkness. A figure was moving along the line of parked cars in front of the house.

She took out her phone and punched in Cornbread's number. "Coming up behind you."

"Got him," Cornbread said. "Got a surprise for him."

•••

CHARLIE LUNA WAS IN the bushes behind the garage relieving himself after five hours when he saw a man with a shotgun moving across the backyard toward the house. He gripped his primary and slid it out of the holster. The man with the shotgun stopped at Charlie's G-ride, shielding his eyes from the flood lights on the back of the house, trying to see in the SUV.

Thirty feet from the man, now in a shooting stance, Charlie said, "US Marshal, drop your weapon." But the man had another idea and started to pivot with the shotgun. Charlie shot him twice. Going down, the man squeezed the trigger. The shotgun roared and blew a hole through the garage door. Charlie cuffed him and heard gunfire in front of the house. He got in the SUV, grabbed the radio, and said, "Unit 125, emergency situation at 2365 Seminole Street. Need immediate support."

"10-4 125."

•••

TOAD HEARD THE HARD blasts of shotguns sounding like bird season and telling him Emmett and Bud had hit their targets. He knocked out a glass pane with his elbow, reached in, and unlocked the door. He moved through the house checking rooms. No one around. Looked out the kitchen window, saw Bud laid out on the grass and knew he'd better get to it, find the judge and get her done.

When Toad got to the top of the stairs, he saw the girl marshal in the hall coming out of a bedroom, closing the door. She was in a vest, pistol in hand. They made split-second eye contact, Toad surprised by her presence, and by the look of things, she by his. He hesitated for an instant before squeezing the trigger, the high-caliber pistol exploding and kicking, making a racket in the narrow confines of the hallway, his ears ringing. Did the girl really think she was gonna take him?

The foxy marshal had disappeared, dove to the right into a room. Toad went after her, crouching low in the doorway, lights from the hall illuminating part of the floor. He moved through the room into the adjoining bathroom that led to another bedroom, and now he had a pretty good idea what she was up to.

•••

WHY DIDN'T SHE SHOOT the skinhead when she had the chance? You didn't hesitate in a situation like that. But he did too or she wouldn't be standing there. Kate remembered the photos of him, his bug eyes and white body covered with tats, but couldn't think of his name. She crept back to Judge Steve's bedroom and went in. The skinhead was behind His Honor, holding a knife to his throat.

"US Marshal, drop your weapon."

"Drop yours or I promise you I'll gut this Jew-boy."

"Do what he says," Judge Steve said.

Kate heard sirens and saw flashing emergency lights blinking off the front windows. "You hear what's going on out there? It's all over."

"It ain't over while I got this," he said, indicating the knife.

Judge Steve was a different person now, scared to death—not a hint arrogance or self-importance. The skinhead noticed it too. "What happened to the hard-ass, loud mouth? Big man in the courtroom surrounded by police. Aren't you gonna threaten to put me in prison, I don't leave your house?" The skinhead grinned, seemed to think he was in control.

Kate could see a wet spot appear in the crotch of Judge Steve's faded Levi's, widening, moving down one leg, and running out on the carpeted floor.

"Will you look at that. He ain't even house-broke."

Kate took a breath trying to calm herself. It was a tense situation. The judge's life was in her hands, the outcome her responsibility. "Why are you doing this? 'Cause Vernon Meeks told you to?"

"It's the natural order of things," the bug-eyed skin said, "survival of the fittest."

He pressed his knife against Judge Steve's neck.

"Drop it," Kate said. "Or I'll drop you."

"You got pluck; I'll give you that."

The skinhead was about the judge's height and was directly behind him. Her only target was the man's black boot angled just past Judge Steve's bare foot. Kate took a breath and—fighting her own resistance—raised the Glock and squeezed the trigger. First there was an explosion, then the skinhead dropped the knife and fell back on the floor, holding his damaged foot, face twisted in pain. Kate cuffed him and escorted Judge Gant out of the room.

"McGraw, I owe you an apology."

You owe me a helluva lot more than that, Kate was thinking.

•••

THERE WERE TWO DEAD: Bud Teague and Emmett Parnell. Gary Grabowski was in stable condition and on his way to the Detroit Medical Center with a gunshot wound in his right foot.

Kate stood on the judge's driveway with Charlie, watching the medical examiner leaning over the body of Bud Teague laid out on the lawn.

Charlie said, "You okay?"

"Still wound up."

"You did a helluva job. I don't think you could've handled the situation any better. Judge Gant owes you big time."

"I was nervous."

"Of course you were. Who wouldn't be?"

On the way home at 1:30 a.m., she checked her messages. There was one from Frank saying he had been arrested by the Birmingham police for drunk driving. Kate couldn't imagine how the night could get any worse, but there it was—dear old Dad screwing up again.

She called the PD, identified herself, and was told that Frank Galvin had been taken to the Oakland County Jail and wouldn't be released till the next morning.

Kate got in bed but couldn't sleep, her mind racing. She kept picturing the scenes in the judge's house, hesitating when she saw the skinhead in the hall, which was more surprise than fear, and the tense standoff in the bedroom. But she felt better after talking to Charlie. She'd handled a difficult situation and saved the judge's life.

SEVENTEEN

FRANK WAS WAITING IN front of the jail when Kate pulled up a little after eight a.m. He saw her, moved to the car, and got in without expression or emotion, looking like a bum in his disheveled condition.

"Thanks for coming," he said.

"You look like hell and smell like a brewery."

Frank ignored her looking out the side window at the courthouse complex.

Pulling out of the parking lot she said, "I get the impression you like it in there. No responsibilities. You don't have to worry about anything. They give you a bunk and a hot meal. You felt right at home, I'll bet."

"Yeah, that's it. I tried to get arrested 'cause it's so relaxing and the food's so good."

They rode in silence for a few minutes, passing strip malls on Telegraph. "Last night you said you had something important to tell me."

"I think Ray Skinner and his Japanese girlfriend live in Windsor."

"How do you know that?"

"I saw him at the racetrack, and Thompson and I followed him."

She couldn't believe it. "Are you out of your mind? What if he recognized you?"

"I thought you'd be grateful. This is probably the first solid lead and you're giving me a hard time."

"What was he driving?" Kate was thinking about the cars illegally parked in front of the Bank of America on Griswold.

"A Cadillac with an Ontario plate."

"Did you get the tag?"

"BPTA 362."

"You're sure it was Ontario?"

"Positive. Remember I mentioned that Skinner played the horses? Well, I figured if he was still around there was a good possibility he'd be at the track. I stopped by a couple times looking for him. Ray always went during the day when I knew him twenty years ago, so he could keep his evenings free to have a nice dinner and stop at a few bars. I remember him talking about betting on the thoroughbreds, the excitement of seeing the horses run and the crowd getting into it. And I remember him saying every summer he talked to the jockeys, paid them for the names of the fastest horses." Frank said, "I went to the stables and showed Skinner's photo to the jockeys and a few of them recognized him." Frank looked out the window and back at Kate. "Yesterday afternoon I asked Thompson if he wanted to go to the track."

"Why involve him?"

"I needed a ride. Maybe you forgot, I don't own a car."

Frank sounded like he was feeling sorry for himself.

"We walked around for a while and then went out to the grandstand and watched a race. It was a petite Japanese girl that first caught my eye. I could only see her in profile as she turned her head to watch the horses. I didn't get a good look at the man she was with until after the race. I followed them to the cashier window, and I saw Ray Skinner, no mistake about it. We followed him on the freeway to Detroit, and through the tunnel to Windsor. But nobody told me you gotta have a passport to get into Canada. We were detained by Canadian Customs, sat in a room for a couple hours while they did background checks on us and saw that we're ex-cons, and sent us home." Frank took a beat. "Ray and the girl rob banks and disappear. Where do you think they go?"

"I'll call the Windsor PD, ask them to run the plate and see what turns up."

Kate merged onto the freeway during morning rush hour, tired and stressed, and now she had Frank to deal with. "Listen, I found out that Thompson's car is in an impound lot in Birmingham. You'll have to pay one hundred and seventy-five dollars to get it out."

"What the hell for?"

"Towing and the impound cost."

"Jesus," Frank said, "I don't have that kind of money on me."

"I'm going to loan it to you. But you're going to need more."

"What're you talking about?"

"Drunk driving has gotten serious. Your fine will be about fifteen hundred dollars. And a lawyer could run you a couple grand. I know an attorney who might do it for less. But even with a lawyer you'll do time in county. You'll be on probation for a year, and you'll have to attend AA meetings three or four nights a week."

"Last time I was overserved and stopped, the cop gave me a ride home."

"They don't do that anymore," Kate said. "There's a federal judge that owes me a favor. Whether or not he'll help, I can't say. But I'll try."

"I'll take off before I do time again."

"Do you want to spend the rest of your life looking over your shoulder?"

"I'm not going back."

There was a small brick building and behind it was a dusty lot filled with cars. It was surrounded by chain-link fence topped with razor wire. Kate gave him the money. Frank opened the door and started to get out.

She said, "Why don't you come for dinner tonight? Do you like meatloaf?"

"I love it, but I doubt Thompson will let me use his car again."

The last thing Kate wanted to do was have company for dinner, but she was concerned Frank might do something crazy and wanted to keep an eye on him. She waited till he came out of the building, held up the car keys, and headed into the lot.

•••

KATE PULLED INTO THOMPSON'S driveway a little after six. Frank shuffled out of the house and got in the car. They didn't talk on the way to her apartment until Frank said, "Still pissed off at me or is there something else bothering you?"

"I'm just tired." She was still stressed from what had happened at the judge's house but didn't want to talk about it.

Frank perked up when they walked in the kitchen and Kate asked if he wanted something to drink.

"I'll have a cold one."

"You sure?" Kate said. "After the way you felt this morning?"

"Hair of the dog."

She grabbed a beer from the refrigerator, popped the top, and handed it to him. Frank took a big drink and glanced at her. "This morning you said I was trying to get arrested for free room and board."

"I was kidding."

He made a face. "Ever eat jail food?"

"No, but I've seen what they serve the prisoners waiting to go to court and it looks disgusting." Kate pictured a slice of baloney on a single piece of white bread with a pat of margarine on it. "What were your favorites at Victorville?"

Now Frank smiled. "That's a tough one. Hmmm…let me think. Salisbury Steak with brown gravy was a real crowd pleaser. There was roast turkey and stuffing smothered in poultry gravy. We had chicken six ways from Sunday. Chicken and dumplings, chicken a la king, chicken fajitas, chicken fried rice. And everything tasted the same. It was all terrible. Even the Jell-O was bad. How do you screw that up?"

"What was the worst thing you ate?"

"Nutraloaf. Do something wrong—say you get in a fight or mouth off to a guard—they put you in seg. It's solitary confinement, and that's all they feed you."

"What's in it?"

"Lot of stuff: carrots, beans, cabbage, corn, tomato paste, garlic powder, applesauce. They throw everything in a blender and then bake the contents. Prison system says it has all the nutrition a prisoner needs to stay healthy."

It sounded like a *Saturday Night Live* skit. "What's it taste like?"

"Hard to describe. You might get a spicy blast of garlic powder or bitter tomato paste, but it's the consistency that's so awful. You can't eat it, but it's all you get."

Kate put plates of meatloaf, mashed potatoes, and peas on the kitchen table. They sat across from each other. Frank took a bite of meatloaf and washed it down with a slug of beer. "That's good. What's this on top?"

"Barbecue sauce. That's not part of the recipe. I added it. I like the smokiness."

Frank nodded and ate another forkful of meatloaf and some mashed potatoes, his arm curved around the plate, protecting it.

"Listen, you don't have to worry. I'm not going to try to steal your food."

Frank slid his arm off the table and looked at her. "Force of habit, I guess. Didn't realize I was doing it."

"You haven't said anything about prison, which is understandable."

"What do you want to know?" Frank took a drink of beer.

"Where is Victorville?"

"About eighty-five miles northeast of LA, San Bernardino County."

Kate noticed his plate was clean. "My god, you eat fast."

"They gave us maybe ten minutes."

"Can I fix you up again?"

"That's the best meatloaf I've ever had."

Kate filled his plate and set it in front of him. "Tell me what it was like?"

He took a bite, took his time chewing, and drank some beer. "When you arrive at Victorville—or Victimville as the hacks referred to it—you go to orientation and they give you an inmate handbook, what you can and can't do, that's like fifty pages. They tell you incarceration can be a rewarding experience, one that will lead to a more fulfilling life upon your release."

Frank cut a piece of meatloaf and dragged it through the mashed potatoes and brought the fork to his mouth, chewed, and swallowed. He drank some beer. "During orientation a guard with a military bearing—he reminded me of a marine drill instructor—barked at us, saying, 'Inmates are not allowed to retain more than two newspapers, ten magazines, and twenty-five letters. Inmates are only allowed to place calls to thirty approved phone numbers.'"

"Who would you call?"

"Your mother till she refused to talk to me, my parents, a couple buddies I'd known since grade school and high school, and Thompson after he was released."

"Mom had a tough time after you left."

"I thought she got married again."

"She did, to a guy named McGraw. It lasted two years."

"Why'd you take his name?"

"I didn't have a choice. I was eight. Anyway, they divorced and Mom got busted for selling weed, did twenty-eight months. She died of breast cancer when I was at the academy."

"I heard."

Frank didn't want to talk about it. He wiped his mouth on the napkin and went back to the prison story. "The drill instructor said, 'Inmates are counted five to six times a day: at twelve a.m., three a.m., five a.m., four p.m., and ten p.m. Those were standup counts."

Frank drank some beer and continued. "Inmates had to dress properly in the dining area. Institution-issued uniforms were the only clothing allowed." Frank took a bite of meatloaf. "Inmates weren't allowed to wear shower shoes, house shoes, hair curlers, do-rags, or hats. I got a kick out of that. Some prison official had thought about it and included those particular items in the rules."

"Were hair curlers popular?"

"Certainly among the brothers." Frank finished his beer and Kate got him another one. Frank finished his second helping. "God, that was good."

"Want to go for three?"

"I better not." Frank poured the fresh beer into his glass and drank. "My favorite prison advice was from one of the chaplains. He said, 'Please do not put your life on hold for the period of time that you are with us. Anyone can fall, but the idea is to get up and begin again. Stand and start a new beginning.'" Frank paused and drank some beer. "You believe that?"

"Sure," Kate said. "That's the epitome of bureaucracy. I'll bet most inmates heard it and thought, *What?*"

"After that inspirational advice I was taken to a cell and met my cellmate Sergio Cruz, who went by Checo—a convicted drug trafficker from Sonora, Mexico—who had a bad attitude and bad hygiene. The room smelled like sweat most of the time."

"Why didn't you tell him to take a shower?"

"I did, but he didn't know any better."

"Did Sergio give you a hard time?"

"He was a little guy, about five-five, one twenty. Played tough but wasn't."

Kate finished her meatloaf and sipped some Chardonnay. "I can't imagine sharing a room with someone like that."

"You don't have a choice. I'd open my eyes—I had the lower bunk—and he'd be on the toilet grinning at me."

"Why didn't you hang a sheet?"

"I did later, when Sergio was paroled and Thompson was my cellmate."

"What happens when you're locked in a room and you can't leave?"

"At first you feel angry, anxious, depressed. You're looking for an excuse to take it out on someone. But you learn to stay calm, don't lose your head, do something dumb. 'Cause if you can't cut it on the mainline they send you to SHU, which stands for Special Housing Unit. It's solitary confinement. They put you in a six-by-eight concrete room. And when you're in there you have to keep your mind right or you'll go crazy." Frank took a beat. "I like talking to you. It's so effortless."

"Tell me about last night." Kate poured more Chardonnay in her glass.

"I met someone. First eligible female in a long time." He picked up his beer glass but didn't drink. "We hit it off. At least I think we did."

"Do you have plans to see her again?"

"I said I'd call." Frank took a business card out of his shirt pocket and handed it to Kate.

Hall & Hunter Realtors

Peggy Nolan Realtor

There was a color photo of Peggy, smiling. She was attractive and looked friendly, someone you would like to know.

"She's forty-two," Frank said. "Married twenty-six years, divorced. No brothers or sisters, kids, or pets. Parents passed away."

"She sounds lonely." Kate sipped her wine. "What did you tell her about yourself?"

"I just got out of prison after eighteen years for armed robbery."

"She didn't get up and run?"

"On the contrary, she was interested, asking how I did it and what prison was like."

Kate was thinking about the crazy women who were turned on by the badass glamour of a convict. "What does her ex do?"

"I think he's an accountant."

"Exactly. You're her excitement. She can tell her friends she's seeing an ex-con, helping you readjust, reenter society."

"Aren't you laying it on a little heavy? We haven't gone out yet and we may not. I don't have any money, and I've got this drunk driving thing hanging over my head. So relax, will you? You don't have to worry about me."

Kate wasn't so sure.

"What'd you do last night?"

"I was on protection detail, keeping an eye on a federal judge whose life had been threatened. You don't remember me telling you that?"

"This the one who owes you a favor?"

Kate nodded. "Three men came to kill him. Two are dead and the third one is in the hospital."

"And you saved his life?"

Her phone vibrated. She pulled it out of a jean pocket. "I've got to take this." She stood and walked out of the kitchen.

Frank was doing the dishes when she came back in. He put a plate in the dishwasher and turned to her.

"The Cadillac with the Ontario plate is registered to a Ray Carrick, County Road 42, Windsor, Ontario, Canada."

EIGHTEEN

FRANK DIDN'T SEE AN easy way out of his financial predicament. He didn't have $1,500 for the drunk driving charge—let alone $2,000 to hire a lawyer. He wasn't gonna take money from his daughter, and nobody was gonna hire a forty-six-year-old ex-con with no marketable skills. There was only one sure way to get what he needed.

The note read, "This is a robbery, I have a gun." It was in his pocket as he approached the teller, looking for the surveillance cameras, feeling anxious, sweat popping on his forehead. Frank felt like everyone was watching him, knew what he was going to do.

Moving toward the smiling teller he saw himself in a series of quick cuts: taking shit from gangbangers in the exercise yard, glancing at Checo on the toilet, staring at a tray filled with gravy-colored slop in the mess hall, feeling the white cinderblock walls—the claustrophobic confines of solitary closing in on him.

"May I help you?" the teller said. She was a fresh-faced young girl, early twenties. Frank held her in his gaze, frozen, unable to go through with his plan. "Sir, are you all right?" And now Frank came fumbling out of his trance. "I wanted to open a checking account, but it occurs to me I forgot my wallet."

The girl smiled. "Sir, we're open till five p.m. Please come back. Mrs. Belmont in account services will be happy to help you."

Frank turned and moved across the lobby, conscious of his footsteps on the tile floor, trying to stay cool, in control.

Now, sitting in a bar down the street, drinking Maker's on the rocks, Frank reviewed the stupidity of his actions, wondering if there was more to it than needing money. Did he—as Kate had suggested—subconsciously want to go back to prison, where he didn't have to worry about anything? Go back to the life. No thinking required. But that wasn't it. He'd temporarily lost his head, decided to take a shortcut 'cause that's all he knew.

Frank actually felt lucky for the first time since he walked out of Victorville and got reacquainted with Kate. He'd almost screwed up but caught himself. That was a good sign. He might defy the odds and make something of himself. And although he'd just met her, the realtor had grabbed his attention and occupied his thoughts, Frank going so far as to imagine himself having a relationship and going to bed with her. Would he be any good? It had been a long time. No reason to worry about that now, though. He'd deal with the situation if and when it happened.

He called the number on the card Peggy had given him. It went to voicemail and he said, "This is Frank. We met the other night. I enjoyed talking to you and wondered if you'd have dinner with me." He disconnected and picked up his drink. If she said yes he'd ask her to meet him at a steakhouse in Birmingham.

NINETEEN

R AY SAID, "YOU SURE you can do this?"
Yumi nodded but didn't look at him. They were parked
on Nine Mile Road half a block from the Huntington Bank. "Just
remember, you're in control. The bank doesn't want any trouble.
The money's insured. They don't want their customers to get hurt."

She stared straight ahead.

"Don't hesitate, know what you're gonna say and say it like you
mean it. Walk out but don't hurry, don't call attention to yourself."

"Ray, will you stop? I know what to do," she said, raising her
voice.

Yumi had never talked to him like that. *Well, pardon me for trying
to help,* he wanted to say, but instead he said, "Take a couple deep
breaths. I'll be right here when you come out."

•••

YUMI HAD UNDERESTIMATED HOW difficult it would be. Her heart was pounding and she was sick to her stomach. It was nothing like what she had been doing, casing the banks, getting a feel for the layout and taking photographs. That was fun. She was acting, playing a role.

This time she was committing a crime and could go to prison. Now Yumi, standing at the teller window, was asking herself why she volunteered to do this, why she thought it was going to be so easy.

The teller, a young, nerdy-looking guy, said, "May I help you?"

Yumi slid a hand in her purse, gripped the .22, finger on the trigger, and brought the gun out but kept it low. "Give me your money, big bills, what you have there, and no dye packs."

The teller raised his hands. "Whoa, take it easy."

"Put your hands down."

The teller handed her banded stacks of $100s, $50s, and $20s. Yumi stuffed the money in the bag with her free hand. "You're going to stay right where you are until I walk out. Anyone who tries to stop me will die," she said, saying it in her most serious voice, trying to be dramatic.

She was sweating walking across the bank floor, more afraid than she had ever been in her life. Feeling self-conscious now as the uniformed guard glanced at her. The door was forty feet away... thirty...twenty...ten, and then it opened and a man was holding it for her.

Yumi was on the sidewalk looking for the car—it was right there—when she heard the sirens. Where was Ray? She could feel herself panicking, not sure what to do but kept walking, looking for the car. The sirens were getting louder. A police car, lights flashing, pulled up in front of the bank and another one drove past her and stopped.

At the end of the block she turned right, went into a coffee shop. It was loud and crowded. She stood in the hall that led to the restrooms, pulled the cell out of her purse, hand fumbling around stacks of money and speed-dialed Ray. It rang nine times and went to voice mail.

She hid the money in a trash can in the ladies' room and walked out the back door into an alley, calling Ray again. Trying to decide where to go, what to do, when a police car appeared coming toward her.

•••

KATE WATCHED HER FIDGETING at the table in the interview room. "What's her name?"

"Yumika Sato," a Ferndale detective named Higgins said. "She's Canadian, eh?" Faking an accent, sounding like a hockey announcer. Kate was thinking about Frank saying he had followed Ray and the girl to the Detroit-Windsor tunnel. They rob banks in Detroit and disappear into Canada. On her laptop, Kate brought up bank surveillance photos of the Asian girl and compared them to Ms. Sato. She looked at Charlie. "What do you think, do we have a match?"

"Why's he letting *her* do it?" Charlie Luna said. "Shooter's a control freak. Something isn't right."

"Maybe she's working alone," Kate said. "Showing the man she's as good as he is. Two witnesses said she came out of the bank and walked west on Nile Mile Road, looking around," Kate said, "looking for someone—her driver would be my guess. You don't rob a bank without an exit plan. You don't walk down the street to a coffee shop. That doesn't strike you as odd?"

"Maybe she was going to call Uber," Charlie said.

"How much did she get?" Kate said to Detective Higgins.

"Seventeen grand. It was found in the ladies along with a Ruger LCR-22, matching the gun Ms. Sato pointed at the teller." Higgins handed Kate a cell phone. "She made two calls just after leaving the bank—same number."

"Looks like she started to panic when her ride wasn't there." Kate checked the photographs in Yumika Sato's phone but they had been deleted. There were no contacts, saved numbers, or text messages either.

Kate, Charlie, and Detective Higgins went into the interview room and sat across the table from the suspect.

Kate said, "Where's Ray?"

Yumika stared at the table.

"He was going to pick you up when you came out of the bank," Charlie said. "Wasn't that the way it was supposed to happen?"

No response. Yumika was afraid, who wouldn't be? Two US marshals and a police detective staring at her.

Kate said, "Where's Ray?"

No response.

Kate spread copies of photographs on the table. The girl glanced at them but didn't show any expression. "You know who that is?"

The girl's face was still blank.

"We have you positively ID'd in five Detroit banks two days before they were robbed. Do you think that's a coincidence?"

"I was exchanging money," she said, making eye contact with Kate for the first time.

"The problem with that story, you never approached any of the tellers and there are no records of any such transactions. We have surveillance footage of your visits."

Charlie Luna placed photos of the Shooter over the shots of Yumi. "What's his name?"

"I have never seen him before." The girl said, confident now, eyes on Charlie.

"Why are you protecting this man who left you hanging, left you to get caught? That's who you called when you came out of the bank, when the car wasn't where it was supposed to be." Kate paused. "You're going to take the fall, you're going to do time, and Ray'll be out having fun. He'll find another girlfriend and take her to the racetrack and out for expensive dinners while you're in a cinderblock cell, eating pork and beans."

The girl seemed relaxed, unconcerned.

Kate brought out Yumika Sato's blue-and-gold Canadian passport, opened it, and said, "Ms. Sato, do you still live on Riverside Drive East?"

She stared at the table.

"Isn't that where we'll find your accomplice?" Kate's phone beeped. It was Cornbread telling her the number Yumika Sato called was registered through Telus of Windsor, Canada, to a Ray Carrick. She thanked him and disconnected.

Kate motioned to Charlie and they got up and walked out of the room, leaving Higgins and the girl. "After a few days in county, I have a feeling her attitude is going to improve."

When they left the Ferndale PD, Kate called Windsor Constable Dan Giroux. "Danny, how're you doing? It's Kate McGraw with the US Marshals Service. Do you remember me?"

"Remember you? I can't stop thinking about you. I've been wondering what the heck you're doin', wondering when you were gonna call."

"I'm wondering if you could help me with something?"

"Yeah, I thought you'd never ask."

"We're after a fugitive bank robber who we believe is living in an apartment on Riverside Drive."

Giroux cut in, "So this's business, eh?"

"I'm afraid so." Kate took a beat. "But anyway, he comes across the border, robs a bank, and flees back to Canada. As you know, going through official channels could take weeks, even months. All my partner and I want to do is observe, check the apartment. If he's there, you get the arrest. Danny, this guy is dangerous."

"All right, I'll help you any way I can, but when this is over I want you to have dinner with me. Do we have a deal or what?"

"I'm sure we can work something out."

"Okay then. See you tomorrow. Ten a.m., okay?"

Kate had met Giroux six months earlier when a team of US marshals picked up a fugitive murderer and brought him back to Detroit to stand trial. Giroux was one of the cops involved in the prisoner exchange. He had flirted with her and said if she ever wanted to see the sights of Windsor to give him a call. She had never intended to, but now Kate needed his help.

TWENTY

THE NEXT MORNING KATE and Charlie took the tunnel to
Canada and met Constables Giroux and McGill at customs
and immigration. Giroux beamed when he saw her but didn't say
anything personal until McGill took Charlie into the building to use
the restroom.

"Well, aren't you a sight for sore eyes," Giroux had a smile
frozen on his face.

"Nice to see you too, Danny. We certainly appreciate your
cooperation."

"Well, I'd appreciate your cooperation, if you know what I'm
saying."

Dan Giroux had black hair and a heavy beard that was shaved
close, the shadow visible under his pale skin. He was about thirty-
five and friendly—likable, even—but not her type.

On the way to Ray Skinner's apartment, Kate and Charlie sat in the back of the police cruiser. "So, what can you tell us about this bank robber character?" Giroux said, looking at Kate in the rearview mirror.

"He's hit six banks in two months."

McGill whistled. "What's his darn hurry?"

"He's a gambler," Kate said. "Plays the horses."

"That'll get you in trouble faster than a fat kid chasing an ice cream truck," Giroux said and smiled at Kate in the rearview mirror.

"A witness identified the suspect and copied the license number of his car, and as you know it had an Ontario plate." Kate didn't see any reason to tell them about Yumi Sato robbing a bank.

Then they talked about baseball, McGill saying the Blue Jays were going to win the American League pennant. Charlie said not a chance with Verlander and Zimmerman on the mound for the Tigers and the best batting order with the highest team average in all of baseball. The Windsor cops grinned, bantering with Charlie the way guys do. Kate, gazing out the window, was always surprised how good Detroit looked from the Windsor side of the river.

Giroux pulled into the apartment complex and parked near the entrance. The manager met them in the lobby. He was tall man with a ruddy complexion and a flat top haircut and looked like a high school hockey coach. "These are the US marshals I was telling you about," Giroux said.

"I'm Cam Nylander," the manager said. "Think these folks is bank robbers, eh?"

"That's what we're investigating," Kate said. "How long have Mr. Carrick and Ms. Sato lived here?"

"Gosh, let me think—over a year—fourteen months sounds about right. Time flies, eh?"

Kate showed Nylander three surveillance photographs of Ray Skinner. "Do you recognize this man?"

"Oh, yeah. It's Mr. Carrick, no mistake about it. Why's he dressed like that?"

"They're disguises," Kate said, as if it wasn't obvious.

Charlie said, "What's the man like?"

"Quiet, keeps to himself. Pays the rent first of the month—in cash."

Charlie said, "He give you a check for the security deposit?"

"I believe so. I'll look into that. I imagine you want the name of the bank." Nylander stroked his flat top. "I phoned the apartment earlier, and there was no answer. But we can see if they've returned."

Five of them rode the elevator to the eighth floor in cramped silence. The manager knocked on the door, waited, and said, "Hello the apartment, it's Mr. Nylander. You have visitors." He knocked a couple more times, slid a key in the lock, and opened the door. The apartment was empty, the furniture and furnishings—everything—cleaned out, gone."

Nylander said, "Oh, boy, is this a kerfuffle, or what?"

Kate could see indentations in the carpeting where chairs, tables, and couches had been, and hooks in the walls where frames had hung. She glanced at the manager. "How could they have cleaned the place out and you didn't see it or know about it?"

"I took a couple a' days off. But my secretary, Mary Birney, was here."

Kate said, "They had to have a truck, equipment, and movers. Assuming all the rooms had furniture, it must've taken a few hours at least. Can you find out the name of the moving company?"

"You can talk to Mary yourself. She's down in the office."

"Will you give us a few minutes to look around?"

Kate checked the empty bedroom and bathroom, looked in the closet and saw a piece of paper on the floor wedged into a corner partially concealed by the shoe molding. She crouched and dug out a smudged business card from a discount truck rental company on Dougall Avenue.

Charlie turned when she walked out on the balcony, looking at the Detroit River across the road, eight stories below. Kate handed him the business card. "I don't know if this is anything, but it's all we have unless you found something."

"Nothing." Charlie paused, his gaze fixed on something in the distance.

"What do you make of all this? Man leaves his woman to take the rap, disappears without a trace. Why doesn't he need her anymore?"

"Maybe he's tired of her."

"But in this situation, it's a risky move," Charlie said. "Think about what she's got on him. Not only helped him rob banks, but lived with him."

"She thinks his name is Ray Carrick. Who is he? Where's he from? Do you think the girl knows? I don't. I get the sense Carrick has done this before. He goes through women. There's always another one."

"That's cold, McGraw."

"What can I say? I'm heartless." Kate smiled. "Let's go talk to the secretary."

Still looking across the river at Belle Isle, she saw a man setting up a telescope on a tripod.

•••

CONSTABLE GIROUX SEEMED TO be flirting with an attractive platinum blonde when Kate and Charlie entered the office. Giroux, laughing at something, saw them and composed himself. "Mary, meet US Marshals Kate McGraw and Charlie Luna. This is Mary Birney."

"How do you do?" Mary stood, came around the desk, and shook hands with them. "Let's go to the conference room. I think we'll be more comfortable there."

When they were all seated, Kate said, "Did you know that Mr. Carrick had hired a moving company to clean out the apartment?"

"Oh, yeah, I received this note the day prior." Mary slid the paper across the table." It was addressed to:

Dear Mr. Nylander,

Please be advised that Ms. Sato and I are in the process of redecorating the apartment: painting the rooms, refinishing the floors, and installing new cabinetry in the kitchen. As such, we will be placing our furniture and possessions in storage until the work is completed. We've made arrangements with a moving company that'll be here in the morning.

Best regards,

Ray Carrick

Kate said, "What's the name of the moving company?"

"That's a good question," Mary said. "I don't know. I mean, I saw the truck parked behind the building. It was hard to miss. But I don't recall that it had a company name on the side. And of course I saw the men, the movers rolling furniture across the lobby."

Charlie said, "Did you see Mr. Carrick or Ms. Sato that morning?"

"No."

"How did the movers get in the apartment?" Kate said.

Mary said, "I assume Mr. Carrick gave them a key."

Nylander entered the room and handed Kate a sheet of paper. "Well, here you go. It's a copy of the loan agreement signed by Mr. Carrick and a copy of the check he used as a security deposit."

Kate studied the check. It was from the Royal Bank of Canada on Huron Church Road."

Nylander said, "Did you get what you needed?"

Kate said, "We appreciate your help."

The next stop was the truck rental lot. Constable Giroux went in and brought the owner out. His name was Lou Hanna, a short stocky guy in a tank top. He looked about forty and needed a shave and a bath. "What's this aboot?"

"You rented a truck for a move at the Glendarda apartment building yesterday," Kate said. "Who'd you rent it to?"

"I don't know what you're talking about," Lou Hanna said, on the muscle. "We rent trucks, we don't ask what they're hauling or where they're going."

"But you have a record of who you rented to and a copy of their driver's license," Kate said. "This truck would have to have been big enough to carry an apartment full of furniture. That should narrow it down." How tough could it be?

Kate stood at the counter, watching Lou Hanna bent over on the other side, running his index finger down a list of customers that had rented trucks the day before. He straightened up and said, "Must've been the thirty-two-footer picked up by a fella named Gord Spaling."

Lou handed her a Xerox copy of Spaling's driver's license and Kate studied his face—young guy, early thirties, a surgical scar on his cheekbone and another on his forehead. "What time did he bring the truck back?"

"Three o'clock. Picked it up at eight thirty."

In the car Constable Giroux ran Spaling's name in the criminal database. "He was arrested in 2014 for shoplifting, paid a fine, and was on probation for twenty-two months and clean since. Last known address is County Road 42. It's a little outside the city."

Why did the address sound familiar? Kate searched her brain and remembered. It was the address on Ray Carrick's auto registration. She wondered about the connection between Spaling and Carrick. Were they friends or acquaintances, or maybe business partners?

County Road 42 cut through a rural area, fields of crops, farmhouses, and barns scattered in the hazy distance. The scene reminded her of northern Michigan.

They pulled up to a two-story Victorian house that had seen better days. Kate and Charlie followed McGill and Giroux up the porch steps to the front door. Kate looked through the picture window at the mess inside: beer cans, fast food wrappers, and pizza boxes on the coffee table and floor. The TV was on. She could hear guns and explosions and screeching tires, the sounds of an action movie.

McGill, a tall, lean, geek of a man, knocked on the door. Kate saw a guy come down the stairs and move toward the rear of the house. "Someone's going out the back door."

Giroux took off around the side of the house. He was faster than all of them and caught the man climbing a fence that bordered a cornfield, cuffed him, and set him on the grass behind the house. "Why're you trying to deke out, Mr. Spaling?"

"Why're you arresting me? I didn't do nothing."

"Calm down," Giroux said, "We just want to ask you some questions."

"Why'd you put these on me then, and who're they?" His eyes held on Kate and then Charlie.

"US Marshals."

"What do they want with me? Hell, I ain't been over there in ages."

Kate said, "We understand you rented a truck yesterday and moved furniture out of an apartment on Riverside Drive."

"Since when's that a crime?"

"Who helped you?"

"Couple of friends."

"We're going to need their names and contact information," Kate said.

Charlie said, "You in the moving business?"

"No. I met this guy one night at the Black Horse, sitting next to him at the bar."

"It's a pub," McGill said

"Guy's American. We talked about this and that—Red Wings and Maple Leafs. Seemed like a decent fella."

Kate showed Spaling a surveillance photo of Ray Skinner. "Is this him?"

Spaling stared at the image and said, "Yeah. Who is he?"

Kate said, "Who did he say he was?"

"Ray Carrick. Bought me a pint and asked did I want to make some money moving furniture out of an apartment, asked did I have friends that could help me?"

Kate said, "When was this? Give me a date if you can."

"August third."

"Did you think it was odd, this stranger asking you to work for him?"

"The way it happened, and what he said sounded normal enough. Tell me what the heck's going on here, will you?"

"You rented a truck and loaded it up with Mr. Carrick's furniture," Kate said. "Is that right?"

Gord Spaling nodded.

"Where did you take it?"

"The Storage Mart on Lauzon Road. Mr. Carrick rented two medium-sized units."

"Did Mr. Carrick meet you there?"

"He was away on business. Said he'd call and pick up the keys when he was back in town."

Kate said, "Do you have his number?"

"In my pocket."

Giroux unlocked the handcuffs. Gord Spaling rubbed his wrists and dug a phone out of the right front pocket of his jeans. He scrolled through his contacts, found it, and read the number out loud. It was the same one Yumika Sato had called after leaving the bank.

Kate said, "Why do you suppose Mr. Carrick's automobile registration has your address on County Road 42?"

"I don't know anything about that."

Kate said, "How long have you known Mr. Carrick?"

"About a year."

"Why'd you lie?" Charlie said.

"He must have done something bad or you wouldn't be here, and I don't want to get mixed up in it."

Kate said, "What do you think he did?"

"I don't know and I don't want to."

Kate said, "What can you tell us about Mr. Carrick?"

"He's strange."

"You just said he's a decent fella."

"For a weirdo. Let me just say—you don't want to muck it up in the corner with that one."

"What does that mean?"

"You don't want to cross him. It's the way he looks at you with those dark eyes. Like he'd cut your throat without giving it a second thought. Believe me, you don't want this fella after you. I played hockey and fought a lot of tough guys, but Mr. Carrick's in a different league."

Charlie said, "Did he threaten you?"

"No, sir."

Charlie said, "Did Carrick say why he was putting his furniture in storage?"

"No, sir."

Kate said, "Did he mention his girlfriend?"

"No, but I know he was living with a female. We packed up their clothes."

Kate said, "And you took everything to the storage place?"

"Mr. Carrick told us to get rid of the lady's things. She wasn't going to need them anymore."

Kate said, "Did he say why?"

"No."

"What did you do with her clothes?"

"Put everything in boxes and threw 'em in a dumpster behind a Timmy's over on Wyandotte Street."

"It's a Tim Horton's," Giroux said. "Want to take a look? Maybe it hasn't been emptied yet."

So Ray had been planning to get rid of the girl, had set the whole thing up in advance. Kate felt sorry for Yumi. Taken advantage of, and never saw it coming. "We're going to need the keys to the storage units," she said to Spaling, and to Giroux she said, "can we search it without a warrant?"

"Unofficially," Giroux winked at her. "If you know what I mean."

"When Mr. Carrick calls," Kate said, "I want you to contact Constable Giroux."

"Oh, you can count on it. I hope you find the man and put him away."

•••

As it turned out the dumpster at Tim Horton's had been emptied, so they went to the storage facility.

The door rattled and squeaked in the metal tracks as Giroux lifted it. Kate turned on the light, looking at a room filled with furniture. The second unit had more furniture and a dozen heavy cardboard moving boxes. Kate and Charlie had no authority in Canada. Giroux and McGill had to open the boxes. Two were wardrobe containers that had Ray Skinner's suits and sport coats on hangers.

Kate put on a pair of latex gloves and lifted the garments out one by one, checking the pockets. Twelve minutes later Kate was looking at two VIP parking stubs from Hazel Park Raceway, a matchbook from Joe Muer's restaurant, a couple used Kleenex she sealed in a plastic evidence bag, a pair of readers she sealed in another bag, and two purple Nexium capsules—Skinner evidently had heartburn.

Charlie found a brush webbed with hair in another box, and now they had the man's fingerprints on the reading glasses, and possibly his DNA on the Kleenex and hair samples.

Giroux drove them back to their car and offered to question Gord Spaling's friends that helped with the move. Giroux said he would contact Kate after talking to them. "If these knuckleheads are involved in anything nefarious, I'll tell you, they won't be going out for a ginger ale anytime soon." Danny also said he'd keep her informed about Ray Carrick's reentry into Windsor if that occurred. Now he pulled Kate aside and said, "What about that date? When are we gonna get together?"

"Let me check my schedule and get back to you."

Kate thanked the Windsor Constables and she and Charlie headed for Detroit.

"What was that about with Giroux?"

"He wants to go out with me."

"I think you make a cute couple," Charlie said deadpan.

"You're enjoying this, aren't you?"

TWENTY-ONE

R AY WAS ADJUSTING THE viewfinder, zooming in on Yumi's face when she came out of the bank, looking for the car. He wondered what she was thinking. And when she realized the car wasn't there, he saw fear in her eyes. He watched her speed-walking past storefronts, fighting the urge to run, the sounds of sirens getting louder and closer.

The first time Ray saw Yumi, she had looked radiant in a stylish summer dress. He was having lunch at Nico's in Windsor, salt-crusted branzino and a glass of Gavi di Gavi. He glanced out the window as she was crossing the street, and he did something he'd never done before, got up, walked out, and met her as she stepped onto the sidewalk. "At the risk of making a fool of myself, I have to say you're the most beautiful girl I've ever seen." He had always been attracted to Japanese women.

Surprised and embarrassed, Yumi thanked him in her tiny voice and tried to move past him. "Have lunch with me."

"I have just eaten." She smiled. "Do you always wear a napkin in your shirt?"

"It's a new style I'm trying out. What do you think?" Ray had forgotten about it but left it there tucked in the neck of his light blue Oxford dress shirt. "Have desert with me."

"I have to return to work. I am already late."

"Have dinner with me."

"I really must go."

Ray covered his heart with his hands in a theatrical gesture. "*Watashi no kokoro ga kowarete imasu.*"

"*Dekimasen.*" The girl smiled again. "Where did you learn Japanese?"

"In Japan, Tokyo, have you been?"

"I was born there."

That's how they'd met eighteen months ago. Yumi was an impressionable twenty-four-year old who had recently taken a job at Beam Suntori at the former Hiram Walker Distillery and didn't know anyone in Windsor. Her family, originally from Tokyo, now lived in Toronto, and she missed them terribly.

Ray had taken his time getting to know her, gaining her trust, holding off getting intimate for a few weeks, and four months later, they were living together in the apartment on Riverside Drive.

One night having dinner on the balcony, looking out at the water, Yumi said, "Ray, can I ask you something? What do you do? You don't seem to work, and we have a wonderful life. Where does the money come from?"

"I rob banks."

She smiled and sipped her wine. "If you don't want to tell me that's okay."

"I told you. I rob banks."

Yumi put her wine glass on the table. "Are you serious?"

Ray nodded.

"Why?"

"That's where the money is." Ray sipped his wine.

"What if you get caught?"

"I've been doing it for twenty-seven years." He dipped a shrimp in cocktail sauce, brought it to his mouth, but stopped. "Do you want to help me?"

"What would I do?"

"Go into the banks before I rob them, draw a diagram of the layout, tell me how many teller windows there are, where the manager sits, where the guard stands, where the cameras are positioned. How many ways in and out of the building."

A few weeks later, nervous and afraid, Yumi went into a Detroit bank, looked around, made the necessary observations and walked out. What surprised her was how much she liked doing it. Casing a bank was way more exciting than working at Beam Suntori, where the work was boring and the salesmen, often intoxicated, flirted with her constantly.

The way Ray saw it, bringing the little Jap cutie in with him lessened his risk and made her an accessory.

When they started living together Ray told Yumi to call him *shujin*, which meant house master. Thinking he was serious she nodded and bowed. He told her there was a time when women in Japan weren't allowed to own property and were totally subservient to men. Jesus, they could bring that rule back any time.

Once they were working together Yumi started to change, disagreeing and talking back, always asking for money—they were partners. She deserved a share.

Then, according to Yumi, he was losing too much at the racetrack. Her female instinct to fuck with him coming on strong. In Ray's experience all women seemed to have it—some more than others—and it was just a matter of time till it emerged.

She was also talking about getting married and having kids. Yumi wanted a daughter she could dress up and take to the park. Then they would have a boy. Wouldn't Ray like a son, someone he could play catch with? Yeah, that sounded like a lot of fun. The relationship was going sideways in a hurry, and Ray knew he had to do something but didn't know what, until Yumi—tired of waiting for him to get off his ass—said she could rob a bank and he saw a way out.

Ray set the tripod in the soft grass near the riverbank and aimed the telescope at Canada some five-hundred yards away. A freighter appeared, creeping in from Lake St. Clair, and a couple speed boats zipped by. He felt free, no longer tied down in a relationship that was unraveling fast.

Behind him he could hear the heavy bass line of a hip-hop tune coming from a boom box. A black guy and his girl were sitting close on a blanket, smoking a joint on a hill behind him. Adjusting the viewfinder, Ray brought the apartment building into sharp clear focus. There was a Windsor police car parked near the entrance. He tilted the telescope moving up the facade to his balcony and saw two cops.

This was what he was expecting. The police had arrested Yumi, confiscated her passport and cell phone, checked her phone log, and interrogated her. But what could she tell them? What did she know? His name was Ray Carrick. He had cell phone service with Telus. He lived at 8052 Riverside Drive E, Windsor, Canada. The cops went inside and now a blonde-haired girl in street clothes came out and stood at the railing and appeared to be looking across the river at him.

"Dude, I like your 'scope, bet you can see the planets with that, huh? Big Dipper, Milky Way, and such. That's some *Star Wars* shit."

Ray stood and turned, looking at a cut black guy in a wife beater, early twenties, dreads, and muscles.

"What do you want?"

"Look through your 'scope."

"You want to see Windsor? Drive over, check it out."

"What's your problem, man?"

Ray's guess: the guy wanted more than the telescope. He started for the car and the guy moved with Ray, trying to cut him off.

"Where you going? I ain't finished yet. Give me your money, motherfucker. Like a tariff. I let you go, let you off my island."

Ray reached behind his back, pulled the silenced Beretta .380, and racked it. He looked for the girl but didn't see her.

"What you think you gonna do with that?"

Ray shot him and got in the car. Driving now, he dialed Gord Spaling, let it ring half a dozen times.

A tired voice said, "Hey, there, sir. I was just gonna call you."

"What were you gonna tell me?"

"You're all set, furniture's in storage with just enough room. Let me know when you want to move it back. Have you returned from your business trip? Are you in town?"

"What did you say to the police?"

There was silence for a couple beats, and then, "Wait just a minute. I didn't say a darn thing. Sir, I don't know anything." Gord was defensive now, trying to backpedal out of a lie

"Who was the blonde cop you were talking to?"

"She's a US marshal."

"What'd you tell her?"

"I moved your furniture to a storage facility."

"Did you give them the keys?"

"I didn't have a choice."

"You always have a choice."

"What do you want me to do?"

"It's too late." Ray hung up, picturing the marshals and Windsor police going through his things. The marshals, if they were any good, might find his fingerprints on various personal items. But he'd never been arrested, so the prints wouldn't lead anywhere.

Ray stopped the car and got out. Walking toward the river, the nose of the giant freighter was almost to him. He threw the phone as far as he could and saw it disappear in the blue water. He had one loose end to tie up and decided there was no time like the present.

TWENTY-TWO

D RIVING OUT OF THE tunnel into Detroit, Kate called Melvin Weston. "Melvin, you haven't retired yet, I hope."

"That you, McGraw? What's up?"

"Bank robbery in Ferndale. Japanese girl, Yumika Sato from Canada, is in custody."

"Yeah, I heard about that. What, they don't have banks in Windsor, she's gotta come over here?"

"She lived with a guy named Ray Carrick who fits the Shooter's description. Positively ID'd from bank surveillance photos by the manager of the apartment building where he was living." Kate heard voices in the background. "Where are you?"

"Crime scene on Belle Isle. Homicide. Looking across the water at Canada as we speak."

"What happened?"

"This is a strange one. White man with a telescope set up on the edge of the river shoots a young black dude. Whole thing witnessed by the dude's girlfriend."

"What was the white guy looking at?"

"I don't know."

Was that who Kate had seen from the apartment balcony? At the time she didn't think anything of it. But now it might mean something. "We'll be right there."

•••

THE MEDICAL EXAMINER WAS crouched next to the body as Kate and Charlie got out of the car and moved toward the crime scene where three Detroit uniforms stood outside the yellow tape, talking and smoking. Melvin saw them and said, "What, you've apprehended all the fugitives, got nothing else to do but help us with our murders?"

"Melvin, you know Charlie."

"How're you doing?"

Charlie gave him a nod.

Kate glanced at the dead man. "Who is he?"

"Darnell Hicks," Melvin said. "Small timer tryin' to stay clean. Now it's not gonna be a problem."

Kate turned her head to the riverbank and saw the telescope. She walked down the slope, crouched and peered in the viewfinder, looking at the balcony of the apartment building where she had stood hours earlier.

Charlie walked up behind her. "What you got?"

"Take a look."

Charlie went down on one knee, looked through the lens, studying the scene across the river. "You believe this guy? He's a freak."

Kate said, "Why did Skinner leave the telescope?"

"I don't know," Charlie said. "Maybe 'cause the dead guy was trying to hold him up."

"He's aware we're onto him," Kate said. "Wants to know what we know."

Melvin walked down the slope and joined them. "Wanna talk to the girlfriend? Better do it now. She's getting restless, wants to go home."

"Where is she?" Kate said.

Melvin pointed at an old Plymouth sedan parked on the road.

"What's her name?"

"Da Shae Morrison. Just graduated high school, taking it easy with her man on a hot summer day. Smokin' a blunt, sippin' on some 'Sco."

Kate sat in the backseat of Melvin's car across from the girl but left the door open. Da Shae had cornrows and wore black horn rims. "Hi, I'm Kate. I'm with the Marshals Service. Mind if I ask you a few questions?"

Da Shae, looking out the window, didn't respond.

"Tell me what happened?"

Da Shae turned and faced her now. "We was just chill, you know, listening to Kendrick."

"Who were you just chill with?"

"My boo, Darnell. So this white dude's over there with the telescope. Darnell said he gonna check it out."

"Where were you?"

"Up there." She pointed at the top of a grassy ridge.

"Why do you think the man shot Darnell?"

"Was a racist motherfucker."

"Did Darnell try to rob him?" Kate took a bank surveillance photo out of her bag and held it up. "Did you get a good look at the man? Is this him?"

Da Shae studied the image. "I think so." And now trying to convince herself, she said, "Yeah, that's the dude. That's the motherfucker."

"Did you see what kind of car he was driving?"

"Was a Malibu. My sister got one like it."

"Anything else you remember that might help us catch the man?"

"Darnell was shot, right? Didn't know what happen till I saw the man drivin' away and I seen Darnell on the ground. Then he stops, gets out the car, throws something in the water."

"What was it?"

"I think was a cell phone."

"Thanks for your help."

Kate went back to the crime scene. Charlie said, "Get anything?"

"Not much. She thinks it was Skinner but wasn't especially convincing. She did positively ID his car, a Chevrolet Malibu. What about you, Melvin, got anything?"

Detective Weston reached in his sport coat pocket and brought out a plastic evidence bag that had a casing in it. "Head stamp says it's a .380."

"From a Beretta semiautomatic would be my guess," Kate said. "Did you retrieve bullet frags at any of the banks?"

"As a matter of fact," Melvin said.

"And did you dust the telescope?"

"Step ahead of you, McGraw."

"I hope so."

•••

KATE KNOCKED ON THE door to the judge's chambers, opened it, and went in. Judge Steve was at his desk, a Dire Straits tune playing in the background. He glanced at her. "This better be important, McGraw."

She never knew what he was going to say but expected a friendlier reception after saving his life. "Good to see you, too, Your Honor. Did I catch you at a bad time?"

"What do you want?"

"I have a situation. I need a favor."

"Sit down and tell me about it."

Kate sat in one of the chairs in front of his desk. "I have a witness with inside information about a serial bank robber operating in the Detroit area."

"You're talking about the Shooter?"

Kate nodded.

"What's the problem?"

"The witness was arrested for driving under the influence. He's going to trial next week and then—and I'm only guessing—to the Oakland County Jail."

"How many DUIs?"

"I don't know."

"What city?"

"Birmingham."

"Who's presiding?"

"Judge Zimmer."

"I know her, and you do have a problem."

"Is there anything you can do to help?"

"I have no jurisdiction or authority with the state court. I'll have to think about it, think of an angle." Judge Steve looked across the room. "You might have a better chance on your own. Zimmer doesn't particularly care for me. You're a federal officer. Why don't you tell the judge your situation?"

Kate didn't say anything.

"Who's the witness?"

"My father."

"Your father, huh? This is getting good. Why do I get a feeling there's more to it than you're telling me?"

"He's an ex-con, did eighteen years in Victorville for armed robbery."

"Why didn't you tell me?"

"I didn't know. Frank was released about a month ago and looked me up."

"You call your dad Frank?"

"That's his name."

"Not 'dad' or 'father'?"

"I don't think of him that way. He took off when I was six."

"Did your mother tell you what happened to him?"

"All she said was he didn't want to be married anymore, didn't want to be a father. I thought it was my fault. Every time I brought him up she'd say she didn't want to talk about it."

"The marriage fell apart, and you felt partly to blame."

"Now you sound like Judge Judy."

His Honor gave her a dirty look and broke into a smile. "Judge Judy, huh? That's the worst thing you could say to a real judge."

"I knew you'd see the humor in it."

He paused. "Okay, I'll call Zimmer for you."

Kate was surprised by his sympathetic point of view, surprised by his interest and willingness to help. And surprised by what he said next.

"I owe you that at the very least. But I'm not promising anything."

•••

KATE UNLOCKED THE APARTMENT door and heard voices. Walking through the living room she saw Frank and another man at the kitchen table. They were drinking beer and talking loud.

Frank saw her and said, "We've been waiting for you. Honey, this grizzled old fool is Bill Thompson, my benefactor. Bill, my daughter, Kate, the US marshal."

"Kate, nice to finally meet you." Thompson stood and offered his hand and they shook.

"Pour a glass of wine and join us," Frank said.

"I have to take care of a couple things," she said, trying not to sound angry. Kate wanted to take it easy after a long day and now had these two half-drunk ex-cons to deal with.

Feeling relaxed after a hot shower, Kate went back in the kitchen. Frank was where she had left him, still drinking beer. "Where's your friend?"

"Gone. I think Thompson could tell you weren't exactly thrilled to see us."

"It was that obvious, huh?" Kate poured herself a glass of wine. "But *you're* still here."

"I thought there was a forgiveness factor 'cause we're related."

"Don't hold your breath."

Frank shrugged and drank some beer. "What's got you all bent out of shape?"

Kate took him through the events of her day starting with Yumi Sato robbing the bank in Ferndale.

"Why would Skinner let her do it and not be there when she came out unless he wanted her to get caught?"

"That's the way it looks." She told him about Ray Skinner's empty apartment in Windsor, and the storage facility, and about Skinner killing the young black man on Belle Isle. "But the good news: we've got Ray Skinner's fingerprints and DNA."

"I've been thinking about him all day. Suchi, a girl I knew years ago who lived with Skinner, might know something about him if I can find her."

"If you do get something, come to me. Don't do anything stupid. Now that you're back I'd like to have you around for a while."

Frank looked surprised. Like he wasn't expecting that.

•••

RAY DIDN'T WANT TO risk entering Canada through Windsor. If Canadian Customs was involved they were probably circulating a photo of him as Ray Carrick.

Instead he drove to Port Huron and took the Blue Water Bridge to Point Edward, showed his passport and told the Canadian border agent he was going to the casino. That's all it took.

It was dark as he approached the farmhouse. He parked on the side of the road and walked. There were lights on downstairs and he could hear a TV. Ray looked in the window but didn't see anyone. He moved along the side of the house and saw Gord Spaling in the window that was open a couple inches, the smell of grilled onions wafting out.

Ray opened the back door, went up a couple steps, and moved into the kitchen. Gord, standing at the stovetop, shaking a skillet, turned when he heard the floor creak.

"What the…? Sir, you scared the heck out of me." Gord turned a knob on the range and the flame went out. "Hungry, Mr. Carrick? You're just in time for dinner. How 'bout a nice juicy burger?"

There was a mound of ground beef on white butcher paper on the counter.

"What else did the marshals ask you?"

"They wanted to know how long I've known you, and I said we'd just met at the Black Horse on August third. Then they wanted to know why your car was registered to this address." Gord picked up a bottle of beer and took a drink, eyes holding on Ray. "Can I get you something?"

"What'd you tell them about the car?"

"I admitted I've known you for about a year."

Ray gave him a hard look. "You can't keep your mouth closed, can you?"

"I didn't tell them anything they didn't already know."

"You can stick to that if you want. Tell me, where're the keys?"

"Huh?"

"To the storage facility."

"Oh, yeah. Up in my room. Hang on a sec, I'll get them."

•••

GORD WALKED OUT OF the kitchen and up the stairs, wondering what he should do. He didn't like the look on Mr. Carrick's face or his tone of voice. To be honest, the man scared him. Gord took the pistol out of his desk drawer, checked the clip. It was full. He hadn't shot the darn thing for close to a year and had thought about selling it, but now was glad he hadn't.

He remembered putting the keys to the storage facility in the Du Maurier ashtray on his desk. But they weren't there now. He turned on the light, opened the top drawer, and ran his hand over loose change, cigarette packs, random pens, and note paper. Where were the darn keys at? The Levi's he was wearing yesterday were on the floor. Gord picked them up and checked the pockets. Nothing but a half-smoked roach. What was he gonna tell Mr Carrick?

His heart was racing now. Thought about going out the window, climbing down to the yard and making a run for it. He might get away tonight, but he knew Carrick wouldn't give up, would find him eventually. So what was he gonna do? And the answer was surprise him.

Gord entered the kitchen, holding the pistol down his left leg, smelled something burning, saw that the flame was on and meat was sizzling and smoking in the skillet. He turned off the range, glanced to his right, looking for Mr. Carrick. And behind him he heard, "What're you gonna do with that?"

"Nothing," Gord said, barely able to spit the word out he was so scared.

"Put it on the counter."

After resting the gun next to the ground beef, he turned. Carrick was aiming a gun at his chest. "Where're the keys?"

"I can't find them."

"You found the gun okay. Actually, I'm surprised you can find anything in this pigpen," Carrick said. "How can you live like this?"

Gord saw Carrick's finger on the trigger, heard a *pfft*, and felt something punch him in the chest. Now he was trying to hold himself against the counter, feeling light-headed as he slid to the floor.

TWENTY-THREE

J ESUS, NOT YOU AGAIN," Toad said, wrist cuffed to the hospital
bed rail, eyes on the girl marshal in her swat rig. "Doc said even
with therapy I may never walk right."

"You're lucky. That's the only shot I had or we wouldn't be
having this conversation."

The marshal with the mustache said, "You want to help yourself?"

"Help myself do what?"

"Improve your situation."

It was hard to concentrate, his foot hurt so goddamn much.
"What is my situation?" He wiped the white stuff—looked like
grits—out of the corners of his mouth with his thumb and index
finger and rubbed it on the sheet.

The girl, standing at the side of the bed, said, "You're going to
be prosecuted for the attempted murder of a federal judge." She
turned to her partner. "What's the mandatory on that?"

"Life. But due to the seriousness of the crime they'll probably give you life without the possibility of parole."

Kate said, "Do you understand the difference?"

Toad shook his head.

The girl said, "How old are you, Gary?"

"I'll be twenty-seven in a couple weeks."

"You're looking at spending the rest of your life in a six-by-eight-foot cell you'll be sharing with an African American, a Hispanic, maybe even a man of the Arab persuasion," the girl said, pleased with herself. "You have no control over who."

"What do you think?" the man said. "You wanna talk to us?"

Toad pictured himself in a red prison outfit, in a cell with a spook or an Arab, and started feeling sick to his stomach. "What do you want me to do?"

"Tell us about Lowell Hodge's involvement in the attempted murder of Judge Gant," the girl said.

"What're you gonna do for me?"

"We'll put in a good word for you, tell the DA you've been totally co-op," the man said.

Toad shook his head and let out a snort. "You people are something else, you know it? Step all over a citizen's rights, not think a thing about it. But you want me to help you." Toad moved his foot, trying to find a comfortable position. "I got an idea," he said, looking at the girl. "Get me some pain medicine and take me home and I'll think about it."

"You know we can't do that," the girl said.

"Well, then you can bend over and kiss my ass." Toad turned sideways on the bed, pulled the covers down and opened his hospital gown, exposing his white backside. The girl gave him a pained look, and Toad let out a high-pitched laugh. "What's the matter? Never seen a hairy butt?"

•••

DAN GIROUX CALLED AS she and Charlie were driving to question Lowell Hodge, Charlie behind the wheel, Kate next to him on her cell phone.

"Remember Gord Spaling? Of course you do. Well, Mr. Spaling was murdered last night, shot point blank with a .380, one shell casing found, one frag recovered."

"Any witnesses or suspects?"

"No, but an American named Ray Skinner entered Canada via the Blue Water Bridge, Point Edward, Ontario, at six thirty-eight p.m. I'll keep you posted as the investigation progresses."

"What about Spaling's buddies that helped with the move? Have you had a chance to interview them yet?"

"Still trying to track 'em down." Giroux paused. "One more thing. When're we going out? I'm not letting you off that easy."

"Can I get back to you?"

"That's what you said last time."

"I'm in the process of arresting a fugitive. I'll call you later." She disconnected.

Charlie smiled and said, "Let me guess. Dan Giroux, the Windsor constable again. He doesn't give up. Or are you secretly an item?"

Kate gave him a dirty look. "Yeah, he's persistent. I'm trying to be nice. We might need his help again."

"Look, you want to go out with him..." Charlie laughed. "That's up to you."

Kate knew that anything she said would sound defensive, so she let it go.

•••

THE HODGES, LOWELL AND his wife Odette, lived in a ranch house in Canton near the freeway. Kate parked her G-ride in the driveway behind a Dodge Ram pickup with a Rebel decal on the tailgate. "Looks like Lowell's home waiting for us." The blinds covering the front window were closed. Someone pulled up one of the slats and looked out.

Standing on the small concrete porch, Charlie knocked and the door opened. Odette, a busty, hard-looking woman with tat sleeve arms, wearing a denim vest, stared at them through the screen door.

"US Marshals," Kate said. "We're looking for Lowell Hodge."

"You find him, tell him I have a honey-do list for him."

Kate said, "Is Mr. Hodge in the house?"

Odette grinned and looked over her shoulder. "Hey, Mr. Hodge, you in the house?" She seemed drunk or high.

"What can I do you for?" Lowell said, walking up behind his wife.

"We want to talk to you about the attempted murder of Judge Gant."

"Who?"

"Federal Judge Steven Gant."

"Never heard of him."

"Invite us in," Kate said. "We'll refresh your memory."

Odette swung the screen door open. Kate entered a cluttered room that smelled of cigarettes and kitty litter and saw framed pictures of cats on the walls, and two cats walking across a tattered couch, curling up on Lowell's lap as he sat.

"She's the cat lover, not me," Lowell said, making sure they didn't get the wrong idea about him.

Odette smiled and shook her head. "Now that's a crock. Look at them setting on their daddy. Hell, they follow him around and lay down next to him, we're watching TV." She grinned at Lowell. "Hell, they like you better than me."

Kate said, "Mr. Hodge, where were you the night before last between eight and ten p.m.?"

"Right here, watching *Alaskan Bush People*. You seen that show? God almighty, you think life's tough, you don't have a clue till you see how those folks live."

"Mrs. Hodge, were you here with your husband?"

"The two of us, Whiskers, and Bimmer."

Lowell Hodge said, "What's this about?"

"I told you," Kate said.

Lowell slid a pack of cigarettes out of his work shirt pocket, tapped one out, and lit it. "First of all, if I was gonna kill somebody it wouldn't be an attempt, it'd be done," he said with redneck bravado, blowing out a stream of smoke.

"A witness put you at the scene," Charlie Luna said.

"Yeah, well, the witness is full of shit."

"Two of your friends," Kate said, "Mr. Teague and Mr. Parnell, are dead, and Mr. Grabowski's in the hospital."

"What's that got to do with me?"

"You were with them," Kate said.

"Prove it."

"We're gonna do that," Charlie said. "Meantime, we're gonna take you into custody." Charlie pulled the handcuffs off his duty belt. "We have a warrant for your arrest. Stand for me, Mr. Hodge, and put your hands behind your back."

Lowell stubbed his cigarette out in an ashtray, got up, and glanced at his wife. "Call that lawyer. You know the one I'm talking about?"

They escorted Lowell Hodge out of his house, moving him toward Charlie's G-ride. Buck and Cornbread stood sentry at the margins of the property in case Lowell or his wife did something crazy or some armed skinheads appeared.

"You ought to be ashamed," Lowell said. "Takes four of you to bring in one innocent man. What's the world coming to?"

•••

THE WITNESS, A THIRTY-SEVEN-YEAR-OLD African American physician who had positively identified Lowell Hodge the night of the crime, now wasn't completely sure as he studied five men in the police lineup, two on either side of the suspect. An hour later, accompanied by his attorney, Lowell was released from custody.

And that's how it sometimes worked, Kate was thinking as she watched Lowell get into a Ford Fiesta driven by Odette and wondered if the cats were in there too. There wasn't anything law enforcement could do to arrest Lowell unless another witness came forward, which was unlikely, or unless Lowell committed another crime, which Kate believed was just a matter of time.

•••

KATE WAS AT THE table when the guard brought Yumi Sato into the room. She was wearing jail fatigues, hands cuffed to a transport belt. She looked different without makeup and street clothes. Twenty-four hours in lock down, and the defiance had already disappeared, the realization of where she was and what was happening evident in her shell-shocked expression.

"While you were robbing the bank, Ray had your apartment cleaned out."

Yumi wouldn't look at her, stared at the table.

"What's interesting, Ray had been planning the move for some time. Even told the movers to throw your clothes out. You weren't going to need them."

Yumi came out of her trance, dark eyes fixed on Kate. "I don't believe you."

Kate walked around the table, sat next to her, and showed photos of the empty apartment she had taken on her phone.

"That isn't ours."

"It's on the eighth floor and has a river view." Kate showed Yumi shots of the balcony, the park across the road and the Detroit River. "It's yours. You just don't want to admit it." Kate unfolded a piece of paper and handed it to her. "This is a copy of the letter Ray wrote to Mr. Nylander." Yumi glanced at it.

"Ray deceived you. He's a bad guy."

Yumi broke down now, body heaving, tears rolling down her cheeks. "What's going to happen to me?"

"That depends on how much you cooperate; how much you help us. You could conceivably be a witness for the prosecution. You could receive immunity."

"Does that mean you will release me?"

"It's possible, if the information you give helps us find and convict Ray."

Yumi wiped her wet cheeks with a sleeve. "I don't know anything."

Kate slid a card to her across the table to her. "Call me when you do."

TWENTY-FOUR

How do you find someone you haven't seen in a long time? That's what Frank was wondering, thinking about Colleen O'Donnell, the girl he'd had an affair with—the girl who introduced him to Ray Skinner. Colleen was a knockout, a model who lived in an apartment at Lafayette Towers in Detroit when he knew her. "Where's your phone book?" he said to Kate, walking into the kitchen.

"People don't use phone books," she said, looking up from the newspaper. "I'd check the white pages online."

"What's that?"

"It's called the internet. You are out of touch. I'll show you on the computer."

Frank sat next to her, staring at the screen. "How do you turn it on?" Kate showed him and the screen lit up. Now she opened Google Chrome. "Type whitepages.com in the nav bar."

Frank stroked the keys with two fingers.

"Enter the name and address of the person you're looking for."

Frank typed "Colleen O'Donnell" in the box that asked for a name, and "Detroit, MI" in the box that asked for a location and waited while the computer processed the information.

We found 12 possible matches for Colleen O'Donnell.

"Do you see this?" Kate said, pointing at the screen. "The first match is Colleen O'Donnell, age sixty-two. Lives in St. Clair Shores, MI. Knows: Robert O'Donnell, Gerald O'Donnell, and Mary O'Donnell."

"That's not her."

"How old is the woman you're looking for?"

Frank went down the list. "The only possibility is Colleen O'Donnell Hayes, age forty-four, lives in Birmingham, MI."

"Is that her?" Kate said.

"I don't know."

"Click on *view full report.*"

He did, and they waited while a little icon spun in the middle of the screen. Two minutes later he saw: Summary of results for Colleen O'Donnell Hayes.

"She lives on Ferndale Street in Birmingham," Kate said. "Does that mean anything to you?"

"No, she lived in Detroit when I knew her." Frank read down the list of friends and family and noticed a familiar name. "She's definitely the one. See Suchi Tanaka? She's the girl Ray Skinner was dating when I met him at a party at Colleen's apartment."

Now Colleen lived in a big modern two-story chrome and glass house on a small lot. Frank parked on the street and walked to the front door, knocked and waited, saw someone in the window looking at him. When the front door opened, Frank recognized her immediately. She had short blonde hair now and was still as pretty as ever. They stared at each other for a few seconds.

"Frank, what're you doing here? I'm married. I have children."

"I just want to talk."

"I have to pick the kids up at school." Colleen hesitated and then gave in. "Okay, but I only have a few minutes."

They sat in the living room on leather couches, facing each other, separated by a glass coffee table. The furniture and furnishings, like the house, were modern and elegant.

"When did you get out?" Colleen said. She was rubbing her hands and looked nervous, uncomfortable.

"A month ago."

"I couldn't believe it when I heard you were arrested for armed robbery. And you were married. Another small detail you left out." Colleen's eyes held on him. "I really liked you, Frank." She looked away and then back at him to finish what had been on her mind all those years. "You lied and took advantage of me."

"I'm sorry."

"Do you know how lame that sounds?" Colleen gave him a pained look.

"I can't think of anything else to say."

"Frank, what do you want?"

"I'm trying to find Ray Skinner."

"Why would you think I know?"

Frank said, "You still friends with Suchi?"

"She doesn't know either. Wants nothing to do with him, never wants to see him again."

"What happened?"

Colleen made a face. "I'd rather not go into it."

"Will you ask if she'll talk to me? Skinner's the reason I went to prison."

"You didn't have anything to do with it?"

Frank gave her a sheepish look.

"I'll ask, but I seriously doubt it. What's your number?"

He gave it to her and said, "How long have you been married?"

"Frank, you can't come around here. You can't just show up."

"You happy?"

"Listen, I have to go," Colleen said, standing. "I'll call you."

And she did two hours later, saying Suchi would see him.

•••

FRANK MET HER AT a Starbucks in Royal Oak that afternoon. He was at a table drinking black coffee when Suchi walked in, looking around. Frank waved and she came over. He stood and they hugged and then sat, her cute Japanese face looking almost the same as the last time he saw her. "Thanks for seeing me. I got you green tea." He slid the cup over to her.

"Frank, I've missed you. You were fun to be around. I thought Colleen was lucky. I was even a little jealous of her." Suchi lifted the tea bag, wrapped the string around it, squeezed, and put it on a napkin. "I have to tell you, I was shocked when I heard you were in prison. I couldn't imagine you doing something like that. It was totally out of character."

"Ray set it up, knew when the armored truck was picking up a week's proceeds from Tiger Stadium and the route it would take to the bank." Frank sipped his coffee. "Did he tell you how he made his money?"

"Ray said he was a stockbroker, but worked odd hours and spent a lot of time at the racetrack."

Frank handed her a bank surveillance photo.

Suchi studied it for several seconds and said, "It's Ray."

"He's robbing a bank," Frank said. "That's what he does."

"Thinking back, I'm not surprised. He always had money and we went on a lot of expensive trips. One time we flew first class to Paris and stayed at the Ritz for a week."

"What happened, why'd you break up?"

"At first he was the nicest guy in the world, charming and generous, easy to be with. Ray told me I was perfect for him and he wanted to spend the rest of his life with me. I thought he was *the one.* After a month he asked me to move in with him, and then I saw a different side. I thought he was a perfectionist. He'd tell me how to do things a certain way. How to load the dishwasher. How to fold clothes. How to clean the bathroom. It probably sounds annoying and it was, but Ray was polite about it, always said please and thank you." Suchi's phone rang. She took it out of her purse and turned it off.

"One night I went out with a group of girlfriends. I told Ray I'd be back around eleven but didn't get home till almost midnight and he flipped out. Accused me of cheating on him. Called me horrible names. It was the look on his face and the way he said it that was so disturbing. Like he might kill me. I was shocked." Suchi took a breath. "The next day Ray told me we were soul mates. He didn't like it when I went out with my girlfriends. He wanted me all to himself.

"But after that things got worse. Ray was very controlling. He'd call half a dozen times a day to check up on me, wanted to know where I was, who I was with. I never knew what might set him off. He'd freak out if I left hair in the shower or makeup on the counter. I was always stressed on the way home from work, wondering what kind of mood he was in. I walked on eggshells. It was scary."

"I never saw that side of him," Frank said. "Never saw him lose his cool."

"I wasn't a person. I was his possession. It was like he owned me. One time I forgot to pick up his dry cleaning and he went crazy. I said, 'Ray, you're not my boss. I don't work for you.' He went into a rage, hit me, and I went down on the kitchen floor. I left after that, moved out and found my own place." Suchi drank her tea. "Ray found out where I was living. He came over and apologized, asked me to come back. I told him if I ever saw him again, I would call the police. Remember my brother, Hiroshi?"

"The judo expert."

"He stayed with me for a few weeks, I was so afraid." Suchi tucked her straight black hair behind her ears. "Things were okay for about six months, then one day I was buying groceries and I saw Ray coming down the aisle. I left my cart where it was and ran out of the store." Suchi made a face. "After that Ray would appear out of the blue. I would be with a group of friends in a bar and I'd see him. Or he'd walk past me in the mall."

"Did he ever say anything?"

"No. He just stared at me with those dark eyes."

"You're the one that got away," Frank said.

"I'm the one that ran away."

"Have you seen him lately?"

"It's been a couple years. But no matter where I am or who I'm with I always look around expecting to see him."

"What do you know about Ray? Where's he from?"

"He told me he was born in Detroit. He was an only child and his parents were killed in a car accident."

"Where'd he go to school?"

"I don't know. He never said."

"Did you think it was odd this guy you were living with didn't seem to have a background, a past?" Frank sipped his coffee. "Who were his friends?"

"I thought you were."

"I met Ray the night of Colleen's party. I didn't know him."

"I think he was adopted. I was cleaning the apartment one day and found this under a book in the drawer next to his bed." Suchi took an envelope out of her purse and handed it to him. Frank opened it, and took out a sheet of paper that had been stamped and notarized. At the top of the page it read: CERTIFICATE OF LIVE BIRTH. The child's name was Martin J. Dawson, a male born August 7, 1970, at 3:10 a.m., Henry Ford Hospital, City of Detroit, Wayne County. There was a doctor's signature verifying the time and place of birth, and the registrar's signature. The mother's maiden name was Deborah Lynn Dawson. Where the father's name should have been it read "Unknown." Ms. Dawson was born in the state of Michigan. The certificate was signed and stamped by the city clerk.

Frank said, "Why'd you keep it?"

"I don't know. When Colleen called and said you were trying to find Ray, I remembered I had it."

"Do you mind if I make a copy?"

"You can have it."

"Did Ray's birth mother give him up for adoption?"

"I don't know."

"Were his adoptive parents the Skinners? Did you ever ask Ray?"

"No. I was too worried about his reaction. I could hear him accusing me of snooping around, invading his privacy."

"You said Ray's parents were killed in a car accident. How old was he when it happened?"

"He never said."

"Anything else you can tell me?"

"He loved Harsen's Island. We would take the ferry and stay at the Old Club. It's where rich Detroiters have vacationed for a hundred years. I asked him how he knew about it. He said his father took him when he was a kid. I always felt Ray was playing a role when we were there, pretending to be someone else."

"What do you mean?"

"The way he dressed and acted, putting on airs. He'd wear an ascot and use a cigarette holder. It was funny. One time I said, 'Ray, who are you trying to be?' And he got angry."

"Who was he trying to be?"

"This rich guy he knew whose company built yachts. We would always go for a cruise on one of his boats."

"What's his name?"

"Robert Wheeler."

Frank sipped his coffee. "Do you have kids?"

"We can't, but that's okay. Life is good. Listen, I better go. Nice seeing you, Frank."

"If Ray shows up again, call me, will you?"

TWENTY-FIVE

L OOK AT THIS," FRANK said, handing the birth certificate to Kate. She read it and said, "Who's Martin J. Dawson?"

"Ray Skinner. I got it from the girl he was living with when I met him."

"How did she get it?"

"Found it in his apartment." He told Kate what Suchi had said.

"Why did the mother give her baby up for adoption?"

"No idea," Frank said.

"Let's see if Ms. Dawson's in the system."

Frank stared at the screen as Kate entered "Debbie Dawson" into the NCIC database, and now was looking at Debbie's photograph and criminal history.

> **Name:** Deborah Lynn Dawson
> **Race:** White
> **Gender:** Female
> **Hair Color:** Brown

Eye Color: Green
Height: 5′ 3″
Weight: 117
DOB: 7/14/54
MDOC #: 631 2139
Status: Probationer
Assigned Location: Wayne/ Detroit/ Eastern District/ Probation
Security Level: N/A
Scars / Marks / Tattoos:
    Scar: Surgical scar lower abdomen—C-section
    Tattoo: Inside Right Foot—anchor
    Tattoo: Left Shoulder—Marty
    Tattoo: Lower Back—butterfly
    Body Piercing: Right Ear
    Body Piercing: Left Ear

"Debbie Dawson has one inactive sentence for Controlled Substance Delivery / Heroin—50 Grams," Kate said. "And one active sentence for Distribution of a Schedule 1 Drug. Heroin again. Looks like she did time on that one, was released, and is on probation. "Let me make a couple calls, see if I can locate Ms. Dawson. We'll surprise her."

•••

THE APARTMENT BUILDING ON Milwaukee Street just south of Grand Boulevard had once been a stylish gem but had fallen into serious disrepair. Kate parked on the street. She and Frank went in, moved through the crumbling lobby, and walked up a winding staircase, stepping on pieces of plaster that had fallen from the walls and ceiling. They found apartment 304, and Kate knocked on the door.

She could hear a TV inside. When no one came she knocked again. The door opened and she saw a dark-haired woman with bloodshot eyes, checking them out. "Ms. Dawson, I am a US marshal. I'd like to ask you a few questions." She didn't mention Frank, who was standing next to her.

"You have a warrant?"

"We just want to talk," Kate said.

"That's what they said last time. I ended up doing six years."

"We're not here to arrest you," Kate said.

"What do you want to talk about?"

"Your son, Martin, the boy you gave birth to on August seventh, 1970, at Henry Ford Hospital."

Debbie Dawson unhooked the security chain, opened the door, and backed into the room that had cracked, paint-chipped walls that matched the lobby. There was a couch and a small TV on a coffee table.

"I was sixteen when I had Marty. I gave him up for adoption."

Kate said, "Do you remember the name of the family?"

"The Seavys. His name was Jerry, and hers was Carol. I knew where they lived and used to go spy on Marty. Only, they changed his name to Bobby. I'd drive past their house and see him playing in the yard."

Debbie Dawson, sitting on the couch, lit a cigarette. "They lived in Anchor Bay. It's on the north side of Lake St. Clair." Debbie coughed, brought the cigarette to her mouth, and blew out a cloud of smoke. "Jerry and Carol Seavy were killed in a car accident when Bobby was fourteen."

Frank said, "What happened to the boy?"

"Social Services put him in a foster care facility."

Kate said, "Why didn't you take him?"

"I was addicted to heroin and then I went to prison."

Frank said, "What's the name of the foster care facility?"

"Hope House."

Kate said, "Does the name Ray Skinner mean anything to you?"

Debbie's eyes got big. "That's my old boyfriend. How in the world did you know that?" She seemed surprised "He's Marty's father. His given name was Billy Ray Skinner." Debbie Dawson smiled. "He was trouble—a wild man and a charmer. I couldn't say no to him."

Kate said, "Have you seen or talked to Billy Ray lately?"

"Not in forty years."

"Do you know where he might be?"

"He was murdered in prison."

"How would your son know his father's name?" Kate said. "It's not on the birth certificate."

"He asked me, and I told him."

"When was this?"

"I stopped by the house one day after school. The Seavys were working. I said to the boy, 'Do you know who I am?' And he said, 'My mother.'" Debbie Dawson smiled now. "How about that?"

Kate said, "How did he know?"

"He looked like me, probably saw my face in his. And he didn't look anything like his adopted parents. They were short and stocky, and he was tall for his age and good-looking. Marty, that's how I still think of him, was smart, too. He asked why I gave him up and begged me to take him back. Believe me, I wanted to, but it was too late for that."

Kate said, "Have you kept up with your son, do you know where he lives?"

"No idea."

"When's the last time you saw him?"

"Just before the Seavys were killed."

•••

HOPE HOUSE WAS RUN by a Roman Catholic priest named Father Kelly, an earnest disheveled man with dark hair over his ears and dandruff on the shoulders of his black shirt. They sat at a round club table in Kelly's office in east Detroit.

"I can tell you the boy had a tough life," Father Kelly said. "His mother gave him up for adoption. Once he was old enough to understand what happened, he had to wonder why he'd been abandoned. That can have a profound effect on a young person. Why didn't his parents want him? The boy saw himself as a victim. So whatever he did was justified." The priest took a beat. "After his adoptive parents died in a car accident, Social Services brought him to us. We tried placing him with a number of different families. He was off the charts intelligent, had a 155 IQ. He could be charming, but it was superficial. The boy had no feelings of empathy or compassion."

Kate said, "Do you have the Seavys' old address in Anchor Bay?"

"I'm sure we do."

"How did he get along with them?"

"The sense I get is not well. But I think it had more to do with Bobby's behavior than anything. The boy said they abused him."

Frank said, "Do you believe that?"

Father Kelly said, "Bobby had scars on his arms and legs, but I think they were self-inflicted."

Kate said, "Why would he do that?"

"So we'd think he was mistreated."

Kate said, "What were his experiences with the other families?"

"They all liked him at first. Bobby came across as a sweet kid. But eventually they'd catch him lying or stealing money or hurting one of their children. I can't sugarcoat it, he was a problem. We had similar issues with him when he lived here." Father Kelly opened a file folder, took out a photo, and handed it to Kate. "This is what Bobby looked like just before he ran away."

"How old was he?"

"Sixteen. He and another boy—who had his own psychological issues—snuck out of here early one morning and never came back. I haven't seen or heard from either of them since. Of course, I called the police." Father Kelly hesitated. "But you think Bobby's alive, is that right?"

"We know he is," Kate said. "We have his fingerprints. He's graduated from petty theft to bank robbery and murder."

•••

"The pressure's on," Charlie said at the afternoon meeting in the conference room. "The chief and the marshal want this guy found. So what's the latest? What do we know about Ray Skinner we didn't know before?"

"He was adopted," Kate said.

Now everyone looked at her.

"Where's that coming from?" Charlie said.

"I have a CI who knew a girl Ray Skinner dated." She opened her purse and took out Martin J. Dawson's birth certificate and handed it to Charlie.

Then Kate told them what she knew. When she finished, no one said anything for several seconds until Charlie broke the silence. "And you're saying this kid is the Shooter?"

"His prints—on file at Henry Ford Hospital where he was born—match the prints homicide found on the telescope on Belle Isle," Kate said.

Buck said, "Is he in the system?"

Kate shook her head.

"Who's the CI?" Charlie said.

"A guy who knew Skinner back in the day."

Cornbread said, "What's the man's name?"

"Frank Galvin." Kate decided to come clean. They were going to find out sooner or later.

Charlie said, "Who is he?"

"My father." She told them about Frank and Skinner robbing the armored truck in 1997. And Frank doing time at Victorville.

"Why didn't you tell us?" Charlie said.

"I was waiting for the right time."

She told them about Frank taking off when she was six, and Kate thinking he was dead. "Remember the flowers in my hospital room?" she said, looking at Buck and Cornbread. "They were from Frank." And she told them how she found him, and how they had been getting to know each other. "Frank can help us catch Ray Skinner, knows his habits and inclinations."

"Let me think about how to handle this," Charlie said. "In the meantime, let's keep it between us."

TWENTY-SIX

EVERY TIME RAY DROVE through Anchor Bay it was like going back in time. He pictured himself as a boy walking around the dark house at night, eyes adjusting, seeing the deer heads with their trophy racks on the walls. It was quiet—nobody yelling at him, telling him what to do. He'd take money from his mother's purse or his father's wallet and hide it in his bedroom closet under the floorboards. He had a stash of about $1,200, cash he'd need when he ran away.

He'd go into his parents' room, sliding in his socks on the wood floor, smelling the sour air, hearing his father's heavy snoring, which sounded like an engine backfiring. He'd stand on his mother's side, listening to her breathing, a peaceful look on her face. Nothing like the mean, angry expressions she had when she was awake. He'd watch their bodies move under the covers, thinking about what he'd like to do to them.

One time, Carol opened her eyes and caught him. "What're you doing in here?"

"Nothing."

"Go back to your room. Go to sleep."

He walked out and heard her say, "Jerry, wake up."

"What?"

"The boy was in here staring at us."

"Maybe he couldn't sleep."

"No, I'm telling you there's something wrong with that kid. He's crazy and you know it. I'd like to give him back to the agency."

He had an idea what she was talking about, and a few weeks later, going through his parents' desk he found the birth certificate— and based on the date of birth—it had to be his. He never thought Carol and Jerry were his real parents. He didn't look anything like them, and he was smarter than both of them put together.

His birth mother's name was Deborah Lynn Dawson. And his real name was Martin J. Dawson. He couldn't imagine being called Marty; it was a pussy name. Bobby was bad enough. But soon he'd be able to choose his own name, be anyone he wanted.

Ray parked in the Sassy Marina lot and carried supplies to his boat. He pulled the canvas cover off, stowed it below with his gear, and fired up the engines. He released the dock lines, maneuvered out of the marina, and went left on the river to the Pointe Grande Cut that took him to the south channel. He cruised by Tashmoo Marine, where Jerry had been a mechanic and would bring him to work occasionally. Ray would earn a couple dollars washing boats. With his newfound wealth, he'd walk into the village of San Souci and buy a cookie and an Atlas orange soda.

After work Jerry would go to the bar with the other mechanics and drink for a couple hours while Ray sat on the riverbank, watching boats pass by.

Jerry'd come out with a six pack in a paper bag and drink beer on the way home, holding the cans in his grease-stained fingers. He'd finish one, squeeze the can almost flat and toss it on the floor at Ray's feet, belch and say, "What're you waitin' for?" And Ray would pull another one out of the plastic tightener and hand it to him.

Coming home from work on Saturday afternoon Ray would see rich teenagers partying on their fancy boats—thirty or forty of them anchored together in Little Muscamoot Bay. Jerry would glance at them and say, "Look at those rich assholes—Jesus, nothing better to do."

Jerry would be smashed by dinner, getting loud and mean, complaining about what they were eating, complaining about his life and the cards he was dealt, going into poor-me mode. But that part of Ray's life was long gone.

He cruised to the end of the island past the Old Club with its multicolored buildings, tennis courts, and golf course. As always, there were yachts moored against the sea wall.

Ray gunned the Wheeler around the southern end of the island and headed north, straight up the middle channel, the sun high, hull slicing through the cool clean water. It took nine minutes to get to the house. He opened the boat-well door with a remote and eased the Wheeler inside. He secured the dock lines, lowered the door, and walked up the steps into the house that no one had ever been in except him.

•••

THROUGH THE PICTURE WINDOW, Kate watched a freighter creep along the horizon.

"I didn't find the bodies, but I was called to the scene," retired sheriff, Bob Havern, said. "It looked like an accident. Pickup veered off road and hit an oak tree at sixty miles an hour and the oak tree won."

He was a big man with a ruddy complexion and thinning salt and pepper hair. He filled the La-Z-Boy with his doughy girth. Kate sat on the couch next to Frank in Havern's cottage, admiring the stunning view of Lake St. Clair bright and blue in the distance.

"It was an old truck that didn't have airbags, and the Seavys weren't wearing seatbelts. They went through the windshield and were pronounced dead at the scene. It was a sad situation. Doubly so 'cause they had an out-of-control fourteen-year-old kid at home." Havern made a face and massaged his shoulder.

Kate said, "Are you okay?"

"Rotator cuff. I had surgery six months ago, and it's still bothering me." He squirmed in the chair trying to get comfortable. "So as I was saying, it appeared to be an accident. Driver error. But even so, I wondered how it happened. Seavy's blood alcohol level was well under the limit. He wasn't drunk, which was unusual 'cause he was a drinker and known for getting out of control. Had two DWFs."

Kate gave him a puzzled look.

"Driving while fucked up." Havern held his gaze on her. "That's what the sheriff's department used to call it." He shifted his weight in the chair. "So what caused the accident, you're wondering. Did he swerve to miss a deer? They're common enough around here." Bob Havern rubbed his pale meaty face with bratwurst fingers. "Anyway, I had the vehicle towed to a garage in Fair Haven, mechanic I knew. Lo and behold he checks the brakes and sees the brake fluid reservoir is empty."

Kate said, "What does that mean?"

"The brakes didn't work."

"I understand that," Kate said. "How did it happen? Was it willful or neglect?"

"Seavy was in the trade so you'd think he would've known better," Bob Havern said. "But he was working on everyone else's car and probably forgot about his own."

Kate said, "Were there any suspects?" Thinking about the boy now. A smart kid who watched his father work on cars and probably helped him. Did Bobby have the motivation and skill to do it?

"What're you talking about? Like some disgruntled customer was pissed off enough to take the man's life? That's a hell of a stretch, don't you think?"

It was unless you knew something about Ray Skinner's proclivities. "Earlier you said the boy was out of control. Would you explain that, please?"

Bob Havern let out a breath. "Jiminy Christmas, where do I begin?" He shook his head. "A few years before the parents were killed, the boy vandalized the elementary school, throwing rocks at the windows. Caused a few hundred dollars in damage. I'm sure Jerry took a belt to him for that. I'd a' done the same." The big man sat with his mouth open, thinking. "It was one thing after another. Boy was accused of stealing a hunting knife at Kaiser's, the local hardware store. He was accused of setting fire to a mobile home while the owner was at work. All that in addition to fights and disciplinary issues at school."

Kate said, "What were the circumstances of the mobile home fire?"

"Next door neighbor saw the boy in the area right about the time it started."

"Why would he do it?"

"That's what everyone wanted to know. I drove out to the house and talked to Carol, the boy's mother. She said something like, 'It's no secret Bobby gets into his share of mischief.'"

"I said, 'This is way beyond mischief, don't you think?' Carol called the boy's name and he came in the room. I said, 'Son, you know anything about the fire in Mr. Cardell's trailer?' The boy looked me in the eye and said, 'No, sir,' calm as could be, no fear or concern. Now Carol said, 'Bobby, if you had anything to do with it, I want you to tell us the truth.' The kid said he didn't. I said, 'You sure? 'Cause I got a witness saw you in the area about three thirty.' Carol wanted to know who it was. I told her that was confidential information. There was five grand worth of damage, and it could've been a lot worse. It was arson, no two ways about it."

Kate said, "Did you believe the boy?"

"No, I did not."

"Why?"

"It's hard to explain. You had to be there. You had to see his face. There was this cold emptiness about him like he didn't have feelings, didn't care one way or the other."

"Maybe he was afraid," Frank said.

"I didn't see it," Havern said, turning his head from side to side, and rubbing his shoulder. "The boy had a similar reaction when his parents were killed. I stopped by the house to tell him. I said, 'Son, I have some tragic news to share with you.' We sat in chairs across from each other. I was trying to think of how to tell him and said, 'Your folks were in a traffic accident this evening. Ran off the road and hit a tree. They died instantly. There was no pain or suffering, you can rest assured of that. I'm sorry for your loss.'"

Kate said, "What did he say?"

"Nothing. Not a word. Never changed his expression." Bob Havern took a breath. "It was late, and I couldn't just leave him there alone. So I took him to stay with Naomi and me for the night. She gave the boy a piece of pie and a glass of milk, hugged him, took him to the guest room, and put him in bed."

Kate said, "Do you have children?"

"No, just the two of us. It was after three when I heard our bedroom door open. I saw the boy coming toward me, but it looked like he was going for my holstered service revolver on the nightstand. I sat up and startled him. I said, 'What do you think you're doing?' He said, 'I can't sleep,' in that same calm voice."

Kate said, "What did you think he was going to do?"

"I didn't know, but I'll tell you it made me nervous. Here I was, an armed police officer, worried about a fourteen-year-old kid. I took him back to his room and laid awake the rest of the night. First thing in the morning I called a woman I knew at Social Services. She came and picked him up. I have to tell you: I was relieved and figured I'd be hearing more about this kid someday."

Havern labored to lift himself from the La-Z-Boy, breathing hard as he walked them to the door. "You take care now and good luck bringing this boy to justice."

"What do you think?" Frank said when they were in the car. "Was the kid responsible for the deaths of his parents?"

"I was wondering the same thing. But how could a fourteen-year-old kid be capable of that?"

TWENTY-SEVEN

TELL ME ABOUT RAY," Kate said. "What was it like living with him?"

Yumi, sitting across the table, met her gaze. She had dark bags under her red eyes and looked pale and thin in the yellow jail fatigues. "He thought he was the greatest person in the world. Ray loved looking at himself in the mirror, making faces, and he loved talking about himself, telling me I had never met anyone as smart as him. Ray used to say, 'Do you know how lucky you are to be with me?'"

"Did Ray have friends? Did you ever go out with other couples?"

"Never. Ray said we didn't need friends. We had each other."

"Didn't you think that was strange?

"Yes, but Ray said he wanted me all to himself. At first, I was flattered. But after a while, I wanted to get away from him. He smothered me. We did everything together. We would go out to dinner and to the racetrack. He loved to bet on the thoroughbreds. In summer we would spend a couple weekends on Harsen's Island."

According to Frank, Suchi Tanaka had said something similar.

"Where did you stay?"

"At the Old Club. Ray loved it."

"At home did he expect you to cook, clean, and do his laundry?"

Yumi nodded. "And he was very particular. Everything had to be done a certain way. If I didn't fold his clothes right, he would make me to do it again."

"Did he ever accuse you of cheating on him?"

"One time, but it wasn't true. I was out with friends and returned home later than I expected. I walked in the apartment and Ray said, 'Who is he?' I said, 'Who are you talking about?' Ray said, 'The guy you're seeing.' I thought he was kidding."

"Did Ray ever abuse you physically?"

Yumi stared at the table.

"Why did you stay with him?"

Yumi was crying now as she looked up. "I don't know. It was like I was brainwashed, or he cast a spell on me. I knew Ray was bad, but I couldn't bring myself to leave him." She rubbed her handcuffed wrists. "Here's something else. He had cameras installed in the apartment. Ray said it was because he kept a lot of cash. I think it was so he could keep an eye on me, make sure I wasn't seeing someone on the side. I didn't realize it at the time."

"When did things start to go bad between you?"

"When I told him I wanted to get married and start a family."

"What did Ray want?"

"I don't know."

"Have you talked to a lawyer?"

Yumi shook her head.

"Why did you rob the bank?"

Tears were streaming down her cheeks now as she brought her hands to her face.

"Did Ray force you to do it?"

She lowered her hands, wet eyes holding on Kate. "It was my idea."

"Why?"

"We needed money. Ray lost most of our savings gambling."

"I want to help you, but you have to give me something."

She stared at the table.

Thinking the conversation was over, Kate slid her chair back and got up.

"I think Ray has a house on Harsen's Island."

Kate sat, her attention back on Yumi.

"He talked about getting a place on the water and traveling everywhere by boat."

"Where is the house?"

"I don't know."

"You have to give me something or there isn't much I can do to help you."

•••

KATE POURED A GLASS of wine and sat at the kitchen table across from Frank and summarized her conversation with Yumi.

"All right," Frank said. "We've heard about Ray Skinner's Harsen's connection from three different people. Does he have a house there? Who knows. But it makes sense, don't you think? It's a perfect hideaway. He can get there by boat or car, and probably knows every inch of the island. How many people live there?"

"One thousand one hundred and fifty-eight, give or take."

"How do you know that?" Frank sipped his beer. "Let me guess, the internet."

"You're catching on. Harsen's median age is 58.3. And the island is five square miles. There are three restaurants, a post office, and a couple grocery stores. If Ray Skinner has a place there then someone knows him and knows where he lives. I'm getting a list of all the homeowners from the Clay Township Assessing office. If you own a home, you pay taxes, right?"

"Okay, I'm with you so far."

"I think we should go there tomorrow, check it out," Kate said.

"What are you doing tonight?"

"Believe it or not, I have a date."

"Of course I believe it," Frank said. "You should be fighting them off, and I'm not talking about fugitives."

"Spoken like an out-of-touch father."

"Your out-of-touch father has a date, too."

"The realtor?"

"We're meeting at a French restaurant in Birmingham. Beyond that I don't know."

"Just remember you're vulnerable," Kate said, trying not to smile but couldn't help herself. "Don't let her take advantage of you."

•••

"You look good," Adam said, sitting across the table in the loud, crowded restaurant. He flashed a nervous grin.

"Are you saying I didn't the last time you saw me?"

"No, I didn't mean—"

"Relax, will you? I'm kidding."

Now Adam smiled.

"You look good too." He wore an unbuttoned plaid shirt with a blue T-shirt under it. He hadn't shaved in a few days and Kate liked his scruffy look.

"Listen, I'm sorry. I've been an asshole. I know you were just doing your job." He drank some ale and wiped foam off his upper lip with a shirt sleeve.

"When did you decide that?"

"I don't know, a couple days later. I thought you'd call me. You're the one that had to leave."

"I think you've been seeing someone. That's just a guess. You want a girl that's more reliable, someone that doesn't walk out in the middle of a date. I get it."

"I was angry. I wanted to hang out with you." Adam paused. "You may find this hard to believe but I like you."

Adam had never been this open and honest, and it caught her off guard.

"You'd been called away a couple other times, and I took it personally."

"It's going to happen again. When I get a call, I have to go." Kate picked up the sandwich and took a bite, washed it down with a swig of beer. "I don't think I'm the girl for you."

"Then why're you here?"

"I wanted to see you."

"But you said you don't want to go out with me."

"I said you should date someone with a more predictable schedule."

"So let me get this straight. You think you know what I want and you're making the decision for me, is that right?"

"No, I'd like to see you. I just don't know if it's going to work."

"Do you want it to work?"

"Yeah."

"Then you make an effort. You try. You don't give up." Adam bit into a barbecued rib.

All of that from the guy she hadn't spoken to in six weeks.

He said, "What've you been doing?"

"Recovering from a gunshot wound."

"Are you serious?" He put the rib on his plate. "You say it so calm and matter-of-fact. What happened?"

Kate watched Adam, brow furrowed, eyes glued to her while she told him.

"What's it feel like to get shot?"

"It happened so fast. I didn't even know it. I think I was in shock. Never felt a thing till I woke up in the hospital."

"Why didn't you call me?"

"I don't know." But the truth was she kept picturing the look on his face when she got up from the table and walked out of the restaurant. "There was an article about it in the *Free Press*."

Adam said, "What happened to the person that shot you?"

"He's dead."

"Do you feel lucky?"

"I don't think of it that way," Kate said.

"How do you think of it?"

"I don't know."

"I'm glad you're okay."

After dinner, they went back to Kate's apartment. "Find us a movie," she said, heading for the kitchen. "What can I get you?"

"I'm good for now."

She poured herself a glass of wine and went back in the living room. The TV was on. Adam said, "*Full Metal Jacket* or *How to Lose a Guy in 10 Days*?"

"One sounds like my job, the other one sounds like our relationship."

Adam got up from the couch and put his arms around her. "I don't want to watch a movie. I want to see your stitches."

Kate grabbed his hand and led him to the bedroom. She set her glass on the bedside table. And now Adam put his arms around her and his mouth on hers. They made out for a few minutes, standing next to the bed. Kate unbuttoned her blouse, took it off, and let it fall to the floor. He was staring at the gauze and surgical tape that started just below her collarbone and went over her shoulder, covering part of her back.

Kate loosened the tape and pulled the bandage off, Adam made a face as he stared at the bruised skin around the incision, bent his head and lightly kissed the wound. "Does it hurt?"

"When I move a certain way, it feels tight." Kate pulled the covers back on the bed, took off the rest of her clothes, and laid down, watching Adam undress. They had spent the night together once, but tonight there was a feeling of nervousness as if it was the first time. She turned off the lamp, and he was a pale gangly blur getting in next to her. Then feeling the weight and heat of his body, skin on skin, Adam's mouth finding hers. Then he was inside her and they were moving together, finding their rhythm, Kate thinking this's what she needed. Did she ever.

TWENTY-EIGHT

KATE OPENED HER EYES to morning light coming in through a broken slat in the blinds. Adam was gone but there was a note on the bedside table.

Got to work today. Glad we got together. I'll call you.

She pulled the covers back, slid out of bed, moved into the bathroom, slipped on a robe, and brushed her teeth.

There was an email with an attachment from Kelli Davis at the Clay Township Assessing office. Kate opened the file and scrolled down the list of names, homeowners who were paying property taxes on Harsen's Island, but didn't see Ray Skinner's name.

She made coffee and a fried egg and sat at the kitchen table, eating breakfast, reading the sports section. The Tigers were three games out of first place with about three weeks till the end of the season. They had a good chance as long as the pitching held up and Miggy stayed healthy.

A little after ten she picked up Frank at the realtor's house, a big colonial in Bloomfield Village. He smiled as he got in the car.

"You look happy," Kate said. "Or is it satisfaction? Went well, huh?"

"I feel like a high school kid who just got laid for the first time. I think I'm in love."

"I think you're in lust. You don't know the difference 'cause it's been so long. Will you see her again?"

"Are you kidding? I can't wait to see her. We did it twice last night and once this morning."

"TMI."

"That's right, people speak in acronyms now."

"I read an article written by a psychologist that said women should make an emotional connection before jumping into bed. That way it doesn't seem like a hookup or a fling. Sleeping with someone on the first date sends the wrong message."

"Are you putting me on?"

"Uh-huh."

"Good. I'm a little out of practice. Tell me what I should've done."

"What you did. Were you nervous?"

"Do you want the play-by-play?" Frank let out a breath. "How about you? How was your night?"

Kate smiled. "Not bad."

"Did he stay over?"

"I'm not telling."

"You afraid I'll get the wrong idea about you?"

"Check this out, will you?" Kate handed him the list of Harsen's Island property owners.

"Trying to change the subject?" Frank looked at it and said, "Any luck?"

Kate shook her head.

"Maybe he's renting," Frank said. "That shouldn't be too hard to find out."

Kate took I-94 North and fifty-five minutes later pulled up to the dock. The ferry carried Kate's Audi and six other cars across the St. Clair River to the island. The trip took about five minutes. Now Kate drove south on highway 154. She stopped in Sans Souci, a small village that had a bar, a post office, and a couple shops. She parked in front of the bar, and Frank followed her inside.

It was eleven thirty and already crowded. There were big picture windows along the east side of the room with a stunning view of the south channel. "Hungry?" Kate said. Frank nodded and they sat at the bar and ordered cheeseburgers and drinks, a Coke for her and a beer for him. Kate took a photo of Ray Skinner out of her purse. When the bartender, a skinny forty-something blonde approached and set their drinks down, Kate showed her the photo. "Do you happen to know this guy?"

The bartender stared at the photograph and shook her head. "He sure looks familiar, but I don't I know him. Let me get the manager. Phil knows everyone."

A few minutes later a bald heavy-set guy in a Hawaiian shirt came out of the kitchen. "Can I help you?" He glanced at the photo of Ray still on the bar. "This the guy you're looking for? I've seen him in here, I'm sure of it. Couple times with a little Asian gal. But I don't know his name or where he lives or anything like that."

She thanked him and he walked into the dining room, greeting customers.

After lunch Kate went to the post office and showed the photograph of Ray Skinner to a woman behind the counter. She didn't know him but said he looked familiar.

When they were in the car Frank said, "Now where're we going?"

"The Old Club. That's where the high rollers stay and where Ray took his girls. Suchi mentioned it, didn't she? And so did Yumi. The poor orphan boy from Anchor Bay was someone important when he was there. I called, left a message for the manager, identified myself, and told him we were looking for Ray Skinner, who was a member. Never heard back from him. So this'll be interesting."

They were on a narrow road on a narrow strip of land, the bluest water Kate had ever seen on both sides of them. The club was up ahead. As they approached, she could see the multicolored buildings, yachts docked along the sea wall and the manicured golf course. She stopped at the gatehouse and introduced herself. "US Marshal Kate McGraw here to see Mr. Murray." She showed her ID to the security guard. He picked up the phone, spoke in a hushed voice. "Yes, sir, she's here now." The guard hung up the phone. "Mr. Murray will see you. Pull up over there," the guard pointed to a two-story clapboard building, "and go in the office."

James Murray, sixty, wore a seersucker suit and round glasses with tortoiseshell frames.

"I apologize," Murray said, shaking Kate's hand. "It's the end of the season. Let's go to my office." She followed him. "Please make yourself comfortable." He indicated a chair across from his enormous antique desk. There were framed illustrations of fish on the walls, an ancient wooden ship's wheel mounted to a brass helm in the corner of the room. There were brass ship lights and a diving helmet on a table. "To answer your question," Murray said, "in one hundred years no one by the name of Ray Skinner has ever been a member of the Old Club. So if he isn't a member, he must've been a guest. I had to do some digging. That's why I didn't call you back right away." Murray glanced at his computer screen and worked the keyboard. "Turns out Mr. Skinner has been an occasional guest of Robert Wheeler going back twenty years." Murray paused. "Mr. Wheeler'a a yacht builder from Florida, comes here for a month every summer."

"How does he know Ray Skinner?"

"You'll have to ask Mr. Wheeler."

"Where can I find him?"

"On his yacht, or on the golf course."

As it turned out he was on his yacht. Kate stepped on deck and was met by a weightlifter in a yellow golf shirt. "Can I help you?"

"I'm a US marshal here to see Mr. Wheeler." Kate had the star on a chain around her neck and held up her ID.

"What's this about?"

"A bank robber."

He stepped in the cabin, came back a few minutes later. "Mr. Wheeler will see you."

"A bank robber, huh? Sounds interesting. Who is he?" Robert Wheeler was tall and trim, with silver hair and the deep tan of a sportsman who lived in the sun.

"Your buddy, Ray Skinner."

Wheeler grinned. "Did Ray put you up to this?" He shook his head. "You got me."

Kate unfolded the grainy photo of Skinner and handed it to him. Wheeler stared at it for several beats. "Even looks like him. Did you do this in photoshop?"

"It's a surveillance shot of Ray Skinner robbing a bank in Detroit."

Now Wheeler frowned. "Why would he do that?"

"It's what he does." Kate took a beat. "How long have you known Mr. Skinner?"

"Twenty years. I sold him a '46 Garwood and we became friends. Ray's an interesting guy. I invite him to join me here for a couple weekends every summer. Ray brings one of his cute little Asian girlfriends and stays in the hotel."

"How many cute little Asian are you talking about?"

"I don't know—five at least. They're shy little things, sexy and subservient."

"When was the last time you saw Ray?"

"A month ago. He sold the Garwood back to me and picked up his new boat. That's what I do, my company. We build boats and yachts. This is one of mine." He glanced across the luxurious cabin and shrugged as if owning a seventy-foot yacht was no big deal.

Kate nodded. "It's nice."

Wheeler smiled. "Nice, huh? Talk about understated. I'll have to use that in our literature."

"Do you have a photograph of Skinner's boat?"

Wheeler had his phone in his hand, scrolling through images until he found what he was looking for and turned it sideways so Kate could see. The boat had a sleek white aerodynamic shape with blacked-out windows.

"It's a Wheeler 320. What do you think?"

"It's beautiful. What does he call it?" Kate said, remembering every boat she'd ever seen had a name on the stern.

"Sujin of the Seas. It means 'master' in Japanese. Can I build one for you?"

"How much?"

"Prices start at fifty thousand."

So, contrary to what Yumi had said, Skinner didn't seem to have money problems. "You said Ray Skinner came and picked up his new boat."

"He did, and said he was going to a marina in Detroit and that he'd call me."

"Was anyone with him?"

"No. But he'd brought Yumi, the girl he was seeing, a couple weeks before that."

"How did Skinner pay for the boat?"

"With cash. If I remember correctly, with all the options, it was closer to sixty thousand."

"Isn't that unusual? Who carries that much money with them?"

"You'd be surprised. Boats attract crazy wealthy people."

Kate was thinking of the stories she'd heard about million-dollar yachts seized from drug dealers by the US Marshals Asset Forfeiture group. "What did you think Skinner did for a living?"

"I thought he was a playboy with a trust fund, a man of leisure."

"Thanks for your time, Mr. Wheeler. If you hear from Ray, call me, will you?" She handed him a card.

Frank was on a park bench staring out at the river when Kate came back to the car. "How're you doing?"

He turned toward her. "For a guy who lived in a six-by-eight box all those years, this isn't bad. I could sit here all day." He got up and stood facing her now. "What'd you find out?"

"The news about Ray Skinner's financial difficulties have been greatly exaggerated. He just bought a sixty thousand dollar boat and paid cash."

"Business must be good."

On the way to Brown's, Kate slowed the car, looking across stretches of marshland and canals that connected the island to the south channel of the St. Clair River. There were homes with docks lining the banks. The only way in or out, it appeared, was by boat. If you were hiding out, this would be a perfect place to do it.

Kate parked in the lot, went in, and sat on the far side of the horseshoe-shaped bar that was empty except for a couple young guys in Tigers caps drinking beer. Kate stared out at the marina and the wall of cattails bordering the land across the channel. Frank ordered a beer. Kate showed the photo of Ray to the bartender and was surprised when the guy said he was in there yesterday. "Docks his boat and sits at the bar, drinks bourbon on the rocks."

"How do you know his boat?" Kate said.

"It's a classic, an old wooden speed boat."

"Is it by chance a 1946 Garwood?"

"It's a Garwood. I'm just not sure about the year. Lately I've seen him tooling around in a Wheeler sport craft, which, if you know boats, doesn't come cheap."

Frank said, "How often do you see him?"

"It could be a couple times in a week and then not for a month."

Kate said, "Do you know him?"

"Not really, keeps to himself."

Frank said, "Ever see him with a little Asian girl?"

"Not that I recall."

"Does he live on the island?" Frank said.

"I don't know, but when he leaves, I see him go north up the channel."

Frank said, "Where's it go?"

"Runs into the St. Clair River and the mainland. He could have a cottage on Harsen's, or he could live across the way on Dickinson Island."

"What's there?"

"Nothing much. It's mostly marsh." The bartender adjusted his cap that had *Brown's* logotype on the front. "He could live on the south channel or the north channel or dock his boat at a marina in Anchor Bay. There's no telling. Me, I'd look for a house with a custom boat-well. All the money he's got in those boats, he's gonna want to keep them protected."

TWENTY-NINE

LOWELL HAD SWITCHED VEHICLES with Odette. He was driving her Ford Fiesta and she had his Dodge Ram, complaining it was too big, too hard to park, and didn't fit her image. Lowell'd had a good laugh about that one. He said, "Your image? What image is that? Looked in the mirror lately? You're an overweight, over-the-hill bimbo. If anything, the truck's adding to your image."

Lowell felt like a pussy in the little Ford hatchback, imaging guys looking at him and laughing. But as far as blending in, the pussy mobile did the trick. He followed the judge from the courthouse back to his house for a few days. Nothing to it. No marshal security detail. No law enforcement visible anywhere.

That night, watching a Charles Bronson movie on TV, Lowell got an idea about how to take out the judge. All he'd need was two boys with the proper motivation, a pickup truck, and a rifle.

Next morning, he enlisted the services of Sonny and Cooter, two rednecks from the same Easter basket. Lowell told them the objective of the operation was to assassinate the judge, put Vernon away. Any problem? "No," they both said. "Be my pleasure," Cooter added.

"Just be downtown Detroit today at four thirty," Lowell said. "I'll direct you from there."

Sonny was Larry Jennings, an intense, out-of-work pipe fitter, and an ace with a thirty-ought six. Cooter was Earl Tibbits, a retired lathe operator who had time on his hands and liked to stay busy, help the *cause*.

Lowell described the judge's Mercedes and gave them his usual route home, although, of course, you never knew where His Honor might go after his day on the bench, sending God-fearing citizens to federal prison.

What he didn't expect was the judge to make two stops on the way home, taking his time while he went to the market on Gratiot and then a wine store. Lowell was hoping Sonny and Coots were patient and kept their minds on the job.

•••

AN HOUR OR SO after he left the courthouse, after running errands, Steve Gant was driving eastbound on Jefferson, heading home. Traffic was heavy, four lanes going west away from the city and four going east into it, the Detroit River glistening under a hot, late-summer sun. He was thinking about his conversation with Michele Zimmer on behalf of Deputy Marshal McGraw. It had gone about the way he expected. Michele, the sexual intellectual, couldn't just take his word for it. She wanted to see the file. She wanted to make sure Mr. Galvin's testimony was critical to the success of the case. Steve asked her to put Galvin on probation. Michele said she hadn't even seen the record of the arrest and could not promise anything until she had thoroughly reviewed the case. Any other course of action would be unprofessional. She was a pain in the ass when he'd dated her in law school, but in his defense, Michele was sexy then. He remembered taking her to a movie one night and back to his apartment. He was making out with her in the kitchen, trying to get her in bed. Michele pushed away from him and said, "Will you make me scrambled eggs and toast?"

He said, "It's midnight."

"I'm hungry."

So he made her the eggs and when Michele finished eating she was tired and wanted to go home.

A pickup truck cutting in front of him brought Steve back to the present. He jerked the steering wheel and swung into the left lane but the truck cut in front of him again and now there was a car next to him and another one behind him. The Ramones were doing "The KKK Took My Baby Away."

He turned the volume down waiting for the light to turn green. Traffic started to move but the pickup didn't. Steve gave it a couple beats and laid on the horn. Now a man with a rifle rose up from the truck bed and fired a couple times, blowing holes in the windshield. Steve went down as low as he could under a shower of glass, blood rushing from a wound in his chest. Had to be another Vernon Meeks' reprisal. He was faint and losing consciousness as he called 911.

THIRTY

RAY WAS SHAVING, STARING at himself in the mirror, thinking about the US marshals he'd seen on his apartment balcony in Windsor. He wanted to know who they were and what they knew. Ray called Dick Sherry, a personal injury attorney whose name he'd seen on a billboard on I-75. The headline said:

ATTORNEY DICK SHERRY
PUT YOUR TRUST IN A WINNER

There was a photo of Dick Sherry in a solemn pose, and under it, a telephone number.

This guy was perfect: an ambulance chaser who wouldn't ask a lot of questions. He met counselor Sherry in his cluttered office on a freeway service drive. There were stacks of file folders on every available surface: the desk, the chairs, the floor. Ray couldn't imagine hiring someone who looked so disorganized, but this was a unique situation.

Dick Sherry reminded him of Jerry Lewis as a Latin American drug lord in a decorative guayabera shirt and tan pleated slacks, a gold Rolex clamped on one of his hairy wrists. Sherry picked up a stack of folders off a chair, dropped them on the floor in front of his desk, and motioned for Ray to sit. "First, tell me who referred you."

"A billboard on I-75."

Dick Sherry didn't react. "My specialty is personal injury. Car and truck accidents, premises liability, medical malpractice, dog bites, amputations, nursing home neglect, and abuse." He paused for effect. "Something I want you to understand. My clients come first."

"I hear you get results," Ray said.

"Who told you that?"

"I've seen your ads. Very convincing—with just the right amount of sincerity."

"Well, believe me, I try. It's not a job, it's a passion, a calling. What can I do for you?"

"I want you to get me the names of the US marshals on the bank robbery task force, looking for the Shooter."

"I don't do criminal law."

"I want the names and profiles of those involved. That shouldn't be too difficult. You know where their office is?"

"Federal building on West Lafayette, half a block from the Lafayette Coney Island."

"Will fifteen hundred dollars be enough to retain your services?" Ray pulled a wad of hundred-dollar bills out of his sport coat pocket and now Dick Sherry's eyes lit up.

"I'm confident we can work something out."

"You sure? 'Cause if you can't, I'm sure I can find someone that can."

"No, sir. I'm definitely your man."

Ray liked this guy backpedaling, willing to do anything for a payday. "How long's it gonna take?"

"A week or so due to my heavy case load at the moment."

"You've got till the end of the day. Take it or leave it."

"How can I reach you?"

"I'll reach you."

Ray finished shaving, wiped streaks of shaving cream off his face with a towel, and got dressed.

He called Dick Sherry a little after five and got the names of the US marshals: Sam Dodge, Charlie Luna, Terrell Reed, and Kate McGraw.

The next morning Ray drove to the federal courthouse at seven thirty and parked on Lafayette Street just east of Shelby. He drank coffee and ate a Danish, watching the marshals, a dozen or so, arrive in their mismatched vehicles—ten-year-old cars, trucks, and vans. They parked across the street from the courthouse and met on the sidewalk in their duty belts and bulletproof vests, talking, laughing, and drinking coffee. He recognized the dark-haired guy that was on his apartment balcony, and assumed, studying his Hispanic features, the man was Charlie Luna. Kate McGraw, the lone female on the alpha-male task force, was easy to spot. Looking at her Ray would never have guessed she was a US marshal. Didn't seem to fit the profile. She was too girlish and pretty.

Okay, now he saw who he was dealing with. It was time to get back to work.

•••

FIVE HOURS LATER RAY walked into the Huntington Bank at 602 South Monroe Street. It was 1:37 p.m. He wore the navy-blue Brooks Brothers suit, a light-blue shirt, and a striped tie. And an ash brown wig that looked like real hair and a fake mustache.

There were three customers at the teller windows and several more at the island counter in the middle of the lobby filling out deposit or withdrawal slips. Ray was calm and focused, aware of everything around him as he approached the open teller window carrying the soft black laptop bag like a briefcase. "How're you doing today?"

"Fine, thank you." The teller had long straight hair to her shoulders, trying to look younger, but it wasn't working. "Sir, how may I be of assistance?"

"What's your name?"

"Vivian."

"That's pretty. Listen, Viv, this is a holdup." Ray slid the gun out of his case, eyes locked on hers. "Do what you're told and everything will be fine. Press that button you're looking at and I'll shoot you dead."

Her hands were shaking as she stuffed banded bundles of bills into the laptop case. When she finished, Ray took his time, walked out of the bank, and got in the car.

•••

HE WAS BACK IN Detroit, parked on Shelby, when the marshals returned from their work day. They got out of their cars as they had that morning, stood in a group, and talked for a few minutes, Ray's attention holding on the girl before they all crossed the street and went into the federal building.

He saw her again about half an hour later, getting in her Ford SUV, and followed her in rush-hour traffic to an apartment building in Royal Oak. She parked in the lot and went inside. Ray waited a few minutes, got out of the car, walked in the entrance, and stood in the vestibule, scanning names in the directory until he saw K. McGraw in 208.

•••

THE NEXT MORNING, HE watched her come out of the apartment building at seven thirty, get in the SUV, and take off. Ray knew where she was going. He waited twenty minutes, grabbed an empty Starbucks cup, got out of the car, went in the building, and stood in the vestibule. He said good morning to a woman who looked like she was dressed for work, held the door for her as she walked out.

Ray knocked on the door to 208 and waited. Maybe McGraw had a boyfriend or a husband who was still in the apartment. He knocked again, waited, picked the lock, and went inside.

There was a framed Compari poster on the wall in the living room and discount furniture: a couch, chair, and coffee table on cheap taupe carpeting. There was a framed photo of an elderly couple on the credenza against the wall. He picked it up, studied the faces, and put it down.

Ray walked in the bedroom, staring at the unmade bed, clothes draped over a chair. He opened the top drawer of her dresser, running his fingers over panties and thongs in pink and black and white.

He opened the closet and scanned her clothes: blouses, jeans, and dresses. Outfits any girl might have. He opened a velvet jewelry box, picked up a turquoise necklace, and slid it in his pocket.

There were wet towels on the floor in the bathroom, a white terrycloth robe hanging on a hook on the back of the door. There was makeup, perfume, a toothbrush, and toothpaste on the counter next to the sink. Working for the Marshals Service he thought she'd be more disciplined, neater, better organized—and it annoyed him.

Ray opened the medicine cabinet and scanned the shelves, looking at a packet of birth control pills, bottles of Motrin and Aleve, Alka-Seltzer and Tums, Zicam, and a prescription for Ambien. He opened the Ambien, tapped out a couple pills, and put them in his pocket.

The second bedroom was an office. He walked in, surprised to see a dozen photos of him in various disguises, and several of Yumi taped to the wall. There was a stack of folders, a file on each bank robbery. He read the newspaper articles and correspondence and felt relieved. They didn't seem to have a clue who he was. Ray was about to get up and noticed a DVD on the desk. Written in marker on the label it read *The Shooter.*

He tried to boot up her computer but didn't get far without the password. He'd watch it later.

In the kitchen he grabbed a banana from a bowl on the counter, peeled it halfway, and took a bite. It was overripe, and he dropped it in the waste basket under the sink. He opened the refrigerator, scanned the shelves, seeing milk, juice, yogurt, red grapes. There was a bottle of white wine that was half full. He pulled the cork and dropped two Ambien tablets into the chardonnay.

There was a piece of meatloaf in a Ziploc plastic bag. He set it on the counter, slid a knife out of the wooden block, cut off a slice, and ate it cold with his fingers, surprised how good it was.

Ray washed the barbecue sauce off his hand and dried it with a paper towel. He left the knife in the sink and the meatloaf on the counter. That was important. Get in her head. She'd see it and wonder, start to worry.

He checked the rest of the drawers and cabinets, not looking for anything in particular, and saw the Audi key fob, and next to it was a metal ring with two keys on it.

Now he placed the cameras, slid the book cam on a shelf in the living room, and set it in motion detector mode. Ray put the black USB charger cam high on a wall in the office behind the desk. And he positioned a white USB charger cam in the kitchen wall behind the table and walked out of the apartment.

One of the keys on the ring opened the apartment door and the other one opened the building door.

When he got home, Ray slid *The Shooter* DVD into his computer and waited for it to connect.

In the opening scene Ray saw himself enter the bank, stop to write a note on the back of a deposit slip, and then move toward the vacant teller window. It was like watching TV, only better. He was the star. He knew what was going to happen, but it was still exciting. Ray saw himself pull the gun, aim it at the teller, then raise it over his head and squeeze the trigger. After the deafening report there were screams and hysteria as customers and bank employees freaked—everyone staring at him. Ray remembered being calm. Remembered feeling that he was in complete control of the situation as he took the money and walked across the bank to the exit.

THIRTY-ONE

"Y<small>OU HEAR ABOUT</small> J<small>UDGE</small> Gant?" Charlie said as Kate entered the
bullpen. "He's in critical but stable condition at Henry Ford.
Gunshot wound in his chest."

She stood behind him as Charlie scrolled through the crime
scene photographs of the judge's car. First an exterior showing
high-velocity rounds that had cobwebbed the windshield and
gone through the judge's Mercedes and hit the minivan full
of kids behind him—miraculously, nobody was injured. Then
Charlie pulled up various shots of the interior that showed
blood and glass on the dashboard, floor, and driver's seat. Based
on the location of the wound and brutality of the scene, His
Honor was lucky to be alive, if in fact he still was. "Is he going
to make it?"

Charlie said, "I don't know."

"Any witnesses? Anyone come forward?"

"Salesman on his way to Grosse Pointe saw two dudes in a red Ford F-150, one in the bed with a rifle. Got a partial on the tag: CDX 236—missing the last number. Motor Vehicles is checking into it for me."

"What'd we tell him?" Kate said, thinking about Judge Steve, picturing him in a hospital bed, barking orders at the nurses and hospital staff. "He needed protection, but the judge knew better. I think that about sums it up." She paused. "At least we know who is responsible, although proving it might be a little more challenging."

"Well, if you're ready, let's go to the Hodge residence," Charlie said. "Get that over with."

Not surprising, when Charlie pulled into the driveway, Lowell's truck was missing. Odette, still wearing the denim vest, opened the front door and said, "He ain't here, and I ain't seen or heard from him since yesterday morning."

"Your husband is wanted for the attempted murder of Judge Steven Gant."

"As I recall you already tried that, and they let him go. You people don't quit, do you?"

Kate said, "Where do you think your husband went, Mrs. Hodge?"

"I have no idea." She let a grin slip out. "He could be anywhere."

"Let me see your phone," Charlie said.

"You have no right."

Charlie took the warrant out of his shirt pocket and held it up. "This gives us the right. We can search your home and everything in it. Now hand your cell phone over to Deputy Marshal McGraw."

Giving Charlie a dirty look, Odette Hodge pinched the phone out of a vest pocket and handed it to Kate. She checked the log but didn't see any calls from Lowell. Next they searched the house but didn't find anything that indicated Lowell Hodge's whereabouts.

On the way back to the office they stopped at the hospital. Charlie waited in the car while Kate went up to the judge's room. Deputy Marshal Jim Dauer was sitting in a chair outside the room. Kate nodded. "How is he?"

"Asleep when I checked five minutes ago."

"Anyone come to visit?"

"Not that I've seen."

Judge Steve was in bed, eyes closed, hooked up to various tubes that snaked across his body. She saw lights blinking and heard the sounds of machines blipping and beeping behind the bed. Kate listened to the soft wheeze of his breathing and watched his heavily bandaged chest rise and fall. A nurse came in. Kate introduced herself and asked her if the judge had regained consciousness.

"He opened his eyes this morning and seemed to know where he was, which is a good sign, and his vitals are good and getting better."

The nurse replaced the IV bag and examined the wound in his chest. "He's doing well under the circumstances."

The nurse walked out of the room. Kate stood at the side of the bed looking at Judge Steve. In her experience, he had been incredibly difficult, an incredible pain in the ass. Even so, she had gotten used to his insults and grown to like him. Kate reached and took his hand in hers and held it. Judge Steve's eyes blinked open, staring up at her. "McGraw, what're you doing?"

"Holding your hand."

"I can see that," he said, sounding like his old self.

"You've been shot."

"Who do you think called nine-one-one?"

Kate lowered his hand to the bed and released it. "You're lucky to be alive."

"What does luck have to do with it? It's either your time or it isn't."

Kate smiled now. "God, you're something."

"I don't believe in God."

"Of course not, you're a federal judge."

His Honor looked like he was smiling, although it was impossible to know for sure. His sour expression and smile were so similar.

"Judge, do you know what's happening with Frank's DUI?"

"You mean your father? I called Judge Zimmer. She wasn't familiar with the case and wouldn't help. I'll try her again in a few days."

•••

WHEN KATE AND CHARLIE returned to the office, Cornbread, waiting in the bullpen, said, "The little Japanese bank robber wants to talk to you. Evidently remembers something that might help us find the Shooter."

"I'll set it up," Kate said.

"And speaking of the dude, he hit again. But this time it was different. It was a Huntington Bank in Monroe. Check it out."

Kate watched the robbery on Cornbread's laptop. Ray Skinner in a dark suit and sunglasses, carrying a briefcase, approached a teller window, aimed a gun, got the money, and walked out of the bank. It all happened in a couple minutes. No histrionics. No showing off.

Charlie said, "Why'd he change his MO?"

"Maybe he's tired of the old routine," Buck said. "Wants to mix it up."

"Wait, there's more," Cornbread said.

Ray Skinner walked out of the bank and got in the front passenger seat of a Chevy SUV.

"In the dark suit and shades, he looks like one of the Blues Brothers." Cornbread grinned. "I kept expecting him to pull out a harmonica, play 'Soul Man.'"

Kate said, "Did you get any shots of the driver?"

"Couple partials of his face but not enough to ID him," Buck said.

"How about the plate?" Kate said.

"This'll surprise you," Cornbread said. "Car was boosted."

Kate said, "How about surveillance footage in the bank a day or two before?"

"I've got it," Cornbread said. "Haven't looked yet. Wanna see it?"

They watched boring time-coded footage for almost an hour, Kate thinking it was a waste of time till she saw a guy in a camo hunting cap standing at the counter in the center of the bank. There was something familiar about him. He appeared to be filling out a yellow deposit slip, but mostly he seemed to be studying the room. He was there for about ten minutes and left without making a transaction. An exterior camera picked him up coming out of the bank.

"Stop it, will you?" Kate said, "Blue work shirt, camo hunting cap. Anyone recognize him?"

Cornbread froze the frame.

"I don't," Buck said.

"Yeah, you do," Charlie said. "That's Lowell Hodge."

Cornbread shrugged. "You're not saying he's the driver, are you?"

Kate said, "I don't know, but what's he doing in a bank in Monroe the day before it was robbed? Lowell Hodge lives thirty miles away. Does that make any sense?"

Cornbread said, "Hodge being in the bank doesn't prove he was an accessory to armed robbery."

"I've got to check something," Kate said. "Be right back."

She sat at her desk, called Hope House, and asked for Father Kelly. "Tell him it's US Marshal McGraw and it's urgent."

"What can I do for you?" the priest said.

"Who was the boy Ray Skinner ran away with?"

"What's this about?"

"Just tell me his name."

Father Kelly did.

"How'd he end up with you?"

"I know his parents were killed by a drug dealer, but I don't remember the circumstances of how he came to us. He and Ray were roommates."

"Thank you, Father."

"What happened?" Kate heard him say as she disconnected.

She walked back to Cornbread's desk. "If you still think Lowell Hodge's presence in the bank was a coincidence, listen to this." That got everyone's attention. "Lowell and Ray were roommates at Hope House. They ran away together."

Charlie said, "How'd you figure that out?"

"I didn't. It was something Father Kelly said when I stopped by. He never mentioned Lowell's name, but seeing him in the bank got me thinking, and Father Kelly just confirmed it." Kate paused. "How much did they get?"

"Bank says sixteen thousand eight hundred and fifty dollars," Buck said.

Charlie glanced at Kate. "Got anything else for us?"

"According to his most recent girlfriend, Skinner owns a warehouse in the New Center area off West Grand. He boosts cars and keeps them there or did. Used a different one for each robbery."

"Got an address?" Cornbread had a toothpick in the corner of his mouth.

"Ms. Sato said she didn't know the address but could identify the building. With Steve Gant in the hospital we need a federal judge who will release her into our custody. She can help us and help herself at the same time. I feel sorry for her. She seems naive and innocent."

"In my experience," Charlie said, "they can be the most dangerous."

THIRTY-TWO

MIDAFTERNOON, SITTING AT THE bar at Brown's by himself, Ray watched an open boat with an outboard pull into a slip next to his Garwood. A blonde in shorts and a tank top secured the dock lines, stood looking at his boat for a couple minutes, and moved into the bar. Three guys at a table on the deck eating fish and chips checked her out as she walked by. The girl had a ponytail that hung out from the back of a baseball cap. She sat on the same side of the oval bar as Ray, separated by four empty stools.

They looked at each other a couple times—the only customers at the bar—before she said, "Is that your boat out there, the wooden one?"

"Yeah."

"It's a beauty. That's the kind of boat I'd buy if I had the money. What is it?"

"A 1946 Garwood. What're you drinking?"

"Vodka cranberry."

The bartender heard her, made the cocktail, brought it over, and set it down in front of her.

"I'm Sharon, by the way," she said, moving along the bar, offering her small pretty hand that had red painted nails.

"Len."

She stared at him for a couple of beats and went back to her stool. After that she seemed nervous, didn't say much, sipped her vodka drink and stared out at the channel. He'd seen her before. She lived in a small cottage across the channel a couple hundred yards south of him on Dickinson Island. She was nice-looking—in a hard, blue-collar way—and looked about forty from what he could tell. She finished the drink, thanked him, and went out to her boat.

•••

THAT EVENING RAY POURED bourbon over ice, took his drink out to the deck, and sat looking at the sun sinking into the phragmites across the channel. He took out his phone, punched in a number, and listened to it ring several times before a gravelly voice said, "I seen the write-ups about you in the paper. Can't get enough of yourself, can you? What else is new?"

Ray let it go.

"The hell do you want?"

"The services of a wild-man redneck. Know anyone fits that description?"

"I don't know anyone that doesn't. What do you got in mind?"

"I'm lookin' for a driver."

"What's it pay?"

"Thirty percent of the take."

"Last time it was forty."

"That was last time," Ray said. "This is this time."

"We get caught, I'm gonna get the same thing you are. I want half."

"For picking me up?"

"For makin' sure you get away," Lowell said. "I hear they're offering a reward. Maybe I should turn you in and get it all."

"First I'm gonna need you to do a little legwork for me," Ray said.

"What kind of legwork?"

"We can get into the details later. This sound like something you might be interested in?"

"Let me think about it."

"Don't think too long."

Ray disconnected, picturing the day he met Lowell at Hope House. Father Kelly had handed him off to a counselor, a former nun named Shirley McAllister. "Bobby, we're all so sorry for your loss." She squinted and locked her eyes on him. "But you're going to be okay. That I promise you. It's just going to take time and faith in the Lord."

"I'm fine," he said, and meant it. In his mind, he had already changed his identity. And now thought of himself as Ray Skinner, his father's name.

"You're a tough young man, I can see that, but if you ever want to talk about what you are feeling, don't hesitate to contact me. I'm available for you, as is Father Kelly and the other counselors. If you're feeling alone, you can also talk to God. He will listen to you. He will help you get through this difficult time."

Ray didn't feel lonely; he felt relieved, until this motormouth ex-nun started talking and didn't stop.

"Hope House has a dormitory that sleeps seventy-two children from ages eight to eighteen. We have classrooms, a cafeteria, laundry, gym, athletic field, and even a theater where the children put on plays and concerts." The ex-nun gave him a big smile.

"Father Kelly's mantra is 'Hope House is full of hope.' We will help you become the person you want to be."

Ray was thinking about armed robbery as a career even that far back.

After the tour, Counselor Shirley took him to the office to get his suitcase and belongings and then to the dorm where he met his roommate. "Lowell, this is Bobby Seavy, the new boy I was telling you about. Bobby, this is Lowell Hodge."

Lowell, sitting on the side of the bed, glanced at the counselor but didn't say anything.

"I want you boys to shake hands like gentlemen. Go on."

Lowell shrugged and stood. Ray stepped toward him, offering his hand, clamping down on Lowell's mitt like a vise. They locked eyes on each other, both boys squeezing, giving it everything they had.

"That's enough," Counselor Shirley said.

Ray let go and stepped back. Lowell returned to the bed, a hard look on his face.

"You boys will be spending a lot of time together, so try to get along. Be courteous and respect each other's space and boundaries. When you have disagreements, share your feelings and talk things out. And remember to clean up after yourselves. Bobby, that's your dresser." She pointed. "And, of course, you share the closet." She smiled now. "All right, boys, get acquainted. And, Bobby, if you have any questions, you know where to find me."

When the door closed, Lowell stood, pointed at him, and said, "You ever pull that shit again, I'll kick your ass."

Ray stared at him without expression. "We'll see."

"What does that mean?"

"You'll find out," Ray said.

"How old are you?"

"Fourteen."

"Well, I'm sixteen, so you better watch it."

"What does that have to do with anything?" Lowell was bigger and looked stronger, but Ray didn't care. "You think I'm worried about you? Just stay on your side of the room. Stay out of my way and you'll be fine."

"What if I don't?"

Ray grinned and shook his head. This guy was looking for trouble and he was going to get it.

They stayed out of each other's way for a couple days till Ray noticed his money was gone. $1,500. His life savings. He searched the room, paying particular attention to Lowell's side, without finding anything.

It was 3:07 a.m. when Ray duct-taped Lowell's ankles and wrists together with the roll he'd brought from home, fit a piece over his mouth, and aimed the gooseneck reading light in Lowell's face. His eyes blinked and squinted, and his body rocked back and forth. Ray had already opened the pocketknife and now held the blade to Lowell's ear, slicing deep enough to draw blood that dripped down his lobe onto the pillowcase.

Lowell jerked his body and used his arms trying to pull the tape apart. "I'm only going to ask you once. Where's my money?"

Lowell mumbled trying to speak. Ray peeled up a jagged corner of tape and ripped it off his mouth. "Under the dresser." Lowell pointed with his bound hands. Ray retrieved the cash and cut Lowell loose.

To his great surprise they became friends, brought together by their general dislike of people, their resistance to authority and rules, and their propensity to disrupt things for their own amusement and pleasure. Ray had never really had a friend, so this was a new experience.

Lowell, he learned, was an only child whose white supremacist parents were killed by a drug addict that broke into their house. Lowell didn't seem sad or upset that his parents were gone, just as Ray wasn't.

Living at Hope House was no picnic, but it beat the hell out of living with Carol and Jerry in Anchor Bay.

In the evening Lowell would sit at his desk and draw Nazi symbols: swastikas, skulls and cross bones, eagles, and German flags. "The red," he'd say, "represents the social idea of the Nazi movement. The white disk represents the national idea. And the black swastika represents the mission of the struggle for the victory of the Aryan man."

"You don't believe all that crap, do you?"

"Not really, but my parents sure did. I just like some of the designs. I think they're tits."

THIRTY-THREE

Two years later, Hope House felt like a prison. You had to sign out when you left, say where you were going, and sign in when you got back. There wasn't much free time and too many rules. Counselor Shirley told Ray the goal was to be taken in and adopted by a loving family. He'd spent a week or two with three different couples and their children, feeling uncomfortable in the company of these strangers, everyone putting on an act. Ray didn't want any part of it. He'd say something rude or do something inappropriate and they would call Father Kelly, tell the priest to come and get him. It wasn't working and wasn't gonna.

Ray's goal was to be free, to take off and start his new life. He mentioned what he was thinking to Lowell, and Lowell said, "I've got a cousin in Florida who'll set us up."

"You've got a cousin in Florida. What're you doing here?"

"I didn't think I could leave."

"Sure you can," Ray said. "You're about to start your new life. You're about to make your run."

"What does that mean?"

"We're getting the hell out of here and going for it."

They snuck out before sunup two days later. Stuffed their things in backpacks, walked to the Greyhound station, and took a bus to Fort Lauderdale. Ray was sixteen and Lowell was almost eighteen.

The bus stopped every once in a while so people could stretch their legs and get something to eat. And it was interesting to see the scenery change, going through mountains and then seeing the ocean and palm trees.

Lowell's cousin, a tall skinny hippie with pork chop sideburns and a goatee, named Trip, picked them up at the bus station. He lived with Maddy in a motor court efficiency five miles from the ocean. She was a sexy girl with long blonde hair parted down the middle, skinny arms, and breasts that wobbled under her tie-dye T-shirt. Trip said their living arrangement was temporary till a couple things fell into place, which to Ray sounded like bullshit.

"This here's Bobby Seavy, my roommate at the house, and I'm Lowell," he said to Maddy when they walked in the motel.

"Actually, my name is Ray."

Lowell gave him a puzzled look. "The hell you talking about?"

"That's my real name, my father's name: Ray Skinner."

"Why didn't you say so?"

"I was waiting for the right time, and this is it."

Trip moved past them and sat at the kitchen table, rolling a joint that he licked and sealed, examined and lit, taking a big hit he kept trying to suck deeper into his lungs, holding it in till he was about to burst and then releasing an immense cloud of gray smoke. Trip held up the joint now. "Anybody want to get high?" He took another hit, got up, and handed it to Maddy. Lowell took a hit, coughed, and handed it to Ray, and five minutes later they were all buzzed and laughing.

As it turned out, Trip and Maddy didn't just smoke weed; they sold it to tourists in the bars and beaches along Fort Lauderdale's main drag. And they did more than that, as Ray would come to learn.

Ray and Lowell slept on air mattresses on the living room floor. During the day they walked the beach, selling lids of Mexican weed for thirty-five bucks. "Tell your customers it's Acapulco Gold," Trip said. "Tell 'em it'll send 'em to a galaxy far, far away." His eyes held on Lowell and then Ray. "I'll pay you five dollars a bag."

Things were going good. Ray made $100 his first week on the job. Easy money.

He kept at it for almost two years till Trip and Maddy were arrested and Ray didn't know what to do. He searched the rooms at the motel, looking for more weed and found money, a couple thousand, and something better: a gun.

Ray was nineteen when he told Lowell there was a faster, easier way to make money than selling weed on the beach. Lowell looked at him like he'd lost it and said, "Yeah, what's that?"

"Armed robbery. We walk into a drug store, or a 7-Eleven with this." Ray held up the gun from behind his back. "The cashier cleans out the register and hands us the money. We make thousands for a few minutes work, and we won't have to worry about getting sunburned." Ray slid the pistol in his waistband. "One of us goes in first, checks the place out. If it's crowded or we see something that doesn't look right, we abort the mission and go back another time."

"What about the shotgun the guy's probably got behind the counter?"

"That's the first thing we do: disarm the man by creating a diversion."

"What the hell's that mean?"

"Do something to distract the guy, create a problem." Ray could see that Lowell didn't understand what he was saying.

"What if there's someone in the back watching us on the cameras?"

"We wear caps, try not to show our faces, take the money, and run. Look, if you're not up for it, if you're too much of a pussy, I'll go by myself, show you how it's done." Lowell thought he was tough and didn't like it when someone talked to him that way, questioning his manhood.

Two days later, ten at night, Ray entered the 7-Eleven, passed the cashier, a short hairy man of Eastern European descent, went to the back wall of the store where the cooler was, and stopped. There on the shelf to his immediate right was a 1.25-gallon container of 100 percent pure soybean oil. The label said "Use for salad dressings, cooking, baking, and frying." And Ray wanted to add, "Creating a diversion when you're robbing a convenience store."

The problem: Lowell was late as always. Ray waited a couple minutes before unscrewing the cap and emptying the oil on the tan tile floor and dropping the plastic container into the widening pool of liquid.

Lowell was in the candy aisle when Ray moved toward the cashier. "Sir, you have a big problem in aisle three. Someone spilled something and it's a mess."

The cashier looked at him like he didn't believe it, but locked the cash register with a key he slid in his pocket and followed Ray. The man stared at the mess and swore in a hard, guttural language.

Standing behind him, Ray said, "I hear you, but there's another more pressing problem that needs your attention." He aimed the revolver at the man and pulled the hammer back. "Who's in the backroom?"

The man pointed at Ray and said, "fuck you," but with his accent it didn't sound right. Ray stepped forward and drove the butt of the gun into the cashier's head and the man went down into the pool of vegetable oil. Now Lowell appeared, tearing open a candy bar, and said, "What the hell'd you do to him?"

Ray crouched, reached his hand in the cashier's pocket, grabbed a wad of bills and the cash register key. "Take him in back and tie him good." Ray threw him a roll of duct tape he'd found on aisle four.

"What're you gonna do?" Lowell said.

Ray was cleaning out the cash register when a police car parked in front and a cop entered the store and glanced at him. "Where's Kosta?"

"He wasn't feeling well, went home." Ray told himself to stay cool, thinking that if the police knew a robbery was in progress, the cop would've come in with a gun in his hand.

"You new here?"

"Hi, I'm Bobby. I started a few days ago. Kosta asked me to close for him."

"Is the coffee fresh?"

"I think so. Try it. If you don't like it, I'll make a fresh pot." Ray's main concern was Lowell seeing the cop and doing something dumb.

The cop poured a cup, sniffed, and said, "It'll do." The man brought the large coffee and two donuts to the counter and reached for his wallet.

Ray glanced down and noticed a revolver on a shelf under the register. "No charge, Officer. It's the least we can do for keeping our neighborhood safe," Ray said, laying it on heavy.

"Thank you, son. I appreciate that. Give Kosta my best."

Ray examined the matte black .32 pussy gun he found in the store, spun the cylinder that had five rounds, and put the hammer on an empty chamber the way Jerry had taught him. He laid it on the table in front of Lowell and regretted it immediately. He wasn't sure if giving Lowell a gun was such a good idea.

Ray counted the money at the kitchen table while Lowell rolled a joint and took a monster hit. "How much we get?" The words drifting on the jet stream of his exhale.

"Twenty-two hundred and seventeen dollars."

"That's all?"

Lowell handed the joint to him and Ray shook his head. "If this is a typical day, the store makes eight-hundred grand a year. But I agree with you. It isn't enough. Too much risk for too little reward." The other problem was Lowell. He was a wild card. The situation tonight had been a little hinky. Robbing a store was all about timing and Lowell wasn't where he was supposed to be when he was supposed to be there. He also seemed buzzed. "You didn't by chance spark one before our first attempt at armed robbery, did you?"

Lowell, taking another bodacious hit, said, "What do you care?"

Ray didn't say it, but Lowell was part of the problem. This wasn't the time to get into it. Ray wanted Lowell in control of his faculties when he brought it up.

The next morning, after Lowell apologized and promised he'd never get high before a job again, Ray decided to give him another chance. It was easier with two of the them as long as they had their shit together.

Ray, wearing a Miami Dolphins cap low over his eyes, checked out a Walgreens in West Palm Beach. There was a cashier near the front door and an old man in a green vest ringing up a customer's purchases. He walked toward the back, where two pharmacists were working behind a high counter.

There was another cashier at a register next to the pharmacy where customers picked up prescriptions. He had to believe there was a safe somewhere in the store. Ray pretended to look at greeting cards while he watched people pay for their drugs.

Everyone, customers and employees, was old. Ray thought he brought the median age down to about eighty-two.

When he went outside Lowell was sitting on the hood of the car, smoking a cigarette, talking to a cute blonde wearing shorts and a bathing suit top. Lowell saw him, said something to the girl, and she walked away. "How's the store look?"

"You didn't go in?"

"If you like it," Lowell said, "I like it."

"Who's the girl?"

"Little spinner. Name's Caprice. Is that cool or what?"

"What did you tell her?"

"I didn't tell her anything. She walked by, and I said hello. We were just talking. I asked if she wanted to hang out later."

"Did you tell her your name and where you live?"

"Nope. Didn't go there." Lowell dropped his cigarette butt on the parking lot and stepped on it. "You'd like some of that, wouldn't you? Well, you're in luck, 'cause she's got a friend."

Ray's first thought was to wear a ski mask, but where was he gonna find a ski mask in South Florida? His second thought was to wear a fake beard and glasses, and that actually made sense. He bought disguises for both of them at a costume shop on Federal Highway.

Ray put his on in the motel parking lot and walked in the room.

Lowell, startled before he recognized him, said, "Jesus, you look like a homeless dude."

"Then they'll underestimate me, won't they?"

"Seriously, who're you supposed to be?"

"A lumberjack."

"A lumberjack in West Palm? You've got to be shitting me."

"I got one for you too."

"I thought we weren't supposed to attract attention. We walk in the store lookin' like ZZ Top, and you don't think that's a problem?" Lowell lit a cigarette. "I'll do my own disguise."

They hit Walgreens just before closing. Ray parked in the strip mall lot. Still in the car he turned to Lowell and said, "Remember, all you have to do is lock the door, tie up the cashier, and empty the register. If you can see with those sunglasses on."

"Why're you talking at me like I'm some goddamn kid?"

"I want to make sure all the bases are covered before I put my ass on the line."

Ray entered the store, passing the cashier, a girl in her twenties with white blonde hair that had streaks of purple. He moved along the pharmacy area to the register. No one was there. He stepped behind the counter. The two pharmacists, a man in his fifties with readers on the end of his nose, and a younger woman, were preoccupied filling prescriptions.

As he got closer the woman noticed him, and in a condescending voice said, "Sir, what are you doing? You're not allowed back here."

"I think under the circumstances you'll make an exception," Ray said, pointing the .38 at them. "What I'd like you to do is get on the floor." They stood frozen, eyes glued to him until Ray clicked the hammer back and now they went to their knees. "On your stomach." He duct-taped their hands behind their backs and their legs together. "What're your names?"

"Alejandro," the man said with a Spanish accent.

"Natalie."

"I like that. And you can call me Bobby. You see? Now we're friends." Ray paused, looking at the drawers full of drugs. "All right. Aside from the three of us and the cashier up front, who else is in the store?"

"No one," Natalie said.

"Are you expecting anyone? Anyone being picked up?"

"No," she said.

Ray could see her face, eyes straining to see him. "You're sure? 'Cause if someone unexpected suddenly appears, you're the one I'm gonna shoot first."

"I have a daughter."

"Congratulations. You want to see her again, do what I tell you."

"There's no one."

"Hey, Al, she telling the truth?"

"Yes, of course."

"All right, where's the safe?"

Silence.

"It's not your money. Why put yourselves at risk? Think Walgreens gives a shit about you?"

"Is there in the cabinet," Al said, tilting his head toward it. "The top one, push the right edge."

Ray did and it opened and there was a safe in the wall behind it. "What's the combination?"

"We don't know," Al said.

Ray rotated the cylinder and clicked the hammer back.

"Six right, ten left, eight right," Natalie said.

"See how easy that was," Ray said. "How much is in there?"

"We don't know," Al said.

"It doesn't matter. I'll find out soon enough." Ray opened the safe and was stuffing stacks of bills in his backpack when Lowell, wearing mirrored aviators and a Florida State cap, entered the scene.

"The hell's taking so long?"

"I'm sorry to keep you waiting—an important man like yourself. Why don't you make yourself useful, clean out the register behind you and go sit till I'm done."

Ray emptied the safe and zipped the backpack closed. He fit strips of duct tape over the mouths of the pharmacists and walked out. No sign of Lowell. And then he appeared coming down an aisle with a box of Hershey bars.

"What're you doing?"

"You think I'm gonna pass up free chocolate bars?"

They went out the front door and walked to the car. Ray popped the trunk, dropped the backpack in, and closed the lid.

Lowell had a joint in his mouth before they walked in the motel room and lit it as the door closed. "How much you think we got?"

Ray dumped the contents of his backpack on the table. "A lot."

"Ho-ly shit," Lowell said.

"Gimme what you took out of the registers, or better yet, count it yourself." Ray divided the cash into thousand-dollar stacks. When he was finished there were seventeen and a smaller one with $486. Seeing the piles of money reminded him of playing Monopoly. Only this was real.

Lowell sat on the couch counting out loud and swearing.

Ray said, "What's the problem?"

"I keep losing my place."

"That's cause you're high as Zeus. Bring it over here."

When all was said and done Ray glanced at Lowell. "What would you say if I told you we got eighteen thousand three hundred and fifty-one dollars?"

Lowell, still holding what was left of the joint, grinned big. "Are you shitting me?" He shook his head in disbelief. "We're rich. We've got to celebrate. I'll get some party favors and call Caprice, tell her to come by with her friend."

"Don't mention the money."

"Come on. Why would I do that?"

"'Cause you like to show off."

After the girls arrived—Caprice, who Ray had seen, and Lotus, a sexy little Oriental—Lowell popped the cork on a bottle of sparkling wine and poured some into four plastic cups.

"Wow, champagne," Caprice said. "What's the occasion?"

"You're here," Lowell said.

They drank the sparkling wine, smoked weed, and paired off. Lowell and Caprice went into the bedroom. Ray and Lotus sat next to each other on the couch. Lotus was skinny but she had shape, a nice ass and great tits. She was pretty, too, with long dark hair past her shoulders.

Ray told her about running away from the orphanage, and she told him about leaving home when she was eighteen. Her parents believed women should be subservient in the old-fashioned Japanese tradition. Lotus, who had been brought up in Atlanta, thought of herself as an American and wanted to be free.

Now she worked as a secretary at a law firm in Pompano Beach and shared an apartment with Caprice.

"What do you do?" Lotus asked.

"I buy cars, fix them up, and sell them," Ray said. He'd been thinking about it as a way to someday legitimize his life. After all those years helping Jerry, he knew he could do it. All he needed was money, some working capital—which he now had, courtesy of Walgreens.

THIRTY-FOUR

CHARLIE DROVE AND KATE sat next to him. Yumi was in the back of the minivan in a transport cage that had mesh screens over the windows and a steel partition behind the front seats. They had picked her up in the sally port at the county jail. Kate insisted Yumi wear street clothes, wanting her to get a taste of freedom after being cooped up for days and some added incentive to help them find Ray. Judge Gant had arranged to have her released into their custody for the day.

Charlie cruised along Grand Boulevard to the Fisher Building, Yumi staring out the side window, looking at old buildings that had once housed machine shops that made parts for the auto industry.

"Anything look familiar?" Kate said, turning, looking at her through the mesh screen.

Yumi shook her head.

"You sure this is where it's at?" Charlie said, flashing a look of doubt.

Now Kate was wondering why Ray Skinner, who was fanatical about covering his tracks, would show Yumi something that might one day incriminate him. Kate couldn't imagine Skinner trusting her. He didn't trust anyone.

Charlie made a U-turn, drove past the old GM building and past Woodward Avenue. "I think it's up here. Take a right on Brush," Yumi said, pointing at a two-story brick building with glass block windows and a vacant parking lot.

Kate held Yumi in her gaze. "Does anyone live upstairs?"

"No, it's just empty rooms."

"Why did Ray bring you here?"

"He had to drop off a car. I was following him."

Charlie parked on the street and they got out and walked to the entrance. Kate knocked on the door and they waited but nobody came. They had a warrant to search the premises. Charlie went to the car, got the breaching ram out of the trunk, and opened the front door. The lobby was empty. On the other side of a glass partition was a room full of cubicles with desks still in place.

Charlie led them through a door into the shop, a big room with an expansive concrete floor that had faded outlines where machines used to sit.

"What did Ray do here?"

"Changed the license plates and worked on the engines to make sure they were in good shape and wouldn't have problems when we were driving away from a bank."

Kate moved toward a wooden work bench along the far wall and saw tools scattered here and there. Charlie was across the room, opening drawers in an old metal desk.

"I have to use the restroom," Yumi said. "It's through there," she said, pointing toward the hallway that led to the front of the building. Kate followed her to the door, checked the room, and then watched Yumi enter and close the door behind her. She had an idea what was going to happen next but waited for a few minutes before knocking. "You okay in there?" She heard the toilet flush. Kate gave her a little more time and then said, "Yumi." No response. Now Kate turned the handle, but the door was locked.

•••

Yumi unlocked the window and struggled to open it. The frame was warped and it wouldn't budge. She was nervous, trying to hurry, knew she didn't have much time. She grabbed the brass handles. Lifting with her legs and all of her strength, she felt the wood give. The window moved a little and then a little more. Yumi heard Marshal Kate's voice, flushed the toilet, and lifted the window high enough to slide through.

She crossed the street and ran along the sidewalk as fast as she could. At Baltimore Avenue she stopped, lungs burning, bent over, hands on her knees, trying to get her wind back. There was a house that was almost hidden behind trees and overgrown shrubs. The windows and doors were covered with sheets of plywood. A scruffy white man about fifty sat on crumbling brick stairs, smoking and watching her. "You okay? Need some help?" He stood and moved toward her. "What're you doing around here?" Studying her, he said, "Lost, huh? Why don't you come over here. Sit, have a smoke, make you feel good."

Yumi turned, looking back the way she had come and saw the marshals' car and now she ran down the street and hid behind another abandoned house. She was exhausted and afraid. She couldn't go back to jail or she might kill herself.

The marshals didn't see her, their car continuing on, giving her temporary relief until she saw the man again, unsteady, coming toward her through the tall grass.

She took a couple steps to her left, going along the side of the house, and the man moved with her. "You in trouble? I seen the police looking for you." He moved closer to her. "I got a place I can take you, they never find you." The man spread his arms open. She could see his heavy-lidded, bloodshot eyes. And she could smell him, the foul odor of sweat, and something stronger, like decaying meat.

She stepped on something, looked and saw a brick wedged in the grass. Yumi went down on one knee, clutched it in her tiny hand, and stood as the man came at her. She swung the brick into his face. He howled and brought his hands up as blood spurted from his nose, and she ran.

Yumi heard a train and felt the ground shake. She saw it on the overpass, looking down a street called John R. She ran under it and saw the tall buildings of Detroit in the distance. She had to get off the street but was not sure where to go.

The black men were coming toward her three abreast, their bodies gliding over the cracked, rutted pavement. As they came closer, she could see they were teenagers. There was nothing menacing about them, and now she felt relieved. They had no reason to harm her. She had no money, nothing of value.

Yumi studied them as they approached. The first one was a foot taller than the other two and skinny. The second one had a shaved head and a scraggly beard. And the third one wore a small hat with a brim angled on his head.

Smiling, they blocked Yumi's way, surrounding her, saying:

"Look what we got here."

"Yo, what's up?"

"Wanna get high?"

Now another train rumbled by on the overpass behind them and the whistle sounded. They took their eyes off her, and Yumi ran up a hill into a field but didn't get far. The one with the bald head caught her and pushed her down. "Yo, where you going? We gonna have some fun." And now all three of them stood in a circle leering at her.

•••

Yesterday, when they were planning the operation, Kate had said to Charlie, "Let's give Yumi some leeway, see what she does."

"She's Yumi now, huh? What're you gonna do, take her shopping and out to lunch?"

"No, what I'm saying is maybe she'll surprise us."

"Maybe she will."

Given the opportunity, Kate didn't know if Yumi would try to run or not, but it was worth a chance. The chief, initially reluctant, went along with the plan but said, "Keep a close eye on her."

Buck and Charlie would position themselves somewhere in the vicinity with an angle on the building and follow her if she took off.

Now twenty minutes after Yumi had escaped, Kate was in the car with Charlie on the radio talking to Buck. "Where is she?"

"We don't know. She was on Baltimore heading toward John R, and we lost her."

Charlie gunned it speeding under the viaduct, glanced at Kate and said, "How'd you know?"

"Remember the look on her face when we interviewed her?"

"Why didn't she tell us what she knew?"

"Maybe she doesn't know anything,"

"Why'd she run?"

"Ever spent a week in county?" Kate said, and then, "Slow down, will you? I just saw something."

Kate and Charlie walked up a grassy ridge to a field. There were three black guys surrounding Yumi, taunting her. Charlie was five yards to her right, Buck and Cornbread ten yards to her left. The four US Marshals moved into the scene with their weapons. Finally, the black guys noticed them and took off running. Buck fired his shotgun in the air and they froze in their tracks, hands raised over their heads like they'd been there before, knew the drill.

"That was the warning," Buck said in his 'Bama drawl. "Next one won't be."

Buck brought them together, aiming the Remington 870. "On your knees, hands on your head."

Buck cuffed them and Cornbread frisked them, taking small bags of white powder out of their pockets. "What do we have here? Look like possession with intent."

"Found it under the tracks," the dude wearing the pork pie said.

The tall dude had a small nickel-plate semiautomatic in his back pocket.

Cornbread grinned. "Gonna tell me you found this too, I expect."

The tall dude didn't say anything.

Kate holstered her Glock. "Are you all right?"

Yumi nodded.

"Stay here a minute, I'll be right back."

She and Charlie walked out of earshot.

"The PD can come pick up these clowns," Charlie said. "But what about the girl? How do you want to handle this? I mean, you can see her spinning it in her favor. I can hear her telling the prosecutor and the judge that she was helping the Marshals Service, showing evidence that would most certainly help us catch a notorious bank robber. And while in our custody she was kidnapped and molested by three heroin junkies. How would we explain that?"

"I hear your concern, but I think you're overreacting."

Charlie said, "Where was the girl going? You think this was part of a plan?"

"Maybe she knows where Ray is hanging out and was on her way to meet him." Kate looked at Yumi sitting on the grass, arms hugging her legs.

"Even after what he did to her?"

Kate said, "How do you explain love?"

"Oh, you think that's love, huh?"

"I am hardly an expert on the subject, but yeah, I think so."

Kate sat next to Yumi, who was crying softly. "Are you okay?"

Yumi lifted her head and nodded. "What is going to happen now?" she said in her tiny voice.

"Where were you going?"

"I don't know—just trying to get away."

Kate said, "Were you going to meet Ray?"

"If I could."

"What do you mean?"

"I wasn't sure how to get there," Yumi said.

"Are you saying you know where he is?"

"There is one place he might be. If I take you, what will you do for me?"

A week in custody, and Yumi had already learned how to work the system. "I told you I'd talk to the prosecutor on your behalf."

Yumi said, "What does that mean?"

"Try to work out a deal, get your sentence reduced."

"I want a guarantee."

"I can't give you a guarantee," Kate said. "You have two choices: you can go back to jail or you can take us to Ray. Just to be clear, we're not forcing you to do anything against your will."

A Detroit police van picked up Trey Lewis, Eron Hall, and Lonzo Williamson, arrested them for possession of a firearm and possession with intent to distribute what appeared to be about twelve grams of heroin.

THIRTY-FIVE

THE FERRY WAS WAITING when they drove into the lot. The ferry-man guided the two marshals' cars onto the barge. A few minutes later they crossed the St. Clair River to the island. Marshal Kate turned, looking at her through the mesh screen. "Where're we going?"

"It's a cabin off the highway," Yumi said. "I will tell you where to turn. I don't know the names of the roads."

The terrain looked familiar—fields of wild flowers on the left and a wall of milkweeds and marshland on the right. Ray told her the cabin was on the most remote part the island. "If you ever wanted to hide, this is the place to do it." That was the reason she was bringing the marshals here.

She saw the sign and remembered the name Rattery Lane, and she told Marshal Charlie to turn. She was nervous, afraid of Ray and what he would do if they didn't protect her. Yumi's heart was beating faster and then pounding in her chest.

Kate said, "Where's the cabin?"

"Down there," she said, pointing. "At the end of the lane—about four-hundred meters."

"How do you know about this place?"

"I came one time with Ray."

Kate said, "Is there another way in?"

"Just by boat."

"What kind of weapons does he have?" Charlie said.

"Maybe a rifle or a shotgun. Ray brings the guns with him in the car."

Kate said, "Anyone else in the cabin?"

"I don't know. I don't think so. Please don't tell Ray I brought you here."

They left Yumi in the cage. "I'll be back to get you as soon as I can," Kate said. She got out of the car and locked the doors. Buck and Cornbread were in their vests holding long guns. Kate told them what she knew. "There's a hunting cabin at the end of the road. There's a good chance Skinner's in there with a rifle or a shotgun, maybe both."

Buck cracked a tin of Happy Days, filled his lower lip with tobacco, and glanced at Kate. "QD, care for a dip?"

"It's tempting, but I think I'll pass." She was standing at the open trunk putting on her heavy vest.

•••

KATE MOVED THROUGH THE woods, holding the AR-15 across her chest. The sky was overcast, and the air smelled musty, like grass clippings and rotting wood. She heard dry leaves crunching under her boots and saw glimpses of Charlie to her right moving through the trees.

The cabin was in a small clearing ahead. Kate stood just inside the tree line, raised the binoculars, and swept them across the front, holding on the windows and door. Charlie came up next to her, whispering, "See anything?"

Kate shook her head and got a text from Cornbread. "Eye on the back door. No sign of S-1."

"Do you see a vehicle?" Kate texted back.

"Negative."

"They're in position," Kate said. Charlie nodded. Kate texted, "We're going in."

Cornbread texted back, "10-4."

The door was unlocked. Charlie went primary into the cabin, entering the main room that had log walls, a vaulted ceiling and fieldstone fireplace, sweeping the room with the shotgun. Kate followed Charlie and now stood next to him, aiming her AR-15. Buck and Cornbread came in the back door and Buck shook his head. There was a bedroom to the right. Kate pointed. She and Charlie moved toward it and went in. There was a duffel on the unmade bed and men's clothes piled on a chair.

Charlie, gripping the shotgun, went into the adjoining bathroom, slid the shower curtain open with the barrel, looked around, and came back in the bedroom. "Shaving kit on the sink, towel on the floor."

Kate unzipped the duffel, looked in, and saw a bundle of currency held together by a rubber band—hundred-dollar bill on top—"Proceeds from the Huntington Bank of Monroe would be my guess."

"Well, we know he's staying here," Charlie said. "But where's he at?"

"I don't know, but the car sitting in plain sight with Yumi in back troubles me."

"I'll have Buck bring it up to the cabin and keep watch."

Kate left everything where it was and went into the main room and met Cornbread coming out of the kitchen. "There's beer and cold cuts in the refrigerator and a loaf of bread on the counter."

"Skinner left clothes and a pile of money, so I've got to believe he's coming back," Kate said. She moved across the room and looked out at the yard, a short stretch of overgrown lawn that extended to a small lake. She thought she heard the drone of a motor in the distance, walked to the door, and opened it. "Do you hear that?" Kate said, turning toward Charlie.

"I hear something."

Kate aimed her binoculars at the water and saw an open boat appear, its lone occupant sitting in the stern, guiding it toward the cabin.

Charlie said, "Is it Skinner?"

"He's wearing a cap," Kate said, binoculars pressed to her eyes. "I can't see his face, but who else would it be?"

The man steered the boat to shore, tied it to a metal stake, stepped out with a fishing rod and two fish hanging from a line. He moved toward the cabin, semiautomatic in the waist of his Levi's, dropped the fish in a plastic cooler behind the cabin, and opened the door.

Charlie pressed the barrel of the shotgun against his rib cage. "Man, you better play it cool." The man raised his hands, but to everyone's surprise they were looking at Lowell Hodge. "I generally don't argue when there's a shotgun pointed at me."

Cornbread cuffed Lowell's hands behind his back, patted him down, and took his gun and cell phone. Charlie grabbed Lowell's biceps and escorted him to the couch.

"Jesus," Kate said to Charlie. "You believe this?"

"I guess I have to 'cause I'm looking at him."

Cornbread checked the call log on Lowell's phone. "Looks like he and Skinner have been talking. Needed a place to lie low for a while, called his old buddy."

"You've got all the answers, huh?" Lowell said to Cornbread. And then, "Take off the bracelets, let's see what you've got."

"Lucky for you it doesn't work that way," Cornbread said.

"You marshal pussies are all the same—hiding behind your badge."

Kate said, "What time are you expecting Ray?"

"Who says I am?"

•••

BUCK PARKED CHARLIE'S G-RIDE in front of the cabin, nodded at Kate in the doorway, and walked into the woods with his long gun. Kate moved to the car, got in behind the wheel, and slid around so she could see Yumi in the cage. "Where's Ray?"

Yumi tried to look surprised. "You mean he isn't here?"

"You know he isn't. Listen, I've tried to help you. Stop fucking around and tell me where I can find him."

"I don't know."

"Why do you want to protect him after what he did? What's his hold over you?" Some women didn't get it. They'd been mentally and physically abused and kept coming back for more.

"I'm not protecting him," Yumi said. "I'm trying to help you."

"Did you really expect him to be here?" Kate waited for an answer.

"It is the only place I know, the only possibility."

Frustrated, Kate got out of the car.

Charlie came out of the cabin and met her. "She tell you anything?"

Kate shook her head. "What about Lowell?"

"He's been in contact with Skinner; that's obvious looking at his phone. But does he know where Skinner's at? I don't think so. When Skinner took Lowell's calls, tower had him in Royal Oak."

"Do you think he's going to show up here?"

"No, I don't," Charlie said, "but I've been wrong about him more often than not."

"I'd like the opportunity to question Lowell while we have him," Kate said. "Just me and him, see if I can get anywhere."

"Go for it."

Kate walked in the room and set a can of beer on the coffee table in front of Lowell. "What the hell's that?"

"Looks like a can of Miller High Life. You thirsty?"

"Is this where you promise to put in a good word for me with the court if I help you?"

"I don't know that there's a whole lot I can do," Kate said.

"That might be the first honest thing you've ever said to me."

"Turn toward me."

He did and Kate unlocked the handcuffs and put them on the table. Lowell picked up the beer, popped the top and took a long drink. "Jesus, that's better than gettin' laid." He looked behind the couch and noticed they were alone in the room. "Where is everybody?"

"They're around somewhere," Kate said.

"You're not afraid, are you, keeping company with an ex-con?"

Kate smiled. "You think you're my first?"

"What do you want?"

"Tell me about your armed robbery conviction in Florida."

"That's ancient history."

"Was Ray involved? We know you were roommates at Hope House and took off together.

Lowell guzzled the rest of the beer. "Get me another cold one, I'll tell you."

Kate got up, saw Charlie watching from the bedroom, and went into the kitchen. She opened the refrigerator, lifted three beers by the plastic tightener, pulled one off, went back to Lowell, and handed the beer to him. He popped the top and took a drink. "Yeah, we hit a Walgreens in West Palm one night. It was Ray's idea. Got like eighteen grand."

"How'd you get caught?"

"Caprice seen my share of the money and asked where I got it at."

"Who's Caprice?" Kate glanced at his pale muscular arm with tats scattered on it in blue ink.

"Babe I'd hooked up with who looked like a Coppertone model. I said to her, 'Can I trust you? Promise you won't tell anyone?'" Lowell drank some beer. "She says, 'Want me to swear on a Bible?' I remembered seein' one in the drawer of the table next to the bed, and just for fun I went and got it. I said, 'All right, put your hand on it and repeat after me. "I, Caprice Newman, promise to never tell another person where Lowell Hodge got the money at."' Then she tells me she was brought up in one of those strict wacko Christian families and thought it was sacrilegious to make fun of the Bible and wouldn't do it."

"I thought it was her idea?"

"Yeah, but when push came to shove, she freaked." Lowell finished the second beer.

"That's a fun story, but you still haven't told me how you got caught."

"Caprice got busted for possession. She had half a lid in her purse. Gave me up for the Walgreens's job and got probation. And it was all 'cause she wouldn't swear on the Bible."

"But you never divulged the name or whereabouts of your accomplice, Ray Skinner. Why?"

"'Cause you don't rat out your partner." Lowell drank some beer. "How'd you know I was here?"

"We didn't. We thought you were Ray Skinner till you walked in the back door. Is he planning to stop by?"

"Who the hell knows?"

"If you were looking for him, where would you go?"

"What're you gonna do for me?"

"Get you another beer."

"That's a step in the right direction. There's a fifth of George Dickel in the cupboard, why don't you bring that too?"

"If this was me, I'd be trying a little harder to improve my situation. All I can think is maybe you don't understand the trouble you're in or you enjoy spending time in jail."

"Get that beer and the hard stuff and let's see we can come to an agreement."

Charlie followed her into the kitchen and whispered, "What're you doing?"

"Loosening him up, trying to get him talking."

"I think you're getting him drunk."

Kate opened the cupboard, grabbed the bourbon and another can of beer.

"I think he's playin' you," Charlie said.

"Or I'm playing him. We get something or we don't. Either way he takes his buzz back to county and we've arrested a fugitive. I don't see any downside."

Kate handed Lowell his third beer, which he placed on the coffee table, and the bottle of George Dickel that he uncorked and upended, taking a long gulp. He offered Kate a drink.

She shook her head.

"You one of those on-duty, by-the-book people?"

"Or straight whiskey isn't my thing."

Lowell set the bottle on the table and lit a cigarette.

"What'd you do when you got out of prison?"

"Took a bus back to the Motor City. What a fool, huh?" He brought the cigarette to his mouth, inhaled deeply, and blew out smoke that drifted toward the ceiling.

"Did you keep in touch with Ray?"

"I'd get letters from him from different places: Atlanta, Cincinnati, Chicago. He'd sign them with names of guys we knew at the orphanage. Sounding in the letters like they would. It was kind of funny."

"Did Ray say what he was doing?"

"Are you kidding? He's the most secretive son of a bitch I ever met." Lowell hot-boxed the cigarette and tapped it out in the ashtray. "I ran into him a year or so later playing the horses. He was with a tiny Jap girl. At first I thought she was the one he was seeing in Florida. This little dink cutie, given name of Lotus. You believe that?" Lowell reached for the can of beer and popped the top. "Ray had this thing for Orientals."

"Did you work with him again?"

"Yeah, but I'm not gonna get into that—tell you what or when. That's not gonna help either one of us."

THIRTY-SIX

YUMI CRIED MOST OF the way back to Detroit. It was an emotional situation, but there was nothing Kate could do except for maybe putting in a good word with the prosecutor.

After returning Yumi to the Wayne County Jail, Kate was exhausted. She wanted to go home, pour a glass of wine, and take a hot bath, but for whatever reason felt obligated to visit Judge Steve. In her experience he didn't have many friends, and when you were stuck in a hospital bed for days, you needed visitors. At least normal people did. But was Steve Gant normal?

The judge's room was in ICU, the corner of the building where two hallways met. It struck Kate as odd that there were no visitors or hospital staff, no one at the nurse's station, and no one from the Marshals Service was sitting outside His Honor's room providing security.

The judge, still connected to an IV, was asleep when she entered the room. Kate stood at the side of the bed, listening to the sounds of machines monitoring his vital signs. There was a wheelchair on the other side of the bed. She wheeled it over and positioned it next to the bed, lowered the side rail, and shook the judge awake. He opened his eyes, staring up at her. "McGraw, what the hell are you doing?"

"Trying to keep you alive. Put your arms around my neck."

He did without asking why, and she lifted him off the bed and lowered him into the wheelchair. Kate heard the elevator doors open and the sound of footsteps. She looked down the hall and saw two guys in T-shirts and work boots coming toward her, one carrying a bouquet of flowers.

She disconnected all the wires and wheeled Judge Steve into the bathroom. "Don't make a sound." She closed the door.

Standing just inside the room, Kate drew her weapon, holding it behind her back as the two men approached. There was something familiar about these tatted-up, mullet-headed clowns. The one with the flowers said, "We're looking for His Honor, Judge Gant."

"You just missed him," Kate said. "The judge was discharged."

The two guys looked at each other with puzzled expressions till they heard the toilet flush and then they began trying to look around her into the room.

"Why don't you run along." The guy holding the flowers said. "We'll have a look for ourselves."

"Which one of you drives the red Ford F-150?"

The second guy said, "I think you've got the wrong people."

"The way I see it, you've got two choices: you can walk out or be taken down to the morgue."

"That's some strong talk for a little girl. Who do you think you are?"

"A US marshal." Kate brought the Glock up and centered it on the one with the flowers who was closest to her. "Now get on your knees and place your hands on your head."

They grinned at her like she was a schoolgirl playing with a toy gun.

"I'm not going to tell you again."

They both knelt on the spotless beige tile like altar boys.

Jim Dauer, coming down the hall, saw what was happening, set his coffee on the floor, and started running toward her.

Dauer cuffed them and Kate checked their IDs. As it turned out, Larry Jennings—who had "Sonny" inked on his right biceps—owned a 2013 Ford F-150 with a license plate that matched the partial their witness had seen. And Earl Tibbits fit the description of the man with the rifle who shot the judge.

It was seven thirty when Kate got home. The apartment was dark. She turned on lights in the living room and noticed the framed photo of Frank's parents—Mimi and Papa—had been moved to the opposite side of the credenza. She went in the kitchen, turned on the can lights in the ceiling, and opened the refrigerator. She took out a half-full bottle of chardonnay and poured a glass.

The meatloaf was on the counter and a knife smeared with barbecue sauce was in the sink. Stressed from the day, she took a couple gulps of wine, filled the glass, and went into her office. After checking her emails, Kate noticed that The Shooter DVD wasn't on the desk where she left it. She checked her computer. It wasn't there either. She called Frank. "What time did you come over?"

"What're you talking about?"

"You didn't stop by for a piece of meatloaf?"

"Wasn't me. Thompson and I went to a Tigers game. What's going on?"

"I don't know."

"Maybe it was a burglar. He heard how good your meatloaf is."

"I'll talk to you later." She wasn't in the mood for Frank's banter.

"You okay?"

"I don't know."

"Want me to come over?"

"No, I'm fine." But she wasn't. Kate drew her Glock. Someone had been in the apartment. She checked the sliding door to the balcony. It was locked. She checked her bedroom and closet, checked the bathroom. She got the binoculars and stood at the window, scanning cars on the dark street in both directions, but didn't see anyone.

She finished her wine and went in the kitchen for a refill. Sat at the table feeling oddly exhausted. It had been a long day. Five minutes later, Kate walked to the bedroom and laid on the bed. Something wasn't right. She placed her gun on the bedside table next to the clock. It was 8:05. She was groggy, eyes heavy. She couldn't stay awake, started to fade, and heard the phone ringing, sounding far away.

The next thing Kate was conscious of was someone shaking her and calling her name. She opened her eyes, staring at Frank. He looked worried.

"What'd you take? I couldn't wake you, Jesus. I was about to call nine-one-one."

"I didn't take anything." Then she thought—there must've been something in the wine. It was the only thing she'd had since returning to the apartment.

"You didn't sound right on the phone. I tried calling you back about ten times, and when you didn't answer I got worried."

"I'm still whacked out but okay." Kate yawned, sat on the side of the bed. "I feel like I'm going to fall asleep any second."

"I'll be right back." Frank walked out of the room.

Kate was lying down, eyes closed when he returned. She sat up and he handed her a mug of coffee. She blew on the steaming liquid and took a sip.

Frank, sitting on the side of the bed said, "You gonna tell me what's going on?"

"Someone broke in." She told him about the missing DVD.

"You're sure you didn't leave it in your computer?"

"Positive. I think it's Skinner."

"How would he know anything about you?"

"Evidently he's resourceful. You want to find out who's on the fugitive task force, I think it's pretty easy. Skinner wanted to know how close we are to him, and now he does." Kate yawned.

"Listen," Frank said. "I think I should stay with you."

"I'll be fine."

She finished the coffee and went in the kitchen for a refill. After drinking the second mug Kate started to get some energy back. She couldn't help but feel that Skinner was still out there somewhere close by, watching her. Kate grabbed her Glock and slid it in the pocket of her sweatpants. "I'm going out."

"Hang on," Frank said. He looked worried. "I don't think that's a good idea."

"I need to clear my head."

"I'm going with you."

"Just stay here, will you?"

Getting in her car a few minutes later, Kate got another surprise. Hanging from the rearview mirror was her turquoise necklace. Skinner sending another message. Now in a panic she glanced in the rearview mirror, expecting to see him in the backseat. Kate pulled the Glock, opened the door, got out, and walked down the rows of cars in the lot and out to the street. If Skinner was trying to get her attention, he was doing a hell of a job.

Walking back to the apartment, she called Cornbread. Kate felt closer to him than she did Buck or Charlie. She told him what had happened and asked him to keep it between them. "Be cool. I'll be right there.

THIRTY-SEVEN

F RANK WENT BACK TO Thompson's. Bill wasn't there, which was unusual 'cause he didn't go out very often and never at night. Frank's first thought was Bill had taken up with the neighbor lady again and was having his pipes cleaned. That, or he wandered down the street to the bar. Those seemed like the only plausible explanations.

Frank was about to make himself a drink when he heard the doorbell. He moved into the living room, put the porch light on, looked out the window, and saw someone standing there. He thought it was Chuck, their neighbor. Frank opened the door. The man, pointing a gun at him, said, "Mind if I come in?"

"Doesn't matter if I mind or not. I think you're gonna do what you want."

When they were seated across from each other in the living room, the man said, "Who are you?"

"I was gonna ask you the same thing."

"I'll bet you were." He aimed the silenced semiautomatic at Frank's chest.

"You a cop?"

"I'm about the furthest thing from a cop you can get."

"Why were you following me?"

Frank hadn't recognized him at first, his face partially hidden under the cap brim. But now realized he was looking at Ray Skinner.

"Who's your partner?"

"I don't have a partner. You talking about my roommate, Bill?"

"Where is he?"

"Getting laid, I hope."

"Why do you hope that?"

"'Cause he needs it."

"Don't we all." Ray Skinner grinned. "When'd you get out?"

"Month ago. Why'd you turn me in?"

"You've been waiting a long time to ask that. It was either you or me, and I'm gonna win that one every time," Skinner said. "Who's the girl marshal?"

"My daughter."

"Armed robber's kin chooses law enforcement. Think that's ironic?"

"Not if she didn't know what I did. And to my knowledge, she didn't."

"I'm gonna need you to stand, put your hands behind your back."

"What the hell for?"

"'Cause I'm telling you to and I've got the gun." Skinner zip tied his wrists together.

"What do you think I'm gonna do?"

"Nothing. That's the idea."

Now Skinner sat Frank on the couch and bound his ankles. "Never trust anyone. Something you've never learned and never will. Frank, you don't see anything coming until it's too late. So you deserve what you get. I can see dumb surprise on your face. Same expression you had when the police arrested you." Skinner shook his head. "You should've done your time and disappeared." Skinner paused. "Where's the key to that car in the driveway?"

"Kitchen counter."

Skinner walked out and came back in the room a few minutes later and cut the zip ties around Frank's ankles with a pocketknife.

"All right, let's go, on your feet."

Thompson's Honda—with its trunk open—was parked next to the side door. Skinner led Frank to the car, pushed him in the trunk, and closed the lid. The tight quarters took Frank back to seg, the cinderblock room closing in on him like a sardine can. He listened to the whir and drone of the tires on blacktop and the intermittent sounds of traffic, trying to take his mind somewhere else. He was thinking about the situation, wondering why Skinner was going to all this trouble to get rid of him. Frank should've been worried. But what the hell did it matter? He'd been a failure his whole life. All he had to show for forty-six years was a busted marriage, a long stint in prison, and a daughter he was trying to reconnect with.

Frank didn't have any money, didn't own a house or a car, and his job prospects were nonexistent. "Hey, Ray, I've got to thank you for this," he said, raising his voice. "You're doing me a favor. You hear?" Then he thought, *Come on. Don't give up, do something.*

He tried to saw off the zip tie on a strip of metal on the trunk lid. But it was tough to get the right angle. Frank cut his hand in the process but kept at it till the car slowed down and came to a stop. He expected the trunk lid to pop open and Skinner to take him into the woods and shoot him in the back of the head. Frank pictured it happening execution-style.

"You've got to make your own luck," Ray said from the front seat. "That's something else you never learned. And now it's too late."

It was dead quiet for a minute or two and then the driver's door opened. The car lurched forward and started to roll downhill, picking up speed. Frank was slammed on impact as the Honda hit and plunged into what had to be a pond or a lake and started to sink, water rushing into the interior, shocking him by its frigid suddenness. He felt around in the dark, hands bound behind his back, touching the panel where the lock was, feeling for the latch, the water rising up his body to his chest. He tried to sit up, fingers probing the extruded mechanism, head touching the trunk lid, taking a last gulp of air.

•••

IT WAS DARK AS Ray walked along the highway toward the town a couple miles away. He didn't know what the hell he was going to do with Frank, until he saw the lake.

Ray heard a car, turned, saw headlights approaching, stopped, and stuck out his thumb. A pickup passed him, the taillights lit up, and it pulled over onto the gravel shoulder. Ray ran to the truck and climbed in. The driver looked like an aging hippie with round silver glasses and a long gray beard that reminded him of the characters on *Duck Dynasty*. There was a rifle in a metal rack behind the bench seat. "The hell're you doing out here walking in the dark?"

"I need a lift," Ray said.

"Well, count your lucky stars. I'm usually home by now with a glass of Early Times in my hand, but I was working late."

"You're not using the expression correctly."

The old man looked at him with a question.

"Count your lucky stars means be thankful for what you have."

"I don't believe this. You're arguing with the person who, out of the kindness of his heart, is giving you a ride?"

"That has nothing to do with what I'm saying."

The old man rubbed his wild beard with an open hand and glanced at Ray in disbelief.

"Will you do me a favor?" Ray drew the silenced Beretta and aimed it at the man.

"Jesus, what the hell you want with me?"

"I don't want you. I want your truck."

The old man shook his head. "Try to help a fellow citizen and look what it gets you. My God, you can't trust anyone these days." The old man slowed the pickup and pulled over onto the shoulder.

"Leave the keys and get out."

The old man glanced at the rifle.

"I think you'd be dead before you got a hand on it," Ray said.

The old man opened the door and slid off the seat onto the ground. "Now what?"

"Walk toward the tree line."

"I got a daughter and three grandkids I take care of."

"It's about time your daughter stepped up, took some responsibility, don't you think?"

Ray opened the door and stood on the rocker panel, arms resting on the roof, aiming the Beretta. And when the old boy was at the edge of the woods Ray shot him twice and got in the driver's seat.

•••

"I THINK WE SHOULD take you somewhere safe, keep an eye on you." Cornbread was leaning against the kitchen counter, forearm flat on the granite.

"For whatever reason, Ray Skinner seems to have taken an interest in me," Kate said, holding her coffee cup. "I don't want to hide; I want to catch him. I'd rather be in jeopardy than not be involved. Let's take advantage of the situation. Skinner likes the thrill, likes the game. Thinks he's too smart to get caught."

"You can see it from the dude's point of view, though, can't you? 'Cause you're the girl, the lone female. Thinks he can fuck with you and get away with it. De'Ron Griffin—remember him?— probably thought the same thing. We'll talk to the chief about it, see what he thinks."

Kate gave him a look.

Cornbread met her gaze and said, "Come on, QD, how're you gonna get around that?"

"Not say anything."

"I can't let this go. I want to help you but I like my job. I'd like to finish my career with the Marshals Service, not as a security guard working nights at a mall."

"It never happened." She sipped some coffee. "How about that? And if he shows up again, I'm going to shoot him." Kate yawned, still groggy from the spiked wine. "Can we talk about it in the morning? I have to get some sleep. I can't keep my eyes open."

"I can stay if it'll make you feel better. Sleep on the couch."

"I'm okay. Go home."

Kate brushed her teeth and put on a T-shirt. She looked out her bedroom window and saw Cornbread's G-ride parked on the street. She grabbed her phone, punched in his number, and said, "What're you doing?"

"Thinking about your situation."

"What's your conclusion?"

"I'm involved now." He was silent for a couple beats. "We've got to run this by Charlie, see what he thinks."

"Just do me a favor, go home to your fiancée."

Kate racked the Glock, placed it on the table next to the bed, turned out the light, and slid under the covers.

•••

On the way back to town Ray picked up his car in Hazel Park and left the old man's truck on the street. He stopped at a liquor store and bought a bottle of W. L. Weller and a bag of cashews, then cruised by Kate's apartment. The lights were out. He saw one of her marshal buddies, the black guy, sitting in an old Pontiac Bonneville parked on the street, driver's window open, the faint glow of a cigarette. Ray drove to the street behind the apartment building, pulled over, and killed the engine.

He sat for a while, sipping bourbon out of an old coffee cup, checking the cameras he'd installed in Kate's apartment on his phone. The rooms were dark. Ray poured half an inch of Weller into the cup, finished it in two swallows, and got out of the car.

He entered the building through the rear door and took the stairs to the second floor. Ray opened the apartment door and stood in the dark, eyes adjusting. He took off his shoes, walked into the living room, and checked the book cam. It was still operating. Ray downloaded it on his phone and saw a close-up of his distorted face peering into the lens.

He checked the bedroom. Kate was on her side under the covers, snoring lightly. Her Glock was on the table next to the bed. He picked up the gun, ejected the magazine, and put it in his pocket. He glanced out the window. The Pontiac was still parked on the street.

Ray went in the kitchen, wrote a note on the small blackboard, and left the apartment. He drove to the motel and got in bed, lying back on the cushion of pillows, glass of bourbon in his hand. He ate a cashew and washed it down with a slug of Weller, staring out the window at the pink neon sign, too excited to sleep, thinking about what he was going to do in the morning.

THIRTY-EIGHT

K ATE OPENED HER EYES looking at the clock. It was 6:57 a.m. She got up, showered and dressed, went downstairs, got the *Free Press* out of her mailbox, and took it up to the kitchen, scanning the sports section. The Tigers won again and now were only two games out of first place with two weeks to go till the end of the season.

After making coffee and toasting an English muffin, she sat at the table and glanced at the black board and saw *SWEET DREAMS* in white chalk. The simple words sent a shiver through her. Ray Skinner again. How did he know she was alone? It was a risky move. Why would he take the chance? 'Cause it was part of the game. He was toying with her. Kate had her hand on the phone to call Cornbread but hesitated. If she told him what happened that would be it. She'd be taken off the task force. If she didn't tell him it would be withholding information. What was the penalty for that?

Kate glanced at the wall in front of her and noticed a white charging plug in the socket. She'd never seen it before. What was going on? She got up and pulled it out, staring at what appeared to be a lens of some kind, and thought of something Yumi had said. Ray had cameras installed in their apartment. That's what this was. That's how he knew she was alone last night. He was watching her.

She went in the bedroom and picked up the Glock. It felt light. That's 'cause the magazine was gone. The grip was empty. Her heart started racing again, picturing Ray Skinner standing over her while she was sleeping.

Kate unlocked the gun box in the closet, loaded a mag in the Glock, and racked it, chambering a round. Now she stood at the window with binoculars panning cars parked on the street. Cornbread was gone. She searched the apartment and checked the front door. No sign of forced entry. So either Skinner picked the lock or had a key.

In the kitchen, she opened the drawer where she kept her spare keys. They were gone. Kate found another camera in a binder on the bookcase in the living room and a third one in her office. She dumped everything in a plastic garbage bag and sealed the top.

Her cell rang and she answered it, surprised to hear Thompson's voice. "Will you put Frank on?"

"He isn't here, left last night about nine thirty. I haven't talked to him since."

"He isn't here either and I need my car."

"Sorry, I can't help you." Kate disconnected and tried Frank, thinking he was probably at the realtor's house or at a bar having his first drink. The phone rang several times and went to voicemail. "This is Frank, leave a message."

"Call me," Kate said. "It's important."

She was about to leave for work when the phone rang again. The caller identified himself as Detective Shaffo with the Waterford Police Department.

"Am I speaking to Deputy US Marshal Katherine McGraw?"

"What can I do for you?"

"Is Frank Galvin your father?"

"What's this about?"

"I'd like to meet with you and explain the situation."

"Is Frank okay?"

"He's in the hospital for observation, but he should be fine."

Kate was expecting bad news, so that was a relief.

It took forty minutes to get there. Ed Shaffo met her in the lobby. He was lean and pale, with dark hair combed back and sculpted sideburns. After glancing at her ID, he led Kate to an interview room and sat across the table from her, getting right to it.

"Mr. Galvin was found not far from here, walking on Hatchery Road, soaking wet, in a confused, agitated state of mind." Shaffo, the small-town detective, was trying his best to sound official.

"Did you ask him what happened?"

"I questioned him here. At first, he was unresponsive and then said he couldn't remember anything and didn't know what happened to the car he was driving. The way he looked and acted I thought he was drunk, drove off the road into Loon Lake, which is a little more than a mile from here. I had Mr. Galvin breathalyzed and his blood alcohol was under the limit, so obviously something else had caused the accident. Is he taking medication?"

"No."

Shaffo said, "Is he on drugs?"

"No way."

"How do you know?"

"'Cause he's an old-fashioned guy," Kate said. "Still drinks beer out of the bottle."

"Maybe he fell asleep at the wheel. What kind of car does Mr. Galvin drive?"

"A Honda Accord." She didn't tell him the owner was Bill Thompson.

"Mr. Galvin was subsequently taken to St. Joseph Mercy Oakland Hospital for observation, as I mentioned. I questioned him again this morning, and he still didn't remember what happened or the whereabouts of his automobile."

"Is Frank under arrest?"

"No, I don't believe so."

Kate heard doubt in his voice. "You don't sound sure."

"On that same stretch of road where we found Mr. Galvin there was a homicide. Local handyman shot twice. And his pickup truck was stolen."

"And you think these events are related? You think Frank was involved?"

"I'm not saying that."

"What're you saying?"

"The circumstances are unusual, to say the least."

"Did you ask Frank if he witnessed the murder?"

"Says he doesn't remember seeing anything."

Kate said, "You don't believe that either, I'm guessing."

"Not necessarily." Shaffo combed his hair back with long-nailed fingers.

"What does that mean?"

"You have to admit this whole thing is extremely odd."

He didn't know the half of it. "Is Frank being charged?"

"Not as of yet. Mr. Galvin's free to go when the hospital releases him."

"You said a man was murdered last night," Kate said. "Can I see photos of the crime scene?"

"What's your interest in a local homicide?" Shaffo frowned at the thought of a federal agent sticking her nose in police business.

"Did you, by chance, find casings from a .380 Beretta semiautomatic?"

Not expecting that, Shaffo said, "Are you guessing, or do you know something we don't?"

"Let me take a look at the evidence and I'll tell you."

Based on the head stamp on the casings found at the crime scene, they appeared to match the one Melvin found on Belle Isle. There was little doubt in Kate's mind that Ray Skinner was involved, but she had to connect the dots. Kate told Detective Shaffo she'd get back to him.

She parked in the visitor's lot and walked in the hospital lobby. At the reception counter she asked a friendly silver-haired woman in a burgundy blouse what room Frank Galvin was in. The woman checked the computer. "He was in room 436, but Mr. Galvin has been discharged."

"So he's gone?"

"That's what discharged means, honey."

"Did someone pick him up?" Kate was thinking of the realtor, unless he called a cab.

"I have no idea. Mr. Galvin must have arranged for his own transportation."

Kate walked toward the exit trying to remember the name of the woman, trying to picture the business card Frank showed her and the real estate firm where she worked. In the car Kate Googled local realtors, scrolled through three pages of profiles, and saw Peggy Nolan, the good-looking brunette, and it all came back to her. Kate tried Peggy's mobile and it went to voice mail. She left a message and disconnected. A few minutes later her phone rang.

"I should've called you," Frank said.

"You think? Tell me what you're doing. What's going on?"

He told her about Ray Skinner coming to Thompson's house, tying him up and forcing him in the trunk of the Honda. He told her about Skinner rolling the car downhill into a lake.

"How did you get out?"

"I was lucky." He pictured himself in the trunk filling with water, his hand brushing over the lever, pulling it and pushing up on the trunk, feeling it give way and going through the opening. Then swimming to the surface, lungs ready to explode.

"Why did he come after you?"

"He didn't know it was me. He'd seen Thompson and I following him to Canada. Then he recognized me pulling up in front of your apartment, waited for me to come out, and followed me to Thompson's house. He asked what my connection was with you and I told him."

Frank heard Peggy yelling at the maid.

"What's going on?"

"I'll tell you later."

"A man was murdered along that same stretch of road where they found you."

Frank sighed. "The detective told me about it and asked if I saw what happened."

"Did you?"

"No. My guess, Skinner needed transportation, but he was long gone by the time I passed that way. Do the police think I had something to do with it?"

"The detective never said it directly, and you didn't, so don't worry." Kate paused. "Did your girlfriend pick you up? I know Thompson didn't. He's angry, wants to know where his car is."

Frank didn't say anything.

"You still there?"

"I'll have to figure out what to do about that."

"Want me to come and get you?"

"Let me call you back." Frank heard Peggy going after the maid again, using language he couldn't believe. The poor woman was a middle-aged Bulgarian named Tatiana. She had a nice disposition but didn't speak English very well. He felt sorry for her, taking a lot of shit from this wealthy suburbanite for not dusting the molding in the bathroom. "There are cobwebs," Peggy Nolan had said to her. "You can't see that?"

Now Peggy came into the kitchen. "I fired her. She doesn't know how to clean."

"I can't believe you'd talk to someone that way."

"Were you listening to my conversation?"

"It's hard not to when you raise your voice like that."

"I don't see that it's any of your business."

"You're right." He walked out of the room, moving toward the front door, Peggy followed behind him, heels clicking on the tile floor.

"Where do you think you're going?"

"I don't know but I'm not staying here." Frank opened the door.

"You seemed different. I thought I could count on you. Now I'm not sure why. I canceled my appointments to pick you up and this is how you repay me?"

Frank took the sidewalk, heading east on Bradway Boulevard, passing giant red brick colonials. He didn't have a phone or money or any idea where he was going. A few minutes later he noticed a black sedan moving slowly, creeping next to him. The front passenger window went down. "Want a ride?" Kate said.

Frank put his hands on the sill and leaned in. "What're you doing here?"

"I was worried about you. I stopped by your girlfriend's, introduced myself, and she went ballistic. What happened?"

"I saw the real her, and I guess you did too. Now I understand why her husband left. I'll bet he ran out and never looked back." Frank got in the car and closed the door.

"So you broke up with her, huh?" Kate put it in gear and they took off.

"She seemed so normal till today, and then went off on the cleaning lady. I couldn't believe it. She's crazy."

"I guess it's good that you saw it now before spending any more time with her." Kate took a beat. "What're you going to do about Thompson's car?"

"I don't know."

"It isn't your fault, but you've got to tell him what happened. With a police report he probably would've been able to get a settlement from his insurance company." They rode in silence for a couple minutes until Kate said, "I can give you a loan."

"How am I gonna pay you back?"

"Don't worry about it. We'll work something out."

THIRTY-NINE

KATE DROPPED FRANK OFF at her apartment and went to see Father Kelly. The priest was wearing a blue short-sleeve dress shirt, Levi's, and running shoes. They sat at the round table in Kelly's office. "What can I do for you?"

Kate showed him the list of homeowners on Harsen's Island and explained her theory. "We think Bobby Seavy—aka Ray Skinner—owns a cabin on Rafferty Lane in the name Gerald Rowan. Does that ring a bell?"

"Gerry was small for his age and ineffectual, an easy target for Seavy and his roommate."

"Will you check the list, tell me if you see any other familiar names?"

"How many are there?"

"Five hundred and thirty-five."

The priest gave her a questioning look.

"Take you ten minutes at the most and you'll be helping us apprehend a dangerous fugitive."

Father Kelly went line by line, moving his index finger down the left margin.

When he finished, Kelly said, "Here's another one: Leonard Heinle, 4416 Middle Channel Drive." Kelly slid the three single-spaced pages across the table to Kate.

"Why do you think Ray's using names of boys he met here?"

"Maybe because they've passed away," Father Kelly said.

Now it made sense. Who was going to challenge Skinner?

Kate heard her mobile beeping as she approached the car, and she got in but missed the call. She dug the phone out of her bag. She had four messages. The first one was from Cornbread. "Yo, QD, I can't stop thinking about you. I'm concerned." There was a long pause. "I just want to let you know I have to tell Charlie what happened. We can't keep this to ourselves. Skinner's crazy and dangerous. Secondly, you know, if the chief ever found out we were withholding information on a top-fifteen fugitive, we'd both be history. Call me."

Kate wasn't mad at Cornbread. She'd put him in a tough position. But now she had to decide what to do.

The second message was from Charlie. "We have to talk," he said in a serious tone of voice. "I need you to come in as soon as you can."

Frank was number three. "Two marshals stopped by looking for you, a black guy named Reed and a big guy named Dodge. They asked if I knew where you were, and I said no."

The last message was from Adam. "How can we make this work if I can't even get you on the phone? Call me, will you?" Kate didn't need this right now. She had enough on her mind.

Assuming Buck and Cornbread were still in the area, Kate parked on the street behind her building and went in the back way.

Frank was sitting on the couch when she walked in the apartment. He stood and moved toward her. "You gonna tell me what's going on?"

"I'm in trouble."

"That's kind of what I thought when the two deputies stopped by. They didn't seem too happy." Kate moved past him, hurried into the bedroom, grabbed binoculars, and stood, scanning cars parked on the street and saw Buck in the window of his G-ride. She felt bad; they were her friends and partners, and she was deceiving them.

"I know where Ray Skinner is," she said to Frank, walking into the living room. "I want to show you something." He followed her into the office and sat next to her as she booted up her computer, logged onto a map of Harsen's Island, and located the Middle Channel, a tributary that ran north and south along the western side of the island. "Remember what the bartender at Brown's said?"

Frank shook his head.

"Ray always arrived by boat, and when he left, he always headed north." Kate pointed at the map and traced a finger to show Frank what she was talking about. "Ray owns a house somewhere along here. The address at Brown's is 6630 Middle Channel Drive. Ray's address is 4416. This property and the hunting cabin were on the assessment list I showed you. The owners' names are kids Ray knew at the orphanage. They've since passed away and he bought the properties in their names."

"How exactly do you do that?"

"You open bank accounts and hire an attorney to handle the transactions."

FORTY

Ray was sitting at the bar at Brown's when the woman who lived across the channel came in, saw him, and walked over. "Hey, how're you doing? Remember me?"

"Sharon, right? I thought that was you." She looked different without the baseball cap, blonde hair hanging straight to her shoulders.

"Where's your boat?"

"I sold it and got the Wheeler." Ray pointed to it.

"That one's cool too. Mind if I join you?"

"Still drinking vodka and cranberry?"

"You've got a good memory." Sharon sat on the stool next to him.

Ray raised his hand, got the bartender's attention, and ordered Sharon a drink. "How long have you lived in the cottage?"

"Three months. How about you?"

"A few years." Ray sipped the bourbon. "I spend summers here and winters in Palm Beach."

"You're doing something right. Sounds like you've got a good life."

The bartender set a cocktail in front her.

She picked up the glass and took a long drink like she needed it. "Love a ride on that new one if you ever want company. And don't get the wrong idea, I'm not hitting on you. Other than the bartender, you're the only person I've met since I moved here."

"So you're not married," Ray said.

"I was for three months, but that was a long time ago."

"How old were you?"

"Eighteen. Had no idea what I was doing." Sharon sipped her drink. "How about you?"

"I don't believe in it." Ray grinned. "No, I'm kidding. It's just never worked out."

"What're you doing this evening?"

"I don't know."

"Why don't you come by for a drink? We can sit outside, watch the boats, and shoot the shit."

Ray sipped his bourbon, wondering what she wanted and decided she was lonely. "What time you thinking?"

"How about seven?"

"Yeah, I think that'll work." This was the second time he'd run into her. The first time she seemed nervous, didn't say much. But she always waved as he passed by her cottage. More than anything Ray was curious about her. She lived alone on an island that was only accessible by boat. That said a lot. She was running from something and he wanted to find out what.

•••

THEY CAUGHT RUSH HOUR traffic and arrived at the ferry a little after five, and the island a little after that. They switched places in the parking lot. Frank drove and Kate sat in the passenger seat with binoculars in her lap. The blue-green bay was to the left and Middle Channel was to the right. Kate raised the binoculars, looking for addresses on the houses scattered along its banks.

They went a couple miles before she saw it and said, "There it is." Pointing at a two-story cedar cottage. "Let's wait till it gets dark."

Frank drove to Brown's, pulled into the lot, and parked.

"What if he's here?" Kate said, "Then again, why would a guy that keeps a low profile be in a crowded bar at happy hour?"

"I hope he is," Frank said. "I'd like to see the son of a bitch sitting at a table, walk up—hey, remember me?—knock him out of his chair, and drag him out of there."

"I'll bet you would." Kate smiled. "But I think we've got to be a little more subtle than that."

Kate sat with Frank at a table outside. He nursed a couple beers while she searched the happy-hour crowd for Ray Skinner, listening to "Stairway to Heaven" blaring from unseen speakers.

"I forgot to tell you about this." He took a folded piece of paper out of his shirt pocket and handed it to her. "I got it in the mail. It's from a prosecutor with the Forty-Eighth District Court."

"It's a *nolle prosequi* on your DUI. A formal notice of abandonment signed by the prosecutor and the judge. They're dismissing the charges against you."

Frank shook his head. "Jesus, I don't know what to say. I don't know how to thank you."

"Don't thank me, thank Judge Steve. You needed your luck to change and this is a step in the right direction. I'm happy for you. Now you can get a job and get on with your life."

They waited till 7:56 p.m. The sun had set over Dickinson Island. Kate said, "You ready?"

Frank turned, took a last swig of beer, set the bottle on the table, and got up.

•••

WHEN HE GOT HOME Ray checked the cameras in Kate McGraw's apartment on his laptop. All three were turned off, which meant she'd found them. He'd have to take a break for a while, figure out his next move.

Standing on the deck with a glass of W. L. Weller in his hand, Ray watched a pontoon boat pass by loaded with young partiers headed for happy hour at Brown's. He loved living on the island in this house he'd designed and built. He owned two lots on either side of his house, and behind him was the road and behind that was the bay. Over the years he'd had a lot offers from realtors— agents knocking on his door or leaving quotes in the mailbox— asking if he'd sell parcels of his waterfront property and throwing big money at him. He'd always refused. The last thing he wanted were neighbors closing in on him.

•••

"THERE IT IS," FRANK said, as they drove past the house. "Tell me what you want to do."

"I don't know."

He went a few hundred yards, made a U-turn, and pulled over on the soft sandy shoulder and turned to Kate, reading doubt in her expression. "What's the matter?"

"This isn't the way to do it. Although I realize there aren't a lot of options."

"That's just occurring to you, huh?"

"We don't even know if he's there," Kate said. "I didn't see any lights on, and there isn't a car in the driveway."

"Sounds like you're having second thoughts." Frank paused. "You're worried, call your partners."

Kate looked at him but didn't say anything.

"I'm not leaving here without Skinner," Frank said, "I'll do it myself if I have to."

"What's your plan?"

"Knock on the door. He looks out, sees me, it'll confuse him. He thinks I'm dead. You enter from the water side and draw down on him."

"And if he isn't there?"

"We'll wait for him."

"Then what?"

"That's as far as I've gotten."

"Give me the keys," Kate said.

Frank handed them to her. She opened the door and got out, looking south down the dark empty highway, then moved to the back of the car and popped the trunk.

Joining her, Frank said, "What're you doing?"

"Getting ready to apprehend an armed fugitive." Kate slipped the tac vest over her head. Now she unlocked the gun box, took out her back up and two extra magazines.

"Where's mine?"

"You told me you've never fired a gun. I don't think this is the time to start. If there's any shooting, I'm the one that's going to do it."

The house was still dark as they approached on foot. Frank looked in the front window. All he could see were the shapes of furniture in what looked like the living room. He tried the door. It was locked. Of course it was. He could see his idea wasn't going to work.

Frank went around to the channel-side of the house. There was a brick patio and a small dock. Kate, standing at a steel security door, said, "We're not going to get in this way." Above her was a deck that looked like it was built off one of the upstairs bedrooms.

Frank studied the two boat-well doors and noticed a gap between the bottom and the waterline. He took off his shirt and pants, standing in his underwear as Kate walked over.

"Going for a swim?"

Frank lowered himself into the narrow canal that connected the house to the channel. The water was four feet deep and cold. Shivering, he swam under the door on the left. Inside the walls were unpainted cinderblock. There were two lights in the peaked ceiling that were aimed at a sleek white speed boat with blacked out windows on a hoist over the water. The other side of the boat well was empty.

Frank climbed up a short metal ladder onto the deck and walked to an unlocked door that opened to a hallway that led to the kitchen, leaving a trail of wet floor behind him. There was a dish towel on the counter. He spread it out and stood on it, looking through a picture window at Kate on the patio.

He unlocked two deadbolts on the security door and let her in. She handed him his clothes. "One side of the well is empty, so either Skinner has another boat or he drives to the island. Either way he's not here. Give me a minute." Frank went in the bathroom, dried himself with a couple hand towels, and dressed. When he came back in the kitchen Kate was gone. He walked into the living room. She wasn't there either. Then he heard her calling him.

"Frank, come up here. You've got to see this."

FORTY-ONE

RAY SLID THE BERETTA in a grocery bag with bottles of Weller and Grey Goose, moved along the hall to the boat well, pressed the remote, and the door went up. He climbed down the steps into the Saturn inflatable, fired up the engine, untied the mooring lines, and backed out.

Ray putted across the dark water and down the channel, tied his boat to Sharon's dock, took the Beretta out of the bag, and hid it under a life vest in the stern. He didn't think he'd need a gun during cocktail hour. She saw him and got out of her chair, holding a martini glass.

"Here's a present for you," Ray said, handing her the fifth of Grey Goose.

She looked surprised. "What's the occasion?"

"Your drinking pleasure."

"Well, aren't you generous." Sharon stared at the bottle. "This is the good stuff. You don't fool around. And I see you brought your own." Sharon smiled. "Let me get you a glass and some ice."

Ray followed her into the worn-out kitchen with its dirty beige Formica cabinets and counters and beige linoleum floor. There was a framed rocking chair done in needlepoint on the wall with a caption that read "Home Sweet Home."

She took a lowball cocktail glass out of the cupboard, filled it with ice, and handed it to him. Then she dropped a couple cubes into the martini glass and poured Grey Goose to the brim. She was wearing heavy blue eyeshadow, short shorts, and a sequined tank top that looked like Walmart couture.

"To your health," Ray said with a grin.

"To neighbors," Sharon said, taking a big drink, eyes holding on him. "I've been asking myself why you look so familiar. I feel like we met in another life or something."

"Maybe I look like somebody you know," Ray said.

A big black dog with brown markings wandered into the room, brushed against her bare leg, sitting at attention on the floor, its tongue hanging out, staring at Ray like he was a piece of smoked brisket.

"That's Splash," Sharon said, rubbing the dog's head. "'Cause him's a diver and a swimmer, aren't you, boy?" She drank some vodka. "Contrary to popular belief, Rotties are known for being loyal, affectionate, and good-natured."

"He doesn't look too happy to see me."

"You don't have to worry about Splash. He wouldn't hurt a fly, 'less it was bothering me." Sharon sipped her drink. "Let's go outside, I'll leave him here."

They sat in Adirondack chairs in the yard as the sun was setting.

Ray said, "How'd you happen to choose this place?"

"How much time you got?"

•••

KATE MET FRANK AT the top of the stairs, led him into the master bedroom and into the dressing room, and closed the door. There were built-in dressers on one wall. On the opposite side of the room there were hanger racks filled with clothes, shoe shelves, and shelves for luggage. In the center of the room was a dressing table with an Oriental rug in front of it.

Kate held up a folder filled with newspaper articles in plastic sleeves, set it on the Tabletop, and opened it to show Frank. "Looks like Ray started his career in Florida and made his way north. They're all in chronological order." She pointed to a story from the Palm Beach Post. "This one goes back to 1990."

Frank said, "Why would he do this?"

"I imagine he's proud," Kate said. "In Skinner's mind these are his accomplishments. He's robbed sixty-two banks, the armored truck he did with you, and the 7-Eleven and Walgreens he did with Lowell Hodge in South Florida. Lowell admitted it under the influence of beer and bourbon. Lowell got busted, turned in by his girlfriend to beat a drug rap. Went to prison, and according to these newspaper accounts, Ray went north on I-75 and hit banks in Orlando, Atlanta, Chattanooga, Lexington, Cincinnati, Dayton, and Toledo. It reads like a travelogue. The bank robber's guide to fame and fortune."

•••

"WADE, MY EX, WAS a real gentleman at first. He waited till we were living together before he hit me. Wasn't that considerate of him? He'd come home smashed and find something to get mad about. Throw me into walls, kick me." She touched the scar on her cheek. "This little beauty is from the first time he punched me, I had to go to emergency. Took six stitches. I'd leave when he fell asleep, go stay with a girlfriend. He'd call the next morning and apologize, say he was gonna quit drinking, never hit me again. And like an idiot I'd go back to him." She sipped her martini. "There was no shortage of men in my life. The pussy rules and all that, but Wade was different. I think he's mental." She finished the cocktail. "Things got worse, and one night after he hit me I called the police. Wade was arrested and went to court for assault. I testified against him. He's in prison doing two and a half years. Said he'd kill me when he got out, and I believe him. That's why I'm living here with a Rottweiler that weighs more than I do." Sharon held up her glass. "I need a refill, how about you?"

"Sure, I'll have another one."

He opened the door and followed her into the kitchen, poured Weller over shrunken cubes while Sharon grabbed a handful of ice out of the freezer, dropped it in her glass, and poured some more Grey Goose.

"I'm good with faces, and I've got a memory like an elephant. I swear I've seen your picture in the newspaper, the *Free Press.*"

Now Ray knew where she was going. He flashed a fake smile. "I think you've got me confused with someone else."

"We know who you are," a heavyset guy, late thirties, said, entering the room. His hair was high and tight and he had a suntanned face and wore a revolver in a holster on his hip. Ray was thinking, you need a guy that looks like a cop? Call Central Casting and this meathead shows up. The dog went over to him. The guy crouched, rubbed its head.

"Johnny, you believe it? Here he is finally—in the flesh." Then to Ray she said, "This's Sergeant Merritt with the sheriff's department."

There was a laptop on the counter. Sharon uploaded a bank surveillance photo of Ray approaching the teller window. It had been the featured shot in a *Free Press* article.

"There you are about to rob the Huntington Bank in Detroit," Sharon said.

Instead of being worried, Ray felt somewhat relieved. If the police were involved in any official way they would've come to his house and arrested him. "That's not me."

"Sure it is," Sharon said. "You're the Shooter."

"But the good news: I'm not here to bust you. I'm here to offer you a deal, a way out of your trouble." The big man drew a gun that looked like a .38 and aimed it at Ray. "Get on your knees, hands on your head."

He knelt on the warm linoleum and the cop cuffed his hands.

"You can buy your way out of this for five hundred thousand," Sharon said. "Under the circumstances I'd say that's a pretty sweet deal."

Ray didn't see this coming, but it didn't matter. He liked the situation, these two dolts thinking they could take advantage of him. "Well, I guess I don't have a choice." That seemed to take the edge off, lighten the tension.

Sharon smiled. "I'm glad you see it our way."

Ray said, "When did you recognize me?"

"First time I ran into you at the bar. I thought, 'Is that who I think it is?' I get the *Free Press* online, went home, looked up the articles again and there you were plain as day. I called Johnny and the rest is history." Sharon smiled, sipped her martini. "Biggest problem was trying to get you over here. It didn't happen today, we were gonna stop by, knock on your door."

"If you want, I'll go get the money, bring it back," Ray said, thinking they were so dumb they might let him.

"That's a good one," Johnny said, glancing at Sharon. "You didn't tell me he was a comedian."

A little after ten the big man escorted him outside. There were boats passing the cottage heading north. Ray could hear "Purple Haze" blaring from a Chris-Craft Calypso that sped by and then voices and laughter coming from a pontoon boat overloaded with drunk partiers. He thought it was the same one he'd seen earlier.

"We're taking yours, and you're gonna drive," Sergeant Merritt said.

"If that's the plan you're gonna have to take the cuffs off. I can't drive with my hands behind my back."

"Make any kind of move I'll shoot you, get the money myself. Do we understand each other?"

Ray nodded. The cop removed the cuffs and sat on a bench seat in the bow facing him, holding the gun. Ray started the engine, untied the lines, and sat in the stern. He goosed the throttle, pulling away from the dock. He'd left the choke on, and now in the middle of the channel the engine sputtered and quit.

Sergeant Merritt said, "The hell's going on?"

"It's been doing this lately." Ray went down on one knee, released the choke, yanked the pull cord, and restarted the engine. Then he opened the throttle all the way, jerked the steering handle to the right and sent Merritt sideways on the seat. Ray reached for the Beretta and brought it up squeezing the trigger, the suppressor muffling the gunshots. Sergeant Merritt, still trying to find his balance, was hit twice and now was lying in the bottom of the boat.

Ray put it in neutral, stepped over the seat, and knelt next to him. He heard a boat approaching, saw running lights coming behind him as he tried to lift the cop's legs over the starboard side, heaving with all his strength, the boat getting closer, and then

Johnny Merritt hit and splashed, sinking into the blackness of the channel.

A sheriff's patrol boat pulled up next to Ray, a searchlight sweeping across his boat from bow to stern, and when the light was in his face, blinding him, he made a visor with his right hand.

A voice said, "What's the trouble?"

Ray could see two dark shapes, silhouettes on the deck of a twenty-four-foot Boston Whaler. "Engine stalled, it happens, no worries."

"What's your name?" Same voice, one cop doing the talking.

"Len Heinle," Ray said, hoping they weren't gonna ask for ID.

"Where you coming from?"

"Visiting friends down the way." He pointed south.

"Where you going?"

"Home."

"Where's that at?"

"Right up there." He pointed north.

"Been drinking?"

"I've had a couple, but I didn't overdo it, if that's what you're asking."

"Show me you can get it started."

Ray pulled the cord and the engine came to life.

"All right, you have a good night, Mr. Heinle."

The patrol boat took off and when it was out of sight, he eased up on the throttle and turned the boat back toward Sharon's cottage.

•••

THEY'D SEARCHED EVERY ROOM in the house looking for money. Kate even checked the washer and dryer, a crawlspace in the laundry room and vents behind the furnace—places she'd heard of fugitives hiding cash—and came up empty.

Now they were in the boat well. Frank searched the inside of the Wheeler, checked the sleeping area, kitchen, and bathroom while Kate opened every compartment on deck. Again, nothing.

It was nine fifteen when they walked back in the house and went upstairs.

"I know Ray has the money," Frank said, "and it has to be here somewhere."

"Maybe he's got a safe deposit box," Kate said.

Frank wasn't listening. He was looking at the Oriental rug on the dressing room floor. He got on his knees and rolled it to the table. There was a trapdoor with a flush-mounted brass opener in the wood. Frank lifted it and saw a large black duffel bag. He grabbed the shoulder strap and pulled it out of the compartment, surprised at how heavy it was.

Kate unzipped the top, revealing bundles of hundred-dollar bills held together with rubber bands. "How'd you know?"

"I didn't. I knew he had money and we've looked everywhere else. Feels like a couple million."

"You're guessing, huh?"

"A million in hundred-dollar bills weighs twenty-two pounds."

"That sounds like something a bank robber would know."

•••

SHARON WAS AT THE sink, her back to him, washing dishes when Ray walked in the kitchen. "That was quick," she said without looking. "He give you any trouble?"

The dog was standing over a bowl drinking water.

Now she glanced at him holding the Beretta. "What'd you do with Johnny?"

"Who is he?"

"Sheriff's deputy that arrested Wade. We started seeing each other." She sounded buzzed. "I told him about you, thinking he might get a promotion for arresting a high-profile bank robber. He had a different idea, saw an opportunity, and came up with a plan." Sharon sipped some vodka and set the glass on the counter. "It's a shittin' world. You want to put me out of my misery, feel free."

Ray shot her, and she fell back against the counter and dropped to the floor. The dog moved to Sharon, licking her face, and he walked out of the room.

A few minutes later, gliding toward the boat well, he turned off the engine, coasted in, and tied up the Saturn. As he was getting out Ray noticed the cop's gun next to the bow seat. He picked it up, spun the cylinder. It was a Smith & Wesson .38. He slid it in the left side pocket of his khakis.

Now he climbed up on the walkway, went over to the Wheeler, pressed a button on the boat lift remote to lower it into the water. He stepped aboard and went to the controls to warm up the engine, but the key was missing. He didn't remember bringing it in the house, but it had to be in his office.

•••

KATE WAS IN THE kitchen when she heard the boat-well door opening. Frank was still upstairs, said he had to use the bathroom. She moved to the bottom of the stairs, "Frank, I think he's home. Get down here." No response. She wondered if he had fallen asleep. Kate went into the dark living room, knelt behind the couch, gripping her weapon, and waited. She heard footsteps in the hallway and saw Skinner walk by.

•••

FRANK TOOK BANDED STACKS of hundred dollar bills out of the duffel and tossed them on the bed. He counted out two hundred thousand, his share of the heist money and three hundred thousand for spending eighteen years in prison. He felt a rush of excitement thinking about it. The money changed everything. He could buy a car, a Cadillac if he wanted, and get his own place. He could travel and make up for lost time. Kate calling up the stairs to him brought Frank back to reality. She said, "Skinner's home."

•••

RAY SAT AT HIS desk in the office and opened the big drawer, looking for the boat key. The Beretta was digging into his lower back. He reached around, took it out of his waistband, and laid it on the desktop.

"This what you're looking for?"

Ray looked over his shoulder at Kate McGraw aiming a Glock at him and holding up the boat key. "Put your hands where I can see them."

Ray lifted his arms over his head.

"Roll your chair back."

He did. "How'd you find me?"

"We know all about you. Where you were born and where you were raised. We know your mother gave you up for adoption. And your adoptive parents were killed in a car accident when you were fourteen. We know you ran away from the orphanage with Lowell Hodge and you've robbed sixty-two banks. And we know you favor Asian women. It's just taken a while to find you."

"Where're the other deputies?"

"It's just you and me. Lift the Beretta with your thumb and index finger and toss it to me. That's what you used to kill the young black kid on Belle Isle, isn't it? The Canadian in Windsor and the handyman in Waterford? Did I miss anyone? We have casings from all three homicides, and we have your fingerprints."

"You know what I've got?"

She waited for him to continue.

"Money. I'll give you a million dollars. Walk out of here, you'll never see me again. You'll be able to move out of that second-rate apartment and change your life." She didn't take the bait, but it didn't matter. Ray had another idea. He could feel the .38 in his pocket pressing against his thigh, picturing how it was gonna go down. Don't rush, he told himself, take it easy. A foot from the desk, he had a better angle, could see her without twisting his neck and could draw the .38 without getting out of the chair. She was in a shooting stance, two hands on the Glock, aiming it at him.

"All right," Ray said. "I'm gonna pick up the gun. Don't shoot." He lowered his hands, reached for the Beretta with his right, pinched the trigger guard, and tossed the gun. It hit the floor and skidded across the carpeting. Kate crouched to pick it up—lost her balance, put a hand down to steady herself, and took her eyes off him for a second. Ray pulled the .38, turned and had the advantage, trained the revolver on her. "Drop it." She hesitated, and he clicked the hammer back. She laid her gun on the floor and sat back on her legs.

•••

FRANK CREPT DOWN THE stairs and looked into the dark living room. He heard voices, moved along the hall and stopped just short of the office. The door was open. He heard Ray's voice, peeked in and saw a gun in his hand.

He waited till Ray walked Kate through the doorway, hand on her arm. She saw Frank and made a sudden break, moved right and slipped out of Ray's grasp. Skinner went after her, but Frank stepped in and hit him with everything he had. Ray, bouncing off the wall, dropped the gun. Frank hit him again, with a body shot this time, and sent him through the doorway onto the floor in the office.

Ray was conscious but dazed as Kate, on her knees, cuffed his hands behind his back. She helped him up and sat him in the desk chair. His nose was swollen and bleeding but that didn't stop him from working his con. "I've got your share of the heist money and two million dollars more," he said to Frank. "You want to make a deal?"

"Don't say anything else. Don't open your mouth." Frank saw a box of Kleenex on the desk. He grabbed a couple, rolled them into a ball, and stuffed them in Ray's mouth.

Kate stepped out of the room and called Charlie. "You still looking for Ray Skinner?"

"Why didn't you get back to me?"

"'Cause I knew what you were going to say."

"I don't think I can help you."

"Why don't you pick up Skinner and we can talk about it later?" Kate gave him the address.

"How do you know he's there?"

"I'm looking at him."

"You went after that psycho by yourself?"

"Look at the positive side. We just arrested a top-fifteen fugitive who's robbed sixty-two banks. Let's not get hung up on procedure."

"I'll be there as soon as I can."

Kate disconnected and Frank came into the hall. "They're coming for Skinner. I think you should leave." She handed him the car keys. "Take your share of the money and enough to reimburse Thompson for the car."

"What're you gonna do?"

"Hand Skinner over, go home, and have a glass of wine."

FOR MEGAN SULLIVAN